VEIL

of

LIES

A Medieval Noir

Jeri Westerson

MINOTAUR BOOKS ⋈ NEW YORK

VEIL OF LIES. Copyright © 2008 by Jeri Westerson. All rights reserved. Printed in the United States of America. For information, address St. Martin's Press, 175 Fifth Avenue, New York, N.Y. 10010.

www.minotaurbooks.com

The Library of Congress has catalogued the hardcover edition as follows:

Westerson, Jeri.
    Veil of lies : a medieval noir / Jeri Westerson. — 1st ed.
        p.   cm.
    ISBN 978-0-312-37977-3
    1. Knights and knighthood—England—Fiction. 2. Great Britain—History—14th century—Fiction. 3. London (England)—Fiction. 4. Murder—Investigation—Fiction. I. Title.
    PS3623.E8478V45 2008
    813'.6—dc22

                                                2008025097

    ISBN 978-0-312-58012-4 (trade paperback)

First Minotaur Books Paperback Edition: October 2009

D 10 9 8 7 6 5 4 3

VEIL

of

LIES

The Crispin Guest Novels by Jeri Westerson

Veil of Lies

Serpent in the Thorns

To my beloved husband, Craig, whose persistent faith in

me makes all things possible

Acknowledgments

Books don't just happen. And as much as I'd like to think it only takes one brilliant author to sit alone in a room with a keyboard and a monitor, it involves just a little bit more than that. It's been a long, interesting road to get to this point. So many people to thank, especially after fourteen years.

First and foremost, my grateful thanks go out to my husband, Craig, to whom I have dedicated this book. Throughout fourteen years of rejections when I started out writing historical fiction until I buckled down to write historical *mystery*, he has been standing by my side encouraging me. "It will happen someday," he'd say. "I'm sure of it." He was right. And thanks also to my wonderful son, Graham, who happily liked to play by himself all those years ago because Mom was always locked in her office writing.

With historical mystery comes its own set of problems. There is a lot of traipsing back and forth to various libraries, so I am always grateful to the helpful staff of the Tomas Rivera Library at the University of California at Riverside, and also to Nancy Smith and her fine staff at the Sun City Library ("Who is that woman and why is she always here?"). And what I couldn't glean from my local libraries, I garnered from some very helpful scholars, historians, and writers I met online at mediev-l.

Many thanks also go out to my best friend, Marie Meadows, who has been my own personal cheering section. We spent many hours discussing plot and working on Crispin's coat of arms. Thanks also to Luci Zahray, who probably doesn't know how much she encouraged me; to Kat Cormie for giving me a great turn of plot; Henk 't Jong for translation help; Francesco Dall'Aglio at the Istituto Italiano per gli Studi Filosofici in Naples for the embarrassing Italian (sure glad we exchanged e-mails and didn't have to say naughty words to each other over the phone!).

Where would I be without the judicious eyes of my critique groups? First, there was Rebecca Farnbach and Carol Thomas with their sharp red pencils. Later, my Vicious Circle, which consists of Ana Brazil, Bobbie Gosnell, and Laura James, had a crack at it. These indefatigable ladies know how to put me in my place (and that ain't easy!). Their virtual pencils may not be red, but they are sharp enough to pin me down, slap me a little, and make it all work. And thanks also to the online group Guppies of Sisters in Crime, who don't mind answering the same question over and over and are always there to lend a virtual pat on the back.

A big, *big* thanks to my agent, Steve Mancino, who, like a mastiff, would not give up and thrashed my manuscript within an inch of its life. And lastly, a very special thank-you to my superb editor at St. Martin's Press, Keith Kahla, who liked my characters so much he gave them a second chance. Thank you all.

I

London, 1384

THE RAIN DIDN'T BOTHER him, even though London's rain fell thicker and harsher than country rain. Full of the city's stench, the drizzle descended in matted wires, pricking the skin. Crispin's leather hood took the brunt of it. The beaded water ran off his head in long rivulets and pooled at his feet. The cloak did not fare as well, and clung in heavy, wet drapery to his shivering shoulders.

Even this didn't bother him.

What bothered him was standing in this unholy rain while a mere servant boldly appraised him as if he were a stable boy or a tradesman; looked Crispin up and down from his shabby knee-length cotehardie to his patched stockings.

The manservant's face, square and strong, spoke of country stock rather than those hard faces etched by city living. "What do you want?" the servant asked after his prolonged assessment.

Crispin leaned forward. "What I *want*," he said in a clipped tone that made the servant stiffen, "is for you to announce me to your master, the man who summoned me in the first place. The name," he said, advancing to take possession of the threshold, "is Crispin Guest. Do not keep your master waiting."

The servant hesitated before bowing derisively with a "right this way, my lord" that had nothing of respect in it.

They entered a wide hall. Murals of hardworking dyers and weavers decorated both the plaster walls and rich tapestries. The friendly aroma of dried lavender and rosemary censed the cold rooms. The scent reminded Crispin of his long-lost manor in Sheen. Much the same finery adorned those halls and passageways. But that had been some eight long years ago, when he was still a knight.

They came to a door and the servant took a key from his belt. Once they passed through the archway, he stopped, locked the door behind him, and proceeded on.

Crispin watched and frowned. He wanted to ask but doubted he would get an answer. Instead, he simply observed the strange ritual repeated until they climbed a staircase and reached the warm solar. Why would the interview be conducted in the solar? Business discussions usually took place in the parlor. The intimate setting of the solar suited a family's more private society. Crispin shrugged it off as another eccentricity of his wealthy host.

The servant opened the solar's door. White plaster walls were swathed about the room with arcs of rich, blue drapery hanging midheight by pegs. A large, carved buffet stood against one wall, reaching almost to dark ceiling beams marching in a row toward a large window, under which sat a heavy, carved table with parchments and leather-bound accounting ledgers spread across it.

The servant bowed perfunctorily. "My master will be in anon." He turned sharply and then stopped, leaning in toward Crispin. "Don't touch anything." He grinned at Crispin's narrowed eyes and left without locking the door behind him.

Crispin tugged at his tailored coat and sneered in the direction of the receding footsteps. He glanced at the lock and traced his finger around the black iron lock plate. New. And this one only bolted from the inside. Surely the solar was important enough to lock from the outside as well.

He strolled to the fire, luxuriating in its glowing warmth. The hearth, large, almost too big for the room, stood as tall as Crispin. The mantel boasted arms of the mercer's guild chiseled into the stone. "Merchant in cloth," Crispin snorted. He glanced again around the fine room of silver candlesticks and expensive furnishings, and nodded shrewdly. "I am in the wrong profession." He stared at the flagon across the room and licked his lips.

Last night he wondered at such a summons and felt a little trill in his belly. If all went well, this would surely be the richest client of his four-year career, and he needed that fee. The rent was overdue again and he owed Gilbert and Eleanor Langton a lengthy tavern bill as well. Where did the money go? Funny how it had never occurred to him how hard it was to make a living until he had to do it himself.

The door burst open and Crispin instinctively came to attention and faced his wealthy host. The man strode in, his shoulders almost as wide as the doorway. He took command of the space as a general takes command of the field, locking his eyes on Crispin before sweeping his gaze warily around the room. Crispin smiled in spite of himself. There was little doubt in Crispin's mind that such a man was used to barking orders and having them immediately obeyed. It was something Crispin appreciated. Something he had enjoyed himself in years gone by. But this man, this prosperous merchant, was not destined to take his place on any battlefield. His arena was commerce and his soldiers his bolts of cloth.

Crispin looked him over as well, trying to assess the man beneath the confident exterior. On second examination, the man did not appear to have the muscled heft of a mason or smith, but instead the corpulence of a man of leisure. His nut brown fleshy face crinkled at the eyes and met a tidy beard touched by gray. His deep green houppelande made of rich velvet and trimmed with miniver reached to just below his knees. The foliated sleeves touched the floor, and the stiff collar stood up straight and neatly covered the back of a beefy neck.

He wore two gold chains across his wide breast as well as a dagger with a gem-encrusted hilt and a decorated scabbard.

Behind him, the same manservant who met Crispin at the main door followed his master into the room and stood by the door, awaiting instructions.

The wealthy man rested his gaze on Crispin once more and left it there. "Crispin Guest?" he asked.

"At your service, my lord," said Crispin and bowed.

The man nodded briskly before turning to his manservant. "Adam, you are dismissed. We will serve ourselves."

The servant, Adam, threw a suspicious glare at Crispin. He hesitated a moment. But there didn't seem to be any naysaying of this master, and the servant forced a bow before he trudged out, pulling the door shut behind him. The wealthy host strode to the closed door, grabbed the iron bolt, and locked them in.

Crispin glanced at the bolt but said nothing.

The man turned back to Crispin and hastily smiled. "I do like my privacy."

Crispin remained silent.

"Please"—the man gestured toward a cushioned chair—"sit. Will you have wine?"

"Thank you."

The merchant poured and handed Crispin a bowl. Crispin sat and savored the feel of the silver bowl in his hand and almost closed his eyes at the aroma of the sweet berry flavors of good Gascon wine. The man sat opposite in a larger chair. Crispin took only one sip and reluctantly set the bowl aside.

"I have heard of your discretion, Master Guest," said the man at last. "And discretion is utmost in this instance."

"Yes, Master. That is true in most instances."

"Your reputation as an investigator—is it well deserved?"

"For four years I have been known as the 'Tracker.' I have heard no complaints about my service. My clients are well satisfied."

"I see." The merchant smiled with a contented nod, but then his face tightened and he fell into an agitated silence. They measured each other for a long span before the man sprang unexpectedly to his feet and nervously warmed his hands at the hearth.

"Perhaps," Crispin suggested after another long silence, "you should start at the beginning, and then we can discover what it is you would have me do."

The man sighed heavily and glanced once at the closed door. "My name is Nicholas Walcote."

Crispin nodded. This he knew. The richest mercer in London, possibly in all England. Reclusive. Eccentric. It was said Walcote hadn't been seen by his own guild since his boyhood, but his renowned trade in cloth kept his reputation intact. The man seemed always ahead of the trends, always importing just the right merchandise at the right time, cloth that the market seemed enraptured with. The man had a head for business like few others. Crispin mentally shook his head— the cloth trade was a complete mystery to him. There had once been a time when he followed fashions, but he did not have to heed courtly finery today, even if he could afford it.

The thought soured his belly as thoughts of King Richard's court often did. His history made Walcote his better and left Crispin in rags. But not for long. Crispin measured each man these days by the amount of gold they were willing to part with. And by the looks of things, Nicholas Walcote could afford to part with a great deal.

Canting toward the edge of his seat, Crispin schooled his features and pulled the hem of his coat down over his thigh to cover a hole in his left stocking. "What might these discreet matters be, Master Walcote?"

When Walcote met Crispin's gaze his face hardened. "It is my wife. I fear . . . I fear she is unfaithful to me." His eyes filled with tears. Abruptly, he dropped his head into his hands and wept.

Crispin sat back and examined his nails, waiting for Walcote's tears to subside. He waited a long time.

At last Walcote raised his head and wiped his face with large, square hands. "Forgive me." He sniffed and rubbed his nose. "These are disturbing matters. Of course I am not certain. That is why I called for you."

Crispin reckoned where this was heading and didn't like it. "What is it you wish me to do?"

"Surely you have experience in these matters."

He narrowed his eyes. "You wish me to spy on your wife?"

Walcote crossed the room and stood above his untouched wine. The frost-edged window panes added a gray wash of faint light onto the polished wooden floor. The rest of the room lay steeped in shadows or the manicured halos of candle sconces.

"It is driving me mad!" he hissed. "I must know! The business, my estates. I must know that any issue from her is mine. We have been married so briefly and I travel much on business."

Love and jealousy were one thing, but the business of inheritance quite another. "Just so. What are your intentions if you discover an unpleasant truth?"

Walcote's ruddy countenance deepened to red. "That, Master Guest, is my business alone."

"I think you are mistaken. I do not care to be the cause of violence, no matter how justified."

Walcote glared at him, and suddenly the merchant's curled fists opened. He smiled apologetically. "Such personal matters. It is difficult to be rational. There would be words, certainly, and perhaps punitive action. But violence? No. You see, despite it all, I love my wife."

Crispin rose, crossed to the hearth, and warmed his back against the fire. His wet mantle dripped on the floor. "I have no stomach for such business, Master Walcote. I recover lost jewelry, stolen papers, and such like. Adultery? I leave that to clerics." He shook his head and moved to the door, but Walcote scrambled to maneuver in front of him and even spread his arms to cover the entrance.

Walcote weighed a good sixteen stone, but it was all easy living and heavy food. Trim and fit, Crispin did not doubt that if he wished to leave, Walcote could not impede him.

"Please, Master Guest. You know I am a wealthy man. I will pay any price. I cannot tell this story again to another. I beg of you!"

"This is unpleasant and personal business, Master Walcote." Crispin eyed his abandoned wine bowl. "In my opinion, you should talk to your wife." He placed his hand on Walcote's arm and squeezed, moving it easily aside. He reached for the bolt but Walcote grabbed his wrist.

"But how can I believe her answer?"

Crispin offered a smile. "She just might tell you the truth. Stranger things have happened."

"You do not know my wife," Walcote muttered. "I have tried, but the truth with her is different from others."

Walcote tightened his grip on Crispin's wrist. Crispin looked down at it. "Surely there is a servant you can send," he told his host.

"And be the laughingstock of the servant's hall?" He shook his head and released Crispin's wrist. "Have you never been betrayed? Would you not have wanted someone to intervene for you? To warn you?"

Crispin gnawed on words close to his heart. Betrayed? He had been betrayed twice in his life in the worst possible ways. Once by a man he trusted with his life, and the other by the woman he intended to marry. If he had only been warned. If someone had but said—

He lowered his hand from the bolt and stared at the floor, ticking off the advantages both for and against. He stood that way for a while, until a long breath escaped his lips and he pivoted to face Walcote. The man was desperate. No doubt of that. His ruddy face reddened and sweat shined on his nose and forehead. All his wealth was no surety of happiness. Crispin almost snorted at the irony.

Instead, he sighed his frustration, feeling the hollowness of the purse at his own belt. "Very well. What is it you wish me to do?"

Walcote's words spilled out. "Watch the house. See where she goes or who appears when I am out. Report to me what you find. I shall take care of the rest." He wiped the sweat from his upper lip. "What is your fee for such a commission?"

"Sixpence a day, plus expenses."

"I will pay that and more. Here is a good-faith payment." He reached into the purse at his belt and withdrew three coins. "Half a day's wages now. More for however long it takes."

Crispin looked at the coins in Walcote's moist palm. Three silver disks. To refuse them meant starvation. Nothing new. He had starved before. If he accepted them, it meant creeping in shadows, little better than a voyeur. But it also might lead to better appointments, better opportunities. Perhaps even through the Walcote household itself, and a rich household it was.

With a bitter heart, his fingers scooped up the coins and dropped them into his purse.

"How shall I know your wife?" asked Crispin. "May I see her?"

"Oh no! That will never do." Walcote went to the sideboard and opened the doors. He took a small object from a back shelf and cupped it in his hand, gazing at it. Reluctantly he handed it to Crispin. "This is a portrait of Philippa. It is the best likeness."

Crispin examined the miniature. A young brown-eyed woman in her early twenties looked out at him. Her hair was a brassy gold and parted in the middle. Two ring braids draped over her ears. *A fetching lass.* And younger than Walcote, who appeared to be in his late forties. *Little wonder he worries.*

Crispin handed the portrait back, but the merchant shook his head. "Keep that for now. I would have you be certain."

Crispin shrugged and stuffed the small portrait through the opening of his coat.

"I want you to begin tonight," said Walcote distractedly. "And tell me whatever you discover as soon as possible."

"Let us hope your worries are for nought."

"Yes." He wrung his hands and turned his back on Crispin to face the fire. "Adam will let you out."

LEAVING THE WALCOTE COURTYARD, Crispin could not help but look back over his shoulder at the grand stone structure.

He passed through the gatehouse and acknowledged the porter inside with only a curt nod. Pulling his leather hood up, he gathered his cloak about him. The autumn sky hung gray and sullen. He felt grateful the rain had stopped but his breath still fogged his face.

If Walcote wanted him to start tonight then now seemed as good a time as any. He walked across the street to warm himself over a shopkeeper's brazier and nodded to a man already standing there. The man gestured toward the house. "Been looking for a job?" A thick-as-fog Southwark accent, but his manner rubbed a little too feminine for Crispin's tastes.

Crispin gave a brief smile. "Yes. Do you know them?"

"Aye. Me cousin used to work for them."

"Used to?"

"Aye. He says they're a curious lot. I just girded me courage to ask for work there m'self, even though me cousin Harry warned me not to. A man can't be too particular when he needs to earn a living." He was a thin man with a hollowed face, pale hair, a hawk nose, and watery blue eyes. The man pulled his hood down to his brows with long fingers, and stiffly clutched the material closed below his chin.

"And the outcome?"

"I talked to the mistress of the house. She's a stern one, she is. I don't know what she thought. I'm to return on the morrow."

Crispin said nothing. He glanced back at the house. Its proud exterior slowly disappeared behind an encroaching mist, leaving only a hazy gray rectangle with darker rectangles for windows.

The man measured Crispin's shabby rust-colored coat, patched stockings, and worn boots. "Did they hire you?"

Crispin shivered and drew closer to the flames. He shook his head.

"Gluttonous sot," muttered the man. "Walcote has more money than Solomon. You can't take your riches into heaven!" he said to the house, fist raised. He lowered his hand and swiped at the air. "What's one more servant to him?" He leaned toward Crispin. "They say," he said softly, "that he only leaves the house to travel out of the country and buy his cloth. But there's some who say he don't go nowhere at all. Conjures the stuff in his cellar. It's devil's work, that much money."

"Some men are simply good at what they do."

The man sniffed and wiped his fingerless glove across his nose. "Well, I ain't good at much. What are you good at?"

Crispin grinned crookedly. "Oh, a number of things. And none of them pay me enough."

"Ain't that God's truth. And times is hard, ain't they?" The man rubbed his hands and wrapped his cloak over his chest. "I think we should both forget our troubles for now." He put out his gloved hand. "The name's John Hoode. Shall we share a beaker of ale?"

Crispin glanced at the silent house, each door in or out locked tight. He measured the sky. It wouldn't be nightfall for a few hours. Didn't trysts usually happen at night?

Maybe the man had information on the Walcotes he could use. He clasped the man's hand and shook it once. "I *will* accept your kind offer."

"Well now!" The man motioned for Crispin to follow and they walked a block to the nearest tavern.

They settled in. Crispin pushed back his hood, running his fingers through his damp, black hair. Hoode talked merrily about London and his amusing adventures as a workingman. Crispin let him talk, only half-listening. He studied him with slate gray eyes, sipping slowly of his ale. He didn't share as much about himself, saying only that he did a variety of jobs to keep food on the table.

"Tell me," said Crispin, slipping in between the man's chatter. "What was your impression of Madam Walcote?"

The man slurped from his beaker and frowned. "A pretty thing. Young. Steadfast."

Crispin drank. Steadfast? Then why should Walcote suspect her?

"Thinking of getting around *him* and going through *her*, eh?" he asked Crispin. "I wouldn't. She's loyal to the bone. What's good for him is good for her. Like I said. Steadfast."

Crispin dipped his face in his cup and said little else. He wanted to look at the portrait again but that was impossible in Hoode's presence. Perhaps he should have questioned Walcote more rigorously as to why he had his suspicions, but Crispin's personal distaste for this kind of task got the better of him. He shook his head at it. He should know better than that.

What matter could it have been that got Walcote's hackles up? Was there someone loitering near the house, perhaps? Or did she hire servants who were more comely in appearance than Hoode here?

AFTER ALMOST TWO HOURS of nursing a beaker of watery ale and listening to Hoode chatter about this and that, Crispin thanked the man, wished him well, and left the tavern. He sauntered down the chilly street, now black and silver under the indistinct glow of a clouded moon.

He reached the brazier across the avenue from the Walcote gatehouse where he first met Hoode, but the dead fire left only gray ashes swirling at the bottom of the iron cage.

For hours he stood in the darkness. The moon had long gone, making the night seem colder. Finally, a small figure appeared near the gatehouse. If the guard had not brought forth his torch to show her face, Crispin might not have recognized Philippa Walcote, but he saw a flash of brassy gold hair and remembered it from the miniature portrait.

She set out alone along the street, looking back over her shoulder at the house, now dark. Crispin let her get a bowshot away before he ducked his head into his hood and followed.

She walked quickly. The shadows of the narrow lane soon swallowed her slim form, but Crispin's eyes caught the movement. Distantly, he followed her through a stone archway, slick with mist and stinking of mold. Her footsteps echoed within the structure and Crispin waited until they fell away again before he ventured through. She stepped onto a street that gently curved away from the eye, like a river. Tall shops of several stories or lofts towering over one another lined the street, shoulder to shoulder. Their frames seemed squeezed by proximity and they loured over the avenue in stiff indifference to her flight, closing off the black sky. Doors were bolted and shutters closed against the warm, golden light Crispin could just see peeking through the seams. The damp street was deserted, except for the mysterious woman and her shadow.

She stopped and looked back.

Crispin jammed himself against the wall of a stone house, its rugged surface digging painfully into his back. Barely breathing lest the cloud of breath betray him, he quested a cautious eye past his hood to watch her.

She seemed satisfied that she was alone and turned. She gathered her cloak around herself and stepped along the uneven paving stones and sometimes into the mud.

Crispin took a deep breath, allowed her to turn a corner, and hurried, keeping amid the shadows of the eaves like a rat. He slowed when he approached the corner where she had turned and he clutched the lime-washed timber, peering carefully. He saw the hem of her cloak flick as she scurried, watched her tramp across the bridge over the Fleet Ditch, and grimaced. She was making her way south toward parts of London a lone gentlewoman should not go. Crispin snorted. *Foolish woman! You'll get yourself killed. Or worse.*

She trailed her hand along a wattle fence and stepped up onto a granite paving stone situated before a busy inn. She looked once back behind her before ducking inside. Crispin stopped and watched the door open to admit her. A bright rectangle of light briefly lit the dark street before the door closed again.

A few moments later a candle was lit in an upper window, its light streaming through the cracked shutter. Crispin approached and craned his neck, but the sill was too high.

He stumbled through the inn's pitch-dark courtyard, searching for a ladder, and found one leaning against the stable door. Carefully, he carried it back to the window and laid it against the wall, just to the side of the closed shutter. He climbed the rungs—stopped with a wince when they creaked—then made it the rest of the way to the top and peered in through the shutter's cracks.

Philippa Walcote stood facing the window. This time he could see her features clearly. She was, indeed, young and quite beautiful. Her pale skin seemed smooth, almost translucent. Her dark eyes were large under heavy lashes, though they were draped by drowsy lids. He recalled from the miniature that same pert nose and small mouth whose lips were perfectly shaped in two opposing bows. Her hair, redder than in the painting, shone with bright flashes of wheat when the firelight caught it.

Why would a rich woman go to such a low tavern? It seemed a strange place to conduct an affair, if affair it was.

She unhooked the agrafe at her throat that held the cloak in place and tossed the mantle on the bed. Her blue samite dress was decorated with embroidery along the scooped neckline and displayed both her long neck and her high and pronounced breasts, made more conspicuous by the satiny fabric with its shine and shadow.

Crispin almost felt sorry for such a pretty thing, and he wondered why, with Walcote's many locks, he could not manage also to confine his wife.

A shadow passed over the woman, and a man stepped into view. He stood behind her and without preamble ran his hand over the back of her neck. His features were dark, with a wide unpleasant mouth and small eyes. He needed a shave and possibly a bath, for his hair hung about his face in greasy, curled locks.

Crispin watched her passive face. It reflected neither lust nor affection, and kept its steady gaze settled somewhere on the floor, lids at half mast. Not quite the expression he expected. *An unusual tryst, to be sure.*

The man attacked the laces on the back of her gown. He tugged, and her body jerked like a straw manikin, but she did not seem to wish to help him expedite his efforts. He growled, mauling her neck, and the only indication that she acknowledged his presence was a slight wince. The dark hand covering her creamy skin slid to the front of her gown and clawed her breast. At last, the laces opened and her gown slipped, loosened about her shoulders. His long fingers grasped the material and yanked it down. The dark gown crumpled to her waist, revealing her white shift beneath. Those large hands kept roving along her body, pinching and pulling at her. Her eyes betrayed the merest hint of impatience . . . or was it irritation? Those hands bunched the cloth of her shift in two fists and pulled downward. There was a sound of tearing cloth and Crispin suddenly got an eyeful of white, pink-tipped breasts.

He slipped off his rung.

"God's blood!" Arm linked around the ladder, he swung underneath it and hung for a moment, breathing hard. He rested his forehead against a damp tread and waited. Nothing. They had not heard him. No one gave the alarm. They were, no doubt, preoccupied. He shook his head. It had been too long since he had seen a woman that beautiful and in that state of undress. He cautiously pulled himself around to the front of the ladder and made his unsteady way down.

And so. Philippa Walcote *was* an adulteress. No doubt about it. That was a quick sixpence. Too bad it couldn't have been drawn out for a few days for a greater fee.

Crispin returned the ladder and pushed his way into the inn. He sat by the fire with a view of the stairs and ordered wine with one silver coin newly received from Walcote. He did not relish his task in telling the merchant about the misadventures of his wife, but it must be done.

When the liquor arrived he drank a bowlful quickly. He poured himself another and quaffed that, too. The wine warmed his belly and he felt slightly better. After a quarter of an hour he saw the woman descend the stairs and stride across the crowded room.

Crispin scrambled to his feet and left the bowl to follow her. Outside, he looked up at the window and saw the candlelight extinguish, leaving the window dark through the shutters. With her tryst quickly over she hurried home.

It was much too late to go to Walcote's now, especially with such unpleasant news. Home sounded good to him and he left the damp streets for his own bed, dreaming of ladders and open windows.

COME MORNING, HE GLANCED at his ash-filled hearth and frowned, thinking of his empty larder and growling belly. Sixpence a day did not go as far as it once did.

Sixpence. He tried to make light of the whole affair as just another job, but failed. It wasn't just the hiding in shadows and peering through windows like a simpering spy that vexed him. The vision of Philippa Walcote's naked loveliness troubled him far more. He kept seeing her in his mind.

A thump in the shop below drew his thoughts away from her. It was the tinker's family starting their day. Perhaps he'd better do the same. He got up and went to the basin to wash his face and shave. He tied the laces of his chemise, pulled on his socks, drew up and tied his stirruped leggings, and buttoned the cotehardie all the way up his neck.

Crispin reached the Walcote gatehouse within a quarter of an hour. He entered the courtyard and made the long walk across the flagged stones to the wide stairs of an arched portico made of carved granite. He pulled the bell rope and after a few moments encountered the same servant from yesterday.

"Good morrow, Adam," said Crispin, smiling at the servant's agitation at the use of his name. "I have come to see your master. You remember me, do you not?"

The servant returned a wan smile. "Come this way."

The house lay in quiet that early in the morning. No sound lifted from the cold plaster and timbers but their footsteps on the wooden floor and the jangle of Adam's keys.

They arrived at the solar, but when Adam reached for the door ring and pulled, the door remained stubbornly shut. He stared at the door dumbly for a moment before knocking. "Master Walcote," he said, chin raised. "Master Crispin Guest is here to see you."

They both waited for a reply, but none came. Adam glanced at Crispin before he leaned into the door again. "Master," he said louder. "You've a visitor; Crispin Guest."

They waited again. Silence.

Crispin glared at Adam. "Are you certain he's in there?"

Adam's look of bewilderment gave Crispin pause. Adam did not seem the bewildered sort. By his longer gown and ring of keys, Crispin assumed he was the steward and would naturally be the man who knew all goings on in this house.

"He must be," said Adam slowly. "It locks from the inside." He exchanged looks with Crispin. Adam raised his hand and knocked again. The polite knocks turned to pounding and then he turned a desperate expression on Crispin. "Something must be amiss."

Crispin pushed Adam aside and did his own knocking. "Master Walcote!" Foolish to think that his knocking would have more sway over the steward's. An uneasy sensation steeled over his heart. "Get something to break down this door. And get help. Make haste!"

Adam ran down the passageway while Crispin yanked on the door ring. He braced his foot against the wall and with both hands pulled until he was blue in the face. Nothing. His eyes traveled over the door, searching for a means in. The heavy iron hinges were beyond his abilities without tools and the door was made of thick, sturdy oak.

He turned at the sound of footsteps slapping against the floor and moved aside for two men, both with axes. "Master Walcote!" cried one of the men. They turned to Adam for permission and he gave them a desperate nod.

Standing squarely before the door, they hacked at the oak, one hitting the door while the other swung back—a rhythmic thudding of blade on wood precisely timed. The wood splintered little by little, breaking off in long staves and flying chips. Adam danced on the balls of his feet behind them, blinking from each hard blow of the ax. At last they broke through the wood above the door ring. They stopped their swinging and one of the men reached through the tight opening to unbolt the door.

When it swung opened, Adam barked a surprised shout and froze. The two men with the axes searched past their steward and murmured prayers as they crossed themselves. Adam stumbled forward into the room.

A prickle started up Crispin's spine, and when he peered in, his instincts were confirmed. Nicholas Walcote lay on his back on the floor, mouth agape, eyes dilated, with an irregular patch of red beneath him.

2

SHERIFF SIMON WYNCHECOMBE STOOD in the center of the room and surveyed its cloth-draped walls, the cold hearth, splintered door, and finally Crispin. The sheriff narrowed his eyes. "What, by the mass, are *you* doing here?"

Crispin leaned against a far wall. He shrugged. "I happened to be in the parish."

Wynchecombe sneered. "Do you think I'm stupid?"

Crispin opened his mouth to answer but then thought better of it.

Besides Wynchecombe, there was another sheriff of London, John More, but Crispin seldom saw him performing his appointed task for the king. He supposed the man used his authority elsewhere. Perhaps he favored penning writs. On the other hand, Simon Wynchecombe was often on the streets when trouble arose. Crispin suspected it had less to do with sheriffing and more to do with a step closer toward the mayor's office.

Sheriff Wynchecombe, tall and dark-haired, cut a menacing figure. A meticulously coifed black mustache curved downward over his upper lip. A black beard neatly trimmed into two curls sprouted from his chin. He scanned Crispin with his usual irritated scorn before dismissing him.

The sheriff turned to Adam and leaned over him, pressing a finger into his chest in emphasis. Crispin chuckled to himself. He'd been in Adam's shoes many a time, but Adam didn't seem to be faring quite as well.

Crispin turned his attention to the quiet room and to the body of Nicholas Walcote. He'd been stabbed multiple times in the back. There was no sign of a struggle, no cast-over chairs or torn drapery. The blood had stopped running long ago. Such bodies he remembered from battlefields. These were the kind found in the morning after the corpse had lain all night. He could tell that Walcote was killed sometime the previous night by the look of the blood and the gray skin pallor.

Crispin had made a cursory inspection earlier, but Adam had prevented him from a more thorough search of the room, preferring to wait for the sheriff.

He glanced back at Wynchecombe, still pinning Adam to the wall. Smirking, Crispin wagered the servant didn't prefer Wynchecombe's company now.

He stepped over a spilled cup of wine to get nearer. The cup lay rim down. Wine splattered across the buffet. Or was it blood? He crouched down and squinted.

Wine.

He left the cup where it lay and crossed the room to examine the window. It was tightly barred. The dust on the sill told him that it had not been opened in some time. When he moved toward the door to examine the twisted lock, the sheriff's man stood in his way.

Almost wide enough to fill the arch, the man's shoulders blocked the outer gallery's light. His flat nose looked as if someone once flattened it for him. Crispin remembered his name was William.

A commotion at the doorway turned their heads. Philippa Walcote burst into the room trailed by anxious servants, reaching for her. She put her hand to her throat and stared wild-eyed at her husband before she let out a resounding scream.

Wynchecombe motioned to Crispin, and Crispin grabbed the woman's shoulders and dragged her from the room and out into the gallery.

"Now Mistress," he soothed. But when she refused to stop screaming, he opened his hand and slapped her.

She drew up and clamped her lips together. A red mark formed on her pale skin.

"My apologies," he said and released her.

She touched her cheek. Her wild eyes scrambled over Crispin's unfamiliar face, trying to place him. When this proved futile, she took a deep breath, and with it color returned to her face. Her rounded eyes tapered to drowsy slits and she looked at Crispin anew. He returned her gaze with interest, catching the careful relaxing of her shoulders and of her thoroughly taking in the scene before her. It was with surprising calm that she turned to him.

"I don't understand none of this. Tell me what happened," she said. He expected her voice to be high and melodic, but heard instead something low and husky. And arousing. Her accent, too, rubbed unexpectedly coarse on his ear with dropped aitches and a certain edge to the form of her speech.

"We do not know. He was murdered. By the look of the— By the look of him, I would say it was sometime last night."

"How do you know?"

"The blood. It does not run and—"

Her face, so stiff in its attempt at calm, crumpled behind her hand. He felt like kicking himself. "My apologies," he said again.

She shook her head and breathed deeply. Crispin noticed she wore the same gown from the previous night, but now a tiny tear gapped the seam at her shoulder. An impatient lover, her paramour. The rip reminded him he need not be so courteous.

She looked over her shoulder at the hovering servants. "You must have work to do!" she snapped. They stopped chattering and raised their heads before moving down the gallery, looking back and whispering to one another. She closed her eyes and exhaled a tremulous sigh. Cracking her eyes opened again she turned toward Crispin. "What's to be done?"

He admired her spirit. Or was it merely her impatience to get it over with? "Did your husband entertain any guests last night?"

"No. None that I know of."

"You have not seen him since last night?"

"No." Her chin trembled and she pressed her hands to her lips to stop it.

"When he did not come to bed, you did not question it?"

"He often works late with his books."

"Or could it be that you yourself came to bed late?"

She studied him with interest. "Tell me who you are."

He wasn't often disarmed by a pretty face, but he found himself embarrassed by her perusal of his threadbare appearance. "My name is Crispin Guest."

"Are you the sheriff?"

"Indeed, no. Your husband hired me."

"Hired for what?"

He slid his jaw. "I'm called the Tracker . . . among other things."

"Tracker?" Panic struck her voice. "What is lost?"

"Nothing, Mistress. I was hired for personal business."

"Personal? Was your business discharged before . . . before . . ."

"Very nearly."

"May I know what it is?"

He looked for a distraction in the empty gallery, but he saw only a rushlight dropping its burning embers to the floor. He decided to gauge her reaction. "I was following you, Mistress."

She looked askance. A good performance, he thought.

"He hired you to follow me?"

"Yes."

Her hands didn't seem to know what to do; curl into fists, rub her skirt, claw his face. "So these 'other things' you do," she said tightly, "they involve spying on innocent women?"

"Not *innocent* women."

He would have been disappointed had she not slapped him, and she made certain he felt no disappointment. Crispin's ears rang with it and his cheek burned.

"Madam," he said sharply. "Do you deny your infidelity?"

"Aye!"

"Yet I saw you only last night with my own eyes."

"Then your eyes deceive you."

"How can you say—" He shook his head. "I am speechless."

"What does it matter? My husband is dead." Her chin trembled again, and she sucked in her pouting lower lip.

He frowned. *And so are my chances of collecting my thruppence.* "True. My business with you is now over."

"No," she said thoughtfully. "I might need your help."

Crispin's brows rose. "For what purpose?"

"There is more here than you know," she whispered and jumped when a distant step in the gallery echoed. Her rounded eyes searched the shadows. "Not here. Where can I come to speak with you?"

"My lodgings. On the Shambles above a tinker shop. Anyone can tell you which it is."

"An hour's time, then."

She stepped away but he stopped her with a light touch to her sleeve. "It was Master Walcote who hired me. I do not think—"

Her mouth hardened. "Loyal, are you? Good. I can use a loyal man. One I can trust."

"Very well. My fee is—"

"I don't care what your fee is." She glared at him one last time before she wheeled and hurried into the shadows of shuddering tapestries and flickering rushlights.

He watched her shapely form depart and recalled the sight of her breasts from the previous night. A wash of heat warmed his face. *Jesu, Crispin. Is quim all you can think about when her husband lies dead in the next room?*

He walked slowly back into the solar and approached a thoughtful Wynchecombe.

"This is a puzzle," said the sheriff. "The solar was locked from the inside."

"Yes. And the casement is also untouched."

"Then how the hell did the murderer get in or out?"

"Perhaps he was invited in."

"But how did he get out?"

"*That* is the puzzle," Crispin agreed. He walked to the cold hearth and stepped into the gray ashes. Bracing his hands against the inside of the flue, he looked up the chimney.

The sheriff snorted. "Do you think he took to the air?"

"A rope would do. But it looks too narrow for a man. Give me a boost."

"*What* did you say?"

Crispin sighed. Distraction made him forget he was no longer Wynchecombe's better. "I beg your pardon, my lord." He made only a slight bow.

Wynchecombe smirked. "William. Help him."

William smiled and sauntered toward Crispin who took a cautionary step back into the hearth. "What troubles you?" said William, opening and closing his large hands. "Don't you want my help?" William crouched and made a stirrup with his interlaced hands. "Go on," he urged with a chuckle. The big man's fat fingers made a solid step. "Give us your foot. Or do you fear me?"

Crispin had been on the wrong side of William before, and he recalled very well how solid those hands could be. He took a deep breath and placed his foot on William's palms and pushed himself up, balancing his legs across the chimney's opening. He reached for a handhold but found little he could easily grip. The stones radiated warmth, and his nose filled with the stench of smoke. Creosote crumbled and broke off under his groping fingers. He found he could not stand up straight. At his shoulders the chimney narrowed with barely room for his head. He looked up and saw sky but no room for a man to shimmy up the passage.

When he jumped back down into the room, William laughed.

"What's so damned funny?"

"You," said William. "You look like a Moor."

He looked down at his hands covered in black soot and imagined his face looked little better.

"You there!" said the sheriff to Adam. "Get him a basin and water."

Adam moved to comply. Crispin swore at the state of his clothes.

"Never mind that," said Wynchecombe. "What about this body? Stabbed five, six times."

"Not just the back," said Crispin. "He was stabbed on the chest as well. Look here."

The sheriff bent over. A small jagged tear of the cloth at the collar, and a thin strand of blood were all that indicated a wound. "That?" Wynchecombe delicately pulled the cloth aside to examine the small puncture. "This did no damage."

Adam returned and set the basin and jug on the sideboard. Crispin tried to push up his sleeves with his forearms and hoped the servant would help him, but Adam refused to look in his direction. With a muttered curse, Crispin managed, and cleaned his hands and face with the water, soap cake, and towel. He brushed at his clothes with the towel and finally tossed the cloth aside.

He crouched beside the body. "Walcote was stabbed in the back first." He turned the corpse slightly, lifting him from the floor. "See. Most of the blood is here. Probably breathing his last when he hit the floor. Now look at his arms." He lifted the closest one and showed the palms and sleeves.

"Nothing," said the sheriff.

"Precisely. Nothing. If he struggled, his sleeves and palms would most assuredly be slashed and bloodied. He was in no fit state when the attacker came at him from the front."

"Then why this piss-poor stab to his chest?"

Crispin shook his head. "I don't know. The attacker saw no more use in continuing, perhaps. Or maybe he heard a sound." His finger hovered over an almost perfectly round patch of red on the floor beside the body. "See this spot?"

"Only more blood."

"This is a knee mark. The attacker kneeled here to deliver the last blow that never came."

Wynchecombe grunted. From appreciation or confusion Crispin could not tell.

"Well, Crispin. With so much evidence, do you suspect anyone?"

Crispin chuckled. "My Lord Sheriff, I did not come here with the intention of investigating a murder."

"Indeed," said the sheriff with renewed interest. "Why *did* you come here? And no more of your smart-arse remarks."

"That is private."

"Not when the Lord Sheriff asks."

"*Especially* when the Lord Sheriff asks."

The sheriff's gloved hand slammed Crispin's chest and drew him up. "Perhaps you didn't hear me clearly. I asked you why you were here."

Crispin leveled his gaze with Wynchecombe's. "I cannot tell you."

The sheriff released him and stepped back but his elbow jabbed Crispin's belly, bending him in two. Wynchecombe aimed a finger at him and between clenched teeth said, "The next time I ask you a question, I expect an answer."

Crispin waited for his breath to return. It seemed to take a long time. Once it did, he straightened and rubbed his stomach. William chuckled from his place by the door.

"My principles do not permit me to say," he rasped, "even though my client is now dead. It concerned a deeply personal matter."

Wynchecombe adjusted his gloves and glanced sidelong at Crispin. "Principles? When did you acquire those?" He smiled at Crispin's sneer. "Might any of your client's secrets have to do with this murder?"

Crispin took a deep breath and stared at the cold body of his client. "It might have. And I promise to alert you if it should take such a turn."

"You're going to investigate?"

"Do you have any objections?"

"Do I have a choice?"

Crispin grinned but said nothing.

"Then I give my permission." Wynchecombe swung his gaze one last time across the room, toward the locked window and the body getting colder on the floor, before he sauntered toward the doorway. But instead of departing, the sheriff whirled and slammed Crispin hard against the wall, fists curled around the breast of Crispin's coat. With his shoulder blade jammed uncomfortably into the plaster, Crispin winced up into the sheriff's hardened eyes.

"I'll give you a day to fully inform me of your role in these matters, Guest. I think a full day is more consideration than you deserve." His gaze made the circuit of Crispin's face before he released him with a snort. Crispin sagged, pulling the hem of his cotehardie in a fruitless attempt to smooth the wrinkles. Without another glance, Wynchecombe passed through the doorway with William at his heels. The sheriff's man cast a long, mocking sneer in Crispin's direction before succumbing to the corridor's shadows.

Feeling his cheeks warm from shame, Crispin grabbed his belt and squeezed, hooking his thumbs under the leather. It was better than punching the wall. His cheeks flamed all the more when he heard the shuffling step of Adam behind him. Damn Wynchecombe! Did he have to trample Crispin's dignity in front of servants? How was he to ask questions of this man and expect truthful answers if he cannot garner respect?

He turned on his heel and glared at Adam, hoping by the force of his will to gain back control of the situation.

But Adam wasn't paying him any attention. His face was as pale as the sheet he was laying over the body of his master.

Crispin relaxed his wounded pride and took a steadying breath.

He studied the area again, letting his eye sweep from point to point. The only possibilities of entrance or egress were the fireplace, the window, and the locked door that now lay in splinters on the floor. The window was untouched and the chimney was too narrow. That left the door. He went to it and knelt at what remained of the latch on the doorway. He ran his hand over it, hoping to find a string or other device to pull the bolt from the other side, but found nothing. He glanced at Adam before he sauntered toward the window and tested the casement again. He tugged on it, but it did not budge.

Adam stood by, his face growing darker the more Crispin touched the objects in the room. Crispin reached above the window and examined the stone frame. "How long have you been a servant in your master's household?" he cast over his shoulder.

Adam stared at the body and shook his head. "Five years."

"Did you like him?"

Adam said nothing before he abruptly pivoted toward Crispin. He scowled. "What is your meaning?"

Crispin lowered his hand and stood stiffly before the window. "Nothing. What of Mistress Walcote? How long were they married?"

"Three years."

"Did they have rows?"

"Everyone has rows."

"Were they like 'everyone's'?"

Adam rubbed the back of his neck. He glanced again at the body. "I don't know. They were loud."

"Often?"

He shrugged. "Not too often."

"What did they argue about?"

Adam narrowed his eyes. The servant's long nose was turned up at the end like an afterthought. "You are not the sheriff. So why do you ask?"

"I'm a curious fellow. Crime intrigues me. I don't like people getting away with murder. No matter who they are."

"I don't like your implication."

"You are not required to like it."

Adam postured, his fists clenched. He considered Crispin's shabby garb again and the absence of a sword. "Well then?"

"I asked what they argued about."

"I don't know. But I also saw how the mistress and master are— *were* with each other. I never saw a more devoted wife. And she took his abuse, right enough."

"A husband is master in his household."

"Even a master can go too far."

"Did he?"

Adam clenched his jaw and strode to the washbasin. He meticulously wrapped the soap cake in the towel and placed it in the bottom of the basin. "I'll say nothing more until I talk to my mistress." He got halfway over the threshold when he stopped. "If that will be all, I have duties to attend to."

Before Crispin could reply, Adam headed out across the gallery.

"I'll let myself out," Crispin said to the empty room.

CRISPIN WALKED WITH HEAD down into a wet wind that flapped his hood. The chilled air howled through the narrow passage between the two-story shops and apartments, and carried the smell of rain but could not seem to entirely wash away the acrid odor of London's dim streets and trickling gutters.

He hunched further into his cloak with his shoulders nearly up to his ears.

Heading north, he passed St. Paul's, its high, stone walls and spires jutting up into the weak sunshine. The bells suddenly rang out Sext and he cocked an eye back at the bell tower, little believing it was already midday. A growl in his belly reaffirmed this, and as he tread up Paternoster Row, he thought he might stop off at a pie seller on Newgate Market on his way back to the Shambles before its smells of butchering put him off his hunger entirely.

When he reached the corner where Newgate Market became the Shambles, he met a seller with a cart of roasted meat on sticks. Crispin paid his farthing and sniffed at the sour meat. Beggars can't be choosers. He tore the chewy flesh with his teeth while he walked, trying not to think of what animal the meat might have been when alive. It wasn't much and he finished it quickly as he approached the first butcher stalls, tossing the stick into a gutter already running with the days gore.

A house with a stone foundation and an open doorway revealed Dickon, one of the many butchers along this row. His apron was bloody and his face flushed. He was a big man, suited to the task of hauling carcasses about. "Ho, Crispin!" called the man congenially. Crispin raised his hand in answer but did not reply. The fact that he was acquaintances with butchers and tavernkeepers always put him in a sour mood, and even the friendliness of such associates could not assuage that.

He inhaled the cold, hoping that the thickness of the autumn air could stifle the smell. Not so. As he walked deeper into the Shambles, the stench of death and offal and the coppery scent of blood permeated the stones and timbers of the tightly clustered buildings leaning into the streets. Beef carcasses, stripped of their skin, hung in stalls. Farther down the row were the poulterer's stalls. Flightless bodies of birds, their wings frozen outward to mock their captive state, hung beside the glassy-eyed corpses of rabbits and suckling pigs. Crispin ignored the cries of the merchants, the thud of cleavers cutting through bone, the clatter of chickens in stick cages. His only thoughts were of home, or what at least constituted the place he slept and ate.

The tinker shop stood wedged between a butcher and a poulterer. It was a small house. The timbers had aged to gray long ago and the daub between was colored a dull and flaking buff. The ground floor boasted one door and one window that folded down into a stall. Above that was the jutted first floor, easing meekly over the ground floor, cradling an iron kettle that hung on a rod, announcing to all and sundry that this was a tinker shop. Though the second level seemed bigger, the inside was cut in half by a wall, one side being Crispin's entire lodgings, and the other the bedchamber of the tinker and his wife. Though it was not usual to have a tinker situated on the Shambles, it was good business sense on Master Kemp's part. For there was profitable industry in repairing pots for melting tallow and for making hooks.

A narrow stairway led upward to Crispin's first-floor room. The rickety stairs were the only thing separating the tinker shop from the butcher's house beside it. And though it was always dark in the shadow of the neighboring structure, at least it was a private entrance. It was one of the reasons Crispin chose to live there. That, and the rent was cheap.

He plodded to the tinker shopfront and encountered his landlord's plump wife, sweeping off the beaded rain from the unfolded counter. When Alice Kemp spied him withdrawing his key, she placed a pink fist into her ample hip and leaned on the broom. "Well now. If it isn't our lodger. The one who forgets when the rent is due."

Crispin sighed. One day Alice would be found murdered, and no one, including himself, would look too hard for the culprit. "I am aware of how late I am, Madam. Here, then." He reached into the purse hanging from his belt and took out the last of his coins and placed them into Alice's damp, open palm. She closed her fingers over them and popped them into her scrip.

"I should charge you more for that boy that calls himself your servant."

Crispin did not look back while he trudged up the dim stairway. "I do not see why. He is rarely here."

"All the same," she shouted after him, voice like ice. "It's not proper for Master Kemp and me to go uncompensated. Mark me. I shall talk with my husband about it!"

"No doubt," he grumbled, and put the key to the lock, but before it kissed the metal she shouted again.

"I let that woman into your room. She claimed she was a client." She hurled the last shrill words with disdain. "She had better be, Master Guest."

Crispin grabbed his dagger's hilt in frustration. Did she need to shout her insults across the entire lane? He positioned himself before the door as if to block the sound from the client within, but of course it was far too late. Everyone on the Shambles surely heard her mocking voice. How could they not?

He looked down and realized his hand was still on his dagger hilt. How dearly he wanted to use it on Mistress Kemp! He took a deep breath and dropped his hand away, staring at the closed door. How much had Mistress Walcote heard? His dignity seemed to be a rare commodity these days. And what did it matter in the long run? His personal honor could be measured by the number of coins in his purse. With a weak laugh, he realized that purse was presently empty. He shook his head at the irony. The entire situation was disquieting. The one who hired him was now dead, half a day's wage still wanting. And now the wife he was hired to follow wanted his services. For what? It did not feel right working for the wife under these circumstances. But coin was coin.

He opened the door.

3

PHILIPPA TURNED WHEN CRISPIN entered. Poor he may be, but at least he had a servant to keep his meager room as spotless as he could, even though young Jack Tucker often made himself too scarce to be useful. But today, the floor showed no signs of dirt, and the dust was wiped from the few surfaces of shelf and sill. Even the hearth was clean. A small peat fire threw a ripple of gold across the floor, the only gold that room would likely ever see.

The room itself was small, smaller than even the pavilion tents he used to occupy when he marched to war under the old king's banner. One shuttered window overlooked the Shambles and a chipped jug with wine sat on the sill of another window on the opposite wall. It opened to reveal a view of the tinker's courtyard and the many rooftops of London's streets beyond.

The head of a small pallet bed was situated against the common wall he shared with his landlord Martin Kemp and his wife. On the other side of the hearth in a corner lay a pile of straw where Jack slept, presently unoccupied. A bucket of water sat by the wooden chest near the door. Above that was a shelf of meager foodstuffs—a half-eaten loaf of bread under a cloth, a wedge of cheese, two bowls, and a razor. Nailed to the exposed timber above that was a small brass mirror. A worn table with a wobbly leg took up the space in the middle of the room where a tallow candle on a disk of tin offered its weak light. A chair with arms and a back, and a stool tucked beneath the table, served as both his dining hall and place of business.

These meager sticks of furniture were rented along with the room. Crispin owned only the scant bits of clothing and writing tools lying in the plain wooden chest.

He peeled off his damp cloak and hung it on a peg by the door. Pushing back the hood off his head, he bowed slightly to her. "You made mention you wished to hire me. In what capacity?"

She pouted. Her lips were as red as her velvet gown, and his former sourness was forgotten amid lips and gown and sinewy woman. They reminded him that he still carried the miniature painting of her in his purse. He thought of mentioning it and handing it over, but that was as far as he got.

"How lost does something have to be for you to find it?"

The room's dim light illuminated only a stripe across her face, revealing heavily draped lids. Her eyes hid beneath thick lashes, unwilling to reveal all. Slanted and sleepy seemed to be their natural posture.

He measured them through the ribboning black smoke of the candle on the table. "You'd be surprised at the things I've found," he said. "Perhaps even mortified."

She exhaled through her nostrils, blowing the candle smoke toward him horizontally for a moment before the smoke spiraled upward again. "You'd be surprised at the things *I've* seen," she countered. "Perhaps . . . even mortified."

He allowed himself a smile. "I know little about you or your husband—*requiescat in pace*," he said, crossing himself. "What happens behind closed doors does not interest me."

"It should." She strode to the table and leaned her thigh against it. "Kingdoms are bought and sold behind closed doors."

"I own no kingdoms."

"To be sure." She perused the room with mild distaste. "If you are so successful at your profession, then why such poor lodgings? I've seen stables that are better furnished."

His smile faded. "If you do not wish to hire me then don't waste my time."

She waved her left hand. The gold band gleamed insolently in the candlelight. "I merely asked because I do not trust easily."

"Indeed. Then why are you here? Alone."

She turned to look him in the eye. "I trust myself."

He lowered his face. That was more than he could say for himself. He remembered how she looked with her impatient lover. His face grew hot with the memory. "You must trust someone if you are to get the help you say you need." He moved away, putting the table between them. "I have no proof of my deeds except by the word of others. I am not a man to parade my triumphs about my person."

She made a slow measure of him again. She did not smile, but her guarded posture eventually softened. Even weakened. She bit her bottom lip and turned from him. No longer did she wear the expression of the grand lady of the manor, but that of a frightened girl.

"There is something dangerous, something strange hidden in my house," she said in her throaty voice. "I believe it is why my husband was killed. I want you to find it and dispose of it."

He frowned. "Why have you not told the sheriff about this?"

She laughed without pleasure. "I reckon I'm a good judge of character, Master Crispin. And of cunning. Of the two, my choice was you."

He was also a good judge of character, at least he liked to think so. And a good judge of intonation. He again noticed that her accent somehow did not match her status. Her cultivated speech seemed too careful. "There's no need to be melodramatic," he said and crossed the room, took up the iron poker, and jabbed it into the ashes and embers. No fire emerged. He broke some sticks and placed them on the radiant coals, blowing on them to catch a flame. When they did, he poked the small fire to give himself time to think.

She moved slowly toward the hearth, each sinuous step rustling the generous fabric of her gown. "You don't know. You can't imagine. They killed poor Nicholas. I wish it had never been brought into my house." She hugged herself even though the fire now burned warmly.

He walked to the back window and closed the shutter. It did not close all the way, and the wind whistled through the open crack. He moved back toward the fire. "They? Who killed him? Your lover?"

"I have no lover."

He shook his head and crossed his arms over his chest. "Are we to play this game again? Very well. Then I will checkmate you. I saw the two of you together at the Thistle. In the room." He raised his brows meaningfully. "I saw what transpired. Must I go on?"

Her expression did not change except to cool. "I have taken the time, Master Guest, to visit these . . . lodgings. And I have precious little time to give."

"You would protect a murderer?"

She turned her face away and he stared instead at a soft cheek and a braid looped over a pink ear. "I protect no one but my husband. Now he is beyond my protection." She whirled. "What good would it do anyone to kill Nicholas?"

"Why Madam, then your lover could have you for himself."

She shook her head. "Nonsense. He don't want—" She pressed her lips closed. This time one edge of her mouth turned up in a smile.

"Then I have another question," he said, monitoring her reactions. "Did *you* kill him?"

The smile vanished. "No!"

He moved nearer. Her expression remained cool. She seemed aware of his closeness, and like a feral animal, attuned herself to it. One shoulder rose and she tucked her chin down. She looked up at him through a veil of lashes. He detected the faint, sweet scent of elderflowers and found himself leaning closer.

She blinked, slow and even. Her gaze seized him, as if drawing him into a secret she was not yet willing to reveal. He could not help but lose himself in those lustrous eyes.

"I know I can trust you," she rasped. Could those lips truly go unkissed by other men? He tried to imagine what her lips tasted like, how they felt. Were they soft and pliant, or merely flat and moist? He found he wanted to know. He wanted to taste them, to bite them, to feel them like petals running down his flesh. He wondered if she felt the same for him—and then with a jolt he reminded himself of her husband.

He retreated deliberately.

She took a deep breath and the neckline of her gown rose and lowered. Her face grew somber. "What I am about to say, well. It is plainly unbelievable. But you must believe it. If you don't, then I might as well leave now."

"How can I promise before I hear?"

Her eyes searched his. They seemed to drag him forward and shake him, willing him to listen. "Do you believe in the power of holy relics?"

He ran his hand over the back of his neck to wipe away the sweat. "I may have had a run-in or two with relics." He nodded. "But I do not know whether I believe in their power or not."

"But you must believe in this. Have you ever heard of the veronica?"

"Do you speak of Veronica's Veil?"

"Aye. But there are supposed to be many veronicas. They take the words from the Latin and Greek, *vera icona*. It means—"

"True Image," he finished. "Yes, Madam. I know my languages."

She nodded. "There is one veronica's veil that our Lord encountered while on his way to the cross. The woman Veronica offered her veil to wipe our Lord's face, and his image was miraculously imprinted upon it. The other was the shroud from his tomb. But there were others that came before."

"I never heard of these."

"Few have."

"How do *you* know of them?"

"May I sit?"

He motioned her to take the only chair. He sat on the edge of the chest.

Methodically, she folded her hands on her lap. She took her time as if she were recounting exactly how to sit and how to place her hands. Finally she raised her head. "Six months ago Nicholas returned from a long journey on the continent. When he returned, he was a changed man. Nervous. Afraid. Oh, I know what they say. He never leaves the house except to travel. He was always cautious of strangers. But this was different. *He* was different. I begged him to tell me what vexed him but he would not. Soon he had locks affixed to every door, and me and Adam Becton were given the only other keys and told to lock the doors after going through each of them."

"Adam Becton? The steward?"

"Aye. You met him."

He frowned. "Yes. Becton. Go on."

"There isn't much more to tell. Nicholas told me about this Mandyllon, that's what he called it, and that he kept it in the house. I want it gone."

"But why should you fear such a thing? Surely your husband was duped into believing it was authentic. There is much traffic in so-called relics—"

She shook her head. "No. It is authentic. And it is dangerous."

"In what way?"

"It does things to people."

"What sort of 'things'?"

"Please! Can't you find it and rid me of it? I will pay you." She rose and fumbled at her scrip. Crispin watched dispassionately while she spilled a handful of coins on the table, more money than he had seen for a long time. She raised the coins in her cupped hands and thrust them toward him. "Take them! And I will no longer be cursed!" He said nothing and her face became fierce. "You need it, I have it. Take it and do as you are bid! Are you so rich that you would refuse a Walcote?"

The words stung that sore place on Crispin's pride. He lunged forward and grabbed her wrist. The coins jangled and hit the table, some spinning across the floor. He tightened his grip. "I work for myself. I do what I like, when I like. And I need not abide a lying, adulterous serpent of a woman filling my head with straw and nonsense about cursed relics. I care not how wealthy you are. You reek of blood. It could be mine next."

Fear changed her expression to something wild and distant. She stared at his whitened fingers wrapped around her wrist. "You are hurting my arm," she said.

He chuffed his displeasure and threw her hand aside. "Our business is over. Take your coins and be gone."

She blinked hard in succession. Her red lips grew darker when she mashed them together. "You won't help me?"

"Why should I? You come to me with a ridiculous story to hide your own wantonness. I do not wish to waste my time. Good day."

"I cannot go to the sheriff."

"That is not my affair. Good day, Madam."

She raised her chin and gathered the coins. He helped her find those on the floor and dropped them smartly into her open scrip. She said nothing more and strode in harsh steps to the door, yanked it open, and stomped through.

Crispin stood for a moment looking at the open doorway.

"I'm hungry," he decided.

HE SAT BY THE fire in the Thistle and stared up the staircase to the door of Philippa Walcote's most recent tryst. The thick broth he ordered tasted savory, its flavors melting on his tongue, but he found no pleasure in it when considering the possible identity of her dark paramour. With a hunk of brown bread, he sopped the rest of the pottage out of the bowl and looked up from his meal with a belch before he spied a familiar face that had obviously not yet noticed him.

A ginger-haired boy threaded through the crowd, squeezing through with apologies on his lips. Unseen by the patrons, his hand with the small knife slipped down and up, neatly slicing purse from belt on one man after another without detection. It was something quite amazing to behold and Crispin couldn't help admiring the boy's skill even as he grew more annoyed with him. The boy zigzagged quickly through the throng and slipped outside.

Crispin followed hard on his heels, came up behind him, and nabbed his hood. "Jack Tucker."

Jack spun. "*Master!* What are *you* doing here?"

"Working. And so are you, I see."

"W-what? Me?" He tried to hide his hands as if their mere presence made him guilty. "I gave up me thieving ways when you rescued me from the sheriff, remember? All I want in this life is to serve you."

"And I told you I don't want a servant."

"Now, Master Crispin. A man like you ought to have a servant."

"If you would have it so, then why aren't you at home?"

"Well, I just stepped out for a breath of air, didn't I."

"You're a bit far from the Shambles."

Jack smiled. It lifted his entire countenance into an act of revelry with its blunt nose, ginger hair, and array of freckles speckling his cheeks and forehead. "The air's better over here," he said.

"Let's have it." Crispin opened his hand.

Jack tugged uncomfortably on his tunic. "Now Master. I'm hurt, I am. That you should doubt me when I said I'd given it up."

Crispin thrust his hand down the open laces of Jack's tunic and pulled out the money pouches. Three in all. "And how did you come by these?"

Jack pressed his lips together and looked at the ground. "It's a very hard habit to break, sir. And I know you've been low on funds. I was just trying to help."

Crispin laid his hand on Jack's shoulder. The boy winced at first, but relaxed under Crispin's gentle tone. "I do not need this kind of help, Jack. You know my stance on this. You are the one who insists on being my servant, not I. If you truly wish to be worthy, then I suggest you return these to their owners. Now."

"But Master—"

"*Now*, Jack. I will watch."

Crispin handed back the pouches, crossed his arms over his chest, and raised his brows expectantly. Jack withered under his gaze. "Ah now. *All* of them?"

Crispin's frown deepened. "And be careful about it, boy. If they notice you and mistake your purpose, you'll surely hang, and I won't be able to save your neck a second time."

Grumbling, Jack moved back into the inn followed by Crispin. The boy slipped through the crowd and handed each pouch back to its rightful owner, explaining how he'd found them on the floor. The men thanked him and suspiciously tucked them away in their coats, except the last man. He withdrew a farthing and handed it to Jack, thanking him for his honesty.

Jack returned and showed Crispin the coin. "Now look at that! For my honesty. The Lord does forgive!"

"Yes. And you'll repay Him by dropping that in the alms basket next Sunday."

"But Master! What good is an honest living if you can't keep a day's wage?"

Crispin hid his smile by turning away. A day's wage. How hard it was to earn one honestly. He could almost sympathize with Jack. He stared at the boy in all his bland simplicity; a boy who wanted to become what Crispin once was to his former lord John of Gaunt, duke of Lancaster. Crispin, too, had followed his lord about, seeking encouragement and flattering words. He had worked hard in Lancaster's service, though not for a wage, for Crispin had been wealthy enough on his own, being Baron of Sheen. But after Crispin's disgrace eight years ago, Lancaster did not welcome Crispin's company. Yet there was a time when they had been so close. Like father and son. Yet even father and son can have a falling out. Crispin only wished it hadn't involved treason.

Treason. He was the only man he knew who had been found guilty of it and yet lived. By all rights, his body should have been strung up at Smithfield, his entrails dangling from a battered corpse, dead eyes plucked out by ravens. But it was Lancaster who had begged the king. Though he could not save Crispin's knighthood or his title, he had at least saved his life.

He sighed. Ancient history. Best forgotten.

Jack was no page to Crispin's lord. There would be no lands to inherit for him, no battalions to lead in war. Crispin did not even pay the lad, but instead compensated him for his time and his company in food and lodgings, and those were poor wages indeed. In many ways, he envied Jack Tucker his blissful ignorance.

Crispin well remembered the day he had caught Jack stealing Crispin's meager purse. On that day several months ago now, the boy had been more animal than man. Eleven years old, possibly twelve, Jack was dirty with mud and lice. An orphan, a street beggar, and thief. Bound for the gallows, Crispin had rescued him from Sheriff Wynchecombe's clutches only to be rewarded by the boy's unexpected and unflagging devotion. One day he found the boy in his lodgings cleaning the place and the next thing he knew the knave had moved in. An opportunist, was young Jack.

Crispin turned from the boy's concentrated gaze and looked back at the inn's hall with its revelers and quiet sorts drinking at their places, stuffing their mouths with food.

Philippa's lover was lodged here. The more he thought about him the tighter the knot in his neck became. Who was he? Did she harbor a murderer? He could call in the sheriff, but the thought left a sour taste in his mouth. He couldn't merely forget it or leave it to the sheriff, especially when his client was killed right under his nose.

That was bad for business.

He pushed his way deeper into the room, searching for the innkeeper. Jack scrambled to keep up with him. "What are we doing, Master?"

Crispin jabbed his finger at Jack's nose in warning. "*You* are being quiet." He hailed the innkeeper.

The innkeeper's plain face resembled a hound's with its long features and jowls. His oversized hands hung from hairy forearms. "Aye, good Master. What can I do for you?"

"I would know who is staying in the room at the top of the stairs," said Crispin. "I think it is an old friend of mine. Dark hair, ruddy complexion . . ."

The innkeeper glanced up the stairs and turned a perplexed expression back on Crispin. "But Master, there is no one staying in that room."

"Nonsense, man. I just saw him there not too long ago."

"Good Master," he said with a chuckle. "Someone plays a jest on you. There is no one in that room, today or yesterday."

"Well now," said Crispin good-naturedly. "A jest. That must be it. What a fool I've been, eh?"

"Not at all, not at all. And you are a good fellow to take it so well. Is there anything else?"

"No, thank you. I've had my wine."

The innkeeper left and Crispin's smile quickly fell away.

"What's that all about?" Jack whispered.

"Jack, I have a task for you. Go up the stairs to that room and go inside."

Jack blanched. "What? Me?"

Crispin sat at a vacant table and toyed with an empty wine bowl. "Yes. You. You're so anxious to commit larceny, I thought you would jump at the chance."

Jack looked up the stairs and then back at Crispin. He sat beside him on the bench. "What am I supposed to do once I'm in there?"

Crispin smiled a lopsided grin. "The innkeeper is lying. He's let the room to a lodger. I want you to steal his scrip."

"Master! After what you just gone and told me! For shame on you. That's not an honest living, now is it?"

Crispin curled his arm around Jack's shoulders and leaned in. "We're not stealing it for the money, Jack," he said in conspiratorial tones, "but for any information it may contain on the man. Got it?"

Jack sighed and rubbed his nose. "What if it ain't there? What if he's got it with him?"

"Then we'll wait till he returns."

"What if he's there now?"

"You're the thief. Reason it out."

Jack thought a moment, then nodded decidedly. "Right, then!" He leaped to his feet and stomped up the stairs. At the top of the shadowed stairway, he looked both ways down the dim gallery and gently tugged the door ring. When it did not budge, he looked again down the gallery of closed doors, knelt, and worked at the lock until he sprang it.

Crispin glanced to either side of him. No one seemed to notice the boy's covert activity hidden by the gloom and smoke of the gallery above.

Jack winked down at Crispin, gently pulled the door, and looked inside. He raised his thumb to Crispin and, like a shadow, slipped inside, pulling the door closed behind him.

Crispin settled himself and spun the empty bowl to pass the time. He glanced up the stairs now and again. Time dragged. A man with a bagpipe struck up a lively tune. A few men drummed their hands on the table to follow the rhythm. When the piper finished, they tossed him some coins.

Crispin lifted the bowl, forgetting it was empty. With a snort he put it down again and looked up the stairs. At last the door opened and Jack's head appeared. He shut the door softly behind him and took the stairs two at a time and flopped down on the bench beside Crispin.

"Well?"

"Got it!" Jack reached under his shirt and pulled out the scrip.

Crispin snatched it and opened the flap. He pulled out several papers and smoothed them out on the table and stared at the writing.

"What does it say?" Jack whispered, peering over Crispin's arm.

Crispin shook his head. "I don't know. It is close to Latin, but it is not Latin." He ran his finger along the scrawl. "I suspect this is Italian. But I cannot read much of it." The man did not look Italian to him. He looked like a Saracen from the desert countries. It's possible he was a merchant who traveled through the Mediterranean. That would account for the Italian papers. But why would Philippa Walcote take up with a Saracen? Such activities were more than immoral; they were against Church law.

He sat in thought for a moment before he folded the papers again and stuffed them into the scrip. "You'd better take this back now."

"Take it back? But Master—"

"And Jack, put back the coins you took from it."

Jack heaved a bitter sigh and with deadly slow fingers, pulled the coins from the folds of his shoulder cape and slammed them back in the scrip.

"Hurry, now," said Crispin, resting his elbows on the table.

With heavy steps, Jack returned up the stairs and disappeared inside the room. No sooner had the door closed than the inn's door opened with a whoosh of autumn air and crackling leaves swirling in small eddies and collecting in the corners. Ordinarily, such an event would not cause Crispin to take much note of it. But in this instance, he turned and squinted at the man who entered. The man wore a long, dark cloak with a pointed hood. The door shut behind him, blowing the hood low over the man's face. The capering light from the hearth painted the edges of the cloak in a fiery outline and dropped any clue to his features in impenetrable shadows.

Crispin had only snatched a glimpse of the man's face before it disappeared again, but he thought he recognized the man as Philippa's paramour.

Crispin darted a glance up the stairs to the room in which Jack was now trapped.

The man made a cursory sweep of the room—only revealing a shadowy vision of his features—and stomped purposefully toward the stairs, cloak rippling.

Crispin stood. "Jack," he mouthed. What could he do for a distraction? Call to the man? But what? Who was he?

No time to think. The man reached the bottom step and rose up the first tread.

Crispin moved quickly around the table, jabbing his thigh on the corner of the wood. He strode quickly toward the man, but the cloaked figure was at the top of the stairs in a heartbeat. Jack would come out of that door at any moment and be caught. Crispin grabbed for the sword that no longer hung at his side. "God's blood!" His hand went for his dagger instead and he rushed up the first three steps.

"Oi, Master!" said Jack behind him.

Crispin spun, nearly toppling down the stairs. "What the devil are you doing *there*?" Heart racing, blood rushing through his ears, he stared at the smiling boy.

Jack shrugged, still smiling. "I heard someone on the stairs and thought it was our man. So I hightailed it out the window."

Crispin breathed again and grinned. He mussed the boy's already disarrayed curls. Jack ducked away from his touch. "You did well, Jack." Crispin glanced up the stairs. The man had disappeared into his room. The door was shut again. Crispin didn't feel like confronting the man this instant. There was time. Crispin gave the tavern room a final perusal and signaled to Jack.

"WHAT'S THE TASK?" THE boy asked, walking beside Crispin into the street, arms swinging.

Crispin sniffed the cold, damp air. It smelled like the mold at the back of a privy. "Adultery. But I suppose it is now murder."

"Christ Jesus."

"A man hired me to discover if his wife was unfaithful. She was. The next day he's found murdered."

"'Slud! She did it, then!"

"Possibly. But not without help. This morning I saw her in the same gown as the night before. She would have had to divest herself of her gown, killed him, and changed back into it."

"Why, Master?"

"Because I saw a bloody knee print on the floor. It should have been evidenced on her gown."

"Her lover, then?" He thumbed back over his shoulder toward the Thistle, now out of sight around a bend. "He did it."

"Perhaps. The trouble is, her husband was murdered in a room where the door locked from the inside with no other way in or out."

"Blind me! That's a puzzle."

"Indeed."

"Who's the dead man?"

"Nicholas Walcote."

"Not the merchant? 'Slud!" Jack shook his head. His face slowly changed from shock to an expression of pride. "Are you going to find his murderer?"

"I do not like being cheated out of a client. Especially a wealthy one."

After a quarter of an hour they reached the Walcote gatehouse and Jack whistled at the size of the walls and the number of chimney stacks. Upon recognizing him, the porter let Crispin pass through the gatehouse, though he gave Jack a sour eye.

Instead of going directly to the front door, Crispin made a circlet of the outside of the manor, gazing up its encircling garden walls until he spotted the upper-floor window of the solar. Even after walking the length of the enclosure he still found no entrance. He inspected the vines that clung to the wall and experimentally pulled on them, hanging with his full weight.

"Master," said Jack in a nervous whisper. "They've let you in the gate. Why are you trying to break in?"

"I wish to inspect that window," he said, jerking his head upward. He grasped the vines, pushed himself off from the mud, and climbed. Some of the vines were stronger than others. The lesser stems broke off in his hand or snapped under foot, pelting Jack who was climbing directly behind him. With a grunt Crispin reached the top of the wall with his fingers and touched wet granite. He peered over the edge, slid his body out along the top, and jumped heavily to the other side.

Jack fell with a thud beside him, looking unhappy and a little in pain.

"Are you well?" Crispin asked.

Jack got to his feet and rubbed his backside. "Aye. A little worse for wear is all. Garden walls ain't my specialty."

"If I find a purse to cut I'll let you know."

Crispin glanced about the little garden with its short hedges trimmed down to perfect box shapes and other shrubs cut into ornate cones and spirals. The rest lay dead under an early autumn frost. A few fruit trees divested of leaves lined a far wall. A willow stood near the house, draping its long branches like a maiden's hair toward a gravel path.

The earlier mist turned to icy drizzle but Crispin did not put up his hood. Instead, he craned his neck to peer at the window, one of three along the face of the damp stone. Tall, arched, the windows' carved stone sills were dented with ridges and floral carvings.

"Give us a boost, Jack."

Jack looked at him sideways. He was shorter than Crispin by almost two feet and slight of build. Crispin shrugged and climbed as far as he could up the jutting plinth foundation on his own. He examined the stone sill and the wall below the window, running his fingertips along the stone. He could not reach above the arched window, but he looked along the upper perimeter. He could see no telltale scratches, no ropes, no ladders, and no broken tiles from the roof.

Jumping back down to the gravel path, he stared at the window and the one beside it some four feet away. A third window stood only three feet from the solar window. He looked from one to the other and back again.

Jack patted his arms and stamped the ground to keep warm. He blinked away the raindrops though one dangled from the tip of his blunt, reddened nose and seemed to freeze there. "Master, are we done here?"

Crispin studied first the wall and then the windows again without moving.

"Master, we're getting wet. And it's cold."

When he turned at last to Jack, the boy's pleas finally registered. "Of course. Let us go to the house."

Crispin climbed up the wall again. Straddling it, he leaned down, grabbed Jack's arm, and hoisted him over. Together they walked in the drizzle to the front entrance.

Jack's earlier revelry fell subdued under the specter of the enormous entry. "Shouldn't we be going round to the kitchen door?" He peered anxiously at the dark windows.

"No, Jack. We are front-door guests today." Though when he heard the bolt thrown back, Crispin belatedly realized how muddy his foray into the garden made him. He brushed off as much as he could before Adam opened the door.

"I would talk to you, Adam," said Crispin, pushing forward.

Adam tried to close the door on him, but Crispin used his weight to wedge himself forward. He slammed Adam against the wall. "We could do this the easy way or the hard way. Which is it?"

Adam's jaw tightened. "What do you want?" he said between clenched teeth.

Crispin released him and brushed off the man's coat. "Now that's not a very civil attitude. I merely come to seek answers to why your master was killed. Don't you wish to help in this matter?"

Adam pushed Crispin's hands aside. "Aye. I would see justice served."

Crispin measured his brooding countenance. "You told me you served in this household five years. What happened to the previous steward?"

Adam looked once at Jack and then dismissed him. "I don't know. I think he was transferred to my master's estates in the north."

"Is that where you are from?"

"Aye. Though not from his household. I received a missive that I was to be his new steward in London, so I journeyed here and presented the steward with documents from my master stating that I should replace him. And shortly thereafter, I replaced all the servants."

"Replaced all the servants? Why?"

"Because my master wished it. Who knows why the rich do what they do."

"You appear rather insubordinate to me, Becton. You speak of your betters this way?"

"It is no secret about the wealthy. They are all of the same ilk. Doesn't matter where they come from. They all end up the same."

"You did not love your master?"

Adam looked down. "It isn't proper to speak ill of the dead."

"But confidentially, you could do so to me."

Adam snapped up his chin. "And why should I care to do that? You aren't the sheriff."

"Sheriff Wynchecombe and I often work in concert. You would do well to speak to me. *His* interrogations usually involve white hot irons."

Adam's eyes rounded and his jaw slackened. "I do not need to be questioned by the sheriff," he said in a rush. "I've done nought."

"But there may be much you know. Why is it you disliked your master?"

"I didn't hold nought against him, Master Crispin. It's just—" Adam wrung his hands and moved haltingly into the shadows of the vestibule. He glared once at Jack. "He shouldn't have married her, that's all," he whispered.

"I thought you had nothing but admiration for your mistress."

"I do! I mean, I—"

The man's in love with her. Crispin frowned. "It's no good, Becton. She is your better. You must not gaze so high."

Adam broke into an unpleasant laugh. "'Gaze so high'? A jest! I need not gaze high at all."

Crispin took a step closer, hand poised near his dagger. "You'd best watch your tongue, Becton."

"I need watch nought," he said, teeth bared. "Philippa Walcote was the chambermaid for my master before he married her three years ago. She's no better than you or me."

4

ALL THE QUESTIONS ON Crispin's tongue slipped away.

Adam laughed. "Don't have a snappy reply for that, eh?"

.Before he could stop himself, Crispin swung. His knuckles met the flesh of Adam's cheek and the man buckled against the wall. He slid down halfway, but shook his head and unsteadily righted himself.

Adam rubbed his face and grumbled. Crispin couldn't think of anything more to ask. His mind felt numb and he didn't know why; didn't want to know.

He said nothing more and quickly left, massaging his sore knuckles.

Jack chased after, his shorter legs moving twice as fast to keep pace. "That was a right good clout, Master! Set him in his place, I'll warrant." He did his best imitation of Crispin's swing several times. "Master? Master? Did you find out what you needed to?"

Crispin scowled and said nothing. His memory echoed Adam's words: *Philippa Walcote was a chambermaid.*

He wandered down the gray streets toward the Fleet to Gutter Lane without noticing his surroundings or that Jack walked beside him. Even when he pushed through the doors of the Boar's Tusk and sat heavily in his customary corner, he never fully roused himself. He simply sat on the bench and stared at the knife-scarred wood and flinched when Eleanor slapped a bowl of wine in front of him.

"Crispin." She glanced at Jack who smiled in hopeful anticipation of a bowl of wine, and ignored him as usual.

Eleanor set down the leather jug and sat across the table. A white kerchief, neatly draped on her head and expertly tucked about her face, revealed nothing but her hazel eyes, light brows, and stern nose and cheeks, both slightly red from the cold. "What vexes you? You were miles away."

"Was I?" He drew up the bowl in his hands and drank nearly the whole thing.

Eleanor and her husband, Gilbert, were always ready to lend a kind ear. Yet what to say? Why did Adam's news affect him? How could this Walcote woman, this woman he barely knew, mean anything at all to him? He knew little of her, which forfeited any serious consideration.

And yet.

Crispin ran his hand over his forehead and up his scalp, raking his thick hair between his fingers. He glanced once at Jack. "There is nothing to speak of," said Crispin.

"Oh! I'll wager it's a woman!" cried Eleanor.

"Why do you always think it involves a woman?"

"Because nothing can bring out that melancholy look about you but a woman."

Crispin slouched and cradled the bowl in the curve of his arm. "Think what you like."

"Crispin," she said in her best conciliatory tone. "When have I ever left you alone to brood? Come now, out with it. You know it will make you feel better."

"It *never* makes me feel better. It only makes *you* feel better."

She leaned forward and rested her arms on the table, buttressing her ample bosom. "We worry so over you, Crispin. Thank God for Jack Tucker here," and she patted Jack's hand. He smiled grimly and pulled it out from under her attention. "At least someone is looking after you, but I'd rather it were a wife."

"Not this again. I tell you, woman, if you don't let me alone on this matter I will find another tavern to patronize."

"There's none on Gutter Lane that would let you maintain an account month after month like we do, and you know it. Besides, Gilbert and I are your family now. That's the only reason I bring up the subject of a wife time after time."

". . . after time," he muttered into his bowl. He wiped his mouth with the side of his hand and poured more wine. The ruby liquid drizzled into his cup. It swirled around the bowl and settled in diminutive waves. "The thing of it is . . ." He shook his head, amazed that she managed to drag the words out of him. Again. "I don't even know her. Not truly." He let the thought of Philippa ripple in his mind. The thought stayed longer than anticipated. "She's completely unsuitable. But she is intriguing."

"Is she a client?"

"Of a sort . . . no . . . maybe." He chuckled halfheartedly. "I don't know."

"I'm pleased that's settled."

"Truly, Nell, it does not bear discussing."

"Then why do you look so sad?"

"I'm not sad!"

Jack pressed forward. "You would not wonder if you saw the lady," he said, wincing under Crispin's sharp glance. He opened his hands in apology. "It is true. She is something to behold."

"When did you ever see her?" he asked.

"I've seen Madam Philippa Walcote before at market." He whistled and winked at Eleanor. "Rich *and* beautiful."

Crispin measured Jack before he sighed and slowly withdrew the portrait from his scrip and handed it to Eleanor.

"Oh, Crispin, she *is* fair. Is this a good likeness?"

"Yes."

"Where did you get it?"

"From her husband."

Aghast, Eleanor slowly lowered the picture to the table. "Crispin Guest!"

"It's not what you think—God's teeth! I don't know what you think! The husband is dead. He was murdered last night."

She crossed herself and handed back the miniature as if it were the dead man himself. "Bless me! Crispin! Not you?"

His look of disdain mollified her, but only briefly.

"Well you cannot expect a woman who has recently lost a husband to look your way," she said.

"That's not—" He exhaled a long, bitter sigh. "What does it matter?" He clutched the portrait for a moment before he tossed it across the table. It clattered faceup. Philippa's painted face gazed serenely toward the ceiling. "She is, after all, only a servant."

"Only a servant? They do not paint portraits of servants."

Jack made a grab for the jug, but Eleanor easily moved it from his reach. "She was a chambermaid in her master's household," Jack said in a loud whisper, looking back at Crispin. "And he married her! Now that's a right smart lass."

Eleanor nodded knowingly. "There's many a lass who betters herself by marrying the master. It happens more often than you think."

"Perhaps in the merchant class," Crispin mumbled. "But knights do not marry their servants."

Eleanor's kind demeanor darkened. "Oh, it's that again, is it?" She rose, her voice shrill. "It's not that she won't look twice at you; it's that you scorn her class!"

Gilbert arrived at that moment, a barrel-shaped man with dark eyes and brown hair. Crispin glanced at him hopefully while Eleanor postured over him like a Fury, her mouth flapping and her finger wagging.

Flustered, Gilbert frowned at his wife. "What's this? Wife, you're too loud."

"I am not loud enough!" she exclaimed, raising her voice. Some of the patrons turned, but those more used to this exchange slumped back over their cups and edged away.

Gilbert clutched her arm. "You will be still!" He looked at Crispin apologetically.

She shook him off. "I will not be still. This intolerable man, who has lived these eight years in this parish under our care and guidance, still cannot suffer the lower classes, even though he is now one of them."

"Now Eleanor," said Gilbert, lowering her to the bench beside him.

"He'll drink our wine and beg our advice," said Eleanor, "but when it comes to it, *he's* a lord and *we* are peasants, and he will not demean himself with our lowly selves."

Crispin set the cup aside. "Perhaps I should go."

"Now Crispin," said Gilbert, eyeing his wife. "There's no need for that. It takes getting used to," he said to her. "His state, I mean. Even after eight years. He's been a nobleman for far longer than that. It's in the blood."

They talked about Crispin as if he weren't sitting there. It didn't matter. Crispin could not tell whether he flushed more from embarrassment or anger. "It *is* in the blood," he said soberly.

Eleanor picked up the portrait and wagged it at Crispin. "If you have any love for this woman at all, nought should stand in your way. You're not a grand knight any longer. Who could speak ill of you if you sought some happiness? Even amongst the lower classes."

"*I never said I loved her!*" He stood, weaving slightly from the wine. He opened his mouth to speak but changed his mind and swatted the air in a futile gesture. Gilbert took the little portrait from his wife and eyed it with raised brows, but Jack snatched it from his hands when Crispin made no move toward it, stuffed it in his tunic, and scurried ahead to open the tavern door for him.

Crispin called himself a fool ten times over. He never thought of himself as a man who wore his heart on his sleeve. It's the drinking, that's what it was. It loosened his tongue, unmanned him. And in front of Eleanor! His face warmed with a blush. Never again! Philippa Walcote was only a client. A *client*! Nothing more. He didn't need these unnecessary complications in his life. Women. A dog was more satisfying companionship. At least they didn't talk.

He lumbered into the street and soon heard Jack's nimble steps behind. Crispin inhaled the sour odors of London's poorer streets, silently lamenting the lost days where he rode aloft a fine horse, far from the muddy gutters and ingrained poverty of the city's lower class. He used to throw them a few disks of silver in charity, but he never walked among them. And now walk he did.

He scowled the more he thought about his state but owed his temper to the wine and Eleanor's harangue more than a querulous disposition.

They walked silently for a time before Jack nudged him.

Crispin slowed and stopped. The boy held out the little portrait to him. Dammit! He thought he was rid of that.

Jack raised it higher, urging it on him.

Sullenly, Crispin snatched it. He slipped it between the buttons of his coat and felt it slip down his shirt and settle near his midsection where the belt stopped it.

"Where are we going, Master?"

Crispin didn't know. Distracted, that's what he was. And by a silly portrait? His neck flushed. "Tell me, Jack. Is it so wrong?"

"Marrying better, you mean?" he said, not understanding Crispin's question. "A servant marries a master. Their children marry better than they, and onward. Haven't you heard them minstrel songs?"

"But that obscures everything. The race is mongrelized. What point is there at all in being born noble?"

Jack scowled and rolled his shoulders uneasily. "'Mongrelized'? I ain't certain of your meaning." But by the scowl on his face Crispin guessed he was more certain than he let on. "But I see it all around us," Jack went on. "Look at the Lord Mayor. He is a grocer, after all. The one before him was a draper. Nobility don't sprout out of the ground like cabbages, do it? Where'd your family come from, eh?"

Crispin arched a brow. "My family was noble as far back as Adam and Eve."

"'Slud!" Jack lifted his nose mockingly and straightened his shoulders as if they wore ermine. "Course, that ain't the situation no more." He seemed to relish saying it, and Crispin resisted the urge to strike him. "But if you should marry well, say Walcote's widow, then you'd move up again."

Crispin's black mood deepened. "Marry in a class beneath me," he said, voice deadly, "in order to *advance*? You must be mad." He twisted. His cloak spun out around him like a raven's wing.

"The trouble with you—begging your pardon, Master—is that you can't forget yourself; your old self. You can't let yourself be who you are now."

"The only thing different about me is my status," he growled. "I am myself."

"That's your true image, right enough," Jack grumbled.

Crispin halted and Jack ran into him. Swiveling his head, he eyed Jack. "What did you say?"

Jack swallowed and raised his hands to ward off a blow. "Now Master, I don't mean nought. I was raised on these streets and I say what comes into me head. You live here now, and so I think of you as one of us, see. Course your manner and your skills say otherwise, don't they?"

"No. I mean, what did you say? Just now."

"Er . . . y-you said 'I am myself' and I said 'that's your true image, right enough.' But I didn't mean nought by it."

"What made you say 'true image'?"

Jack scratched his flat chin. "Dunno. It just popped out of me mouth."

Crispin's wine-dampened mind rolled the thoughts one over the other. True image. So many "true images" from so many false ones. "I've been distracted." He chuckled, though it came from no place near good humor. "A pretty face will do that. I've been acting like a child." He looked at Jack's eager expression, sometimes as wily as Robin Goodfellow, sometimes as frightened as an infant. "There is a cloth I am supposed to find and it very well may have to do with murder. Let this 'true self' concentrate on that."

INSTEAD OF ENTERING THROUGH the Walcote front door, Crispin and Jack walked around to the servant's entrance situated in a dingy alley smelling of moldy vegetables and rotting bones from past feasts. An old woman with matted hair under a stained kerchief was just opening the door and looked up at Crispin. Her etched features were accentuated by grime and bore a strong resemblance to a castle's stony exterior.

"And who might you be?" She glared at Crispin but aimed an eye at Jack, hiding behind Crispin's left flank. "This is the Walcote kitchens. It ain't Westminster Palace where all come and go as they like." Several of her front teeth were missing and those that remained were black or gray. She brandished a long cooking fork that Crispin didn't like the look of.

"I am Crispin Guest, woman. I am here investigating the heinous crime of your master's murder."

She gave his clothes a quick scrutiny. "You?"

"Bless my soul! Friend Crispin!" John Hoode rushed forward. Surprised to see the man he met at the brazier, Crispin was nevertheless relieved. "Stupid woman! This is Crispin Guest. He's a friend of mine."

"I am glad to be so acquainted," said Crispin. "Master Hoode, I see your fortunes have turned."

"Aye. I'm in the kitchen now. Going to try to give the mistress a chance at hiring *you*, eh?"

"Well, in point of fact, I *am* working for her. I am trying to discover the culprit who killed Master Walcote."

"No! Then I was right about you. You are an educated man."

"Of a sort."

"Oh!" said the woman. "You're that man I seen in the hall with the mistress."

Crispin flicked a nod at her. "Yes. I only wish to ask a few questions concerning your master."

"Oh it's a sad, sad thing, it is. Who would do a thing like that?"

"Indeed. That is what I wish to know."

"He was a good and fair master, m'lord. Always a kind word to all."

"How long have you worked here?"

"Since five years now."

"Has anyone worked here longer than five years?"

"Well now." She put a dirt-blackened finger to her temple and scratched. "Only Master Becton would have been here longer. He's the one what hired me and the others."

Crispin offered a smile bereft of mirth. "I see. May I look in the hall? Is the way locked?"

"The mistress no longer locks all the inner doors. Just go through that passage. Mind your head. It's a low ceiling."

"I will see you again, Crispin," said Hoode, and he glanced at Jack a little suspiciously. Jack glared back.

Crispin entered the kitchens. There were two hearths flickering with light, each tended by a young boy. Other kitchen servants stopped their chopping or dough kneading to watch Crispin and Jack as they passed through, but no one spoke to them. Jack strained his neck looking back curiously when they arrived at a low passageway that led across a courtyard to the rear of the great hall.

"What are we looking for?" asked Jack, once the kitchens were far behind.

"I'm not certain."

"Why did you ask that old woman how long she worked here?"

"Because apparently there is no one in this household who has been here longer than five years."

"Is that unusual?"

"In most houses, Jack, generations serve their masters."

"Aye, but maybe Walcote has not been rich for generations."

"True. I shall have to make inquiries."

They reached the far edge of the hall and passed under its arch only to encounter Philippa Walcote. She and Crispin stood apart in mutual assessment before her face passed from surprise to anger. "Why are *you* here?" she said.

Crispin smiled a lopsided grin. "Why does everyone ask me that in that same uncivil tone?"

"Maybe it's because you don't know when you ain't welcome."

"Seldom am I welcome." He raised his arm and leaned on the archway. His eyes roved insolently over her. "And so, *Mistress Walcote.*" He relaxed against the carved stone. "I've been thinking about what you said. About that cloth. You never finished telling me."

She eyed his casual posture with a frown. "I recall you did not want to have anything to do with it. You refused my coins."

"Perhaps I was rash."

Her frown deepened. She slapped his arm leaning against the arch. He stumbled before straightening. "That's better. When you speak to me in this house, you will conduct yourself with more respect."

"In this house? The house you used to clean, you mean?"

If it were possible for a human to expel flames, Philippa would have done so. Though she did not speak, her lips seemed to form the word "Adam!"

After a pause she said tightly, "I do not care for your manners, Master Crispin."

"I'm not particularly impressed by yours." He straightened his coat and slipped his thumbs into his belt.

She darted a glance at Jack who remained mute and wide-eyed.

"So," she said, "you know who I am. Or rather, who I was."

"It is difficult to disguise that inflection. But you perform it well. You are like a mummer playing a part."

She turned her wedding ring on her finger. "Aye. It is a useful skill."

"So we need play no more games, Philippa."

She raised her chin. "So now you think you may call me by my Christian name?"

Her accent thickened the more he jibed her. "It's not so much the chambermaid, but the adulteress."

She stepped back to gaze at him, or perhaps to get a better swing. Her hand struck his cheek with such force that he teetered. He raised his hand to the welt and smiled. "I beg your pardon," he said.

Her small lips curved. "Now we understand each other."

Crispin continued to rub his cheek. "You have a strong hand, Madam."

"I'm no weakling. I worked hard in this house. I carried water. I did the heavy cleaning. I did more than my share. It was natural that I should catch the master's eye, though I never dreamed it would go so far."

For the first time he noticed a servant in the far corner of the hall pretending to sweep a small square of the floor with a gorse broom. Crispin lowered his voice. "Shall we retire to the parlor?"

She folded her arms over her breasts. "Why? I have no wish to talk with you. You made it clear you would have nought to do with me."

"This is a murder inquiry. If you'd rather speak to the sheriff . . ."

The sparkle in her eye dimmed. Glancing at the servant, Philippa nodded and led Crispin and Jack down a gallery to a warm chamber. She sat in the one large, ornate chair and gestured for Crispin to sit in the smaller one beside it.

Jack stood behind Crispin's chair and wrung the hem of his tunic.

"Can your servant serve the wine?"

Crispin swiveled his gaze toward Jack. Amusement had not left his features since Philippa doled out her slap. "*Can* you serve wine, Jack?"

"Course I can!" Jack's lower lip jutted forward and he narrowed his eyes at Philippa. He searched the room for the wine jug, and when he spied it, he stomped to the sideboard and sloppily poured two bowls. He eyed the silver before he offered a bowl to Crispin first. Crispin shook his head and nodded to the lady. Grumbling, Jack gave her the first bowl and Crispin the second. He retreated to the jug, no doubt wondering how he'd get himself a drink or slip the silver flagon under his cloak.

Philippa drank and studied Crispin over the rim of her bowl.

"So, you caught the master's eye," said Crispin.

She nodded. "A body only hears about such in songs. But I caught his fancy, and before I knew it, I was mistress of this household."

"Did you love him?"

The wine bowl paused at her lips. "A strange question. What does it matter?"

Crispin shrugged. "It doesn't. I merely wondered."

"And I wonder why you wonder."

"You forget." He lowered his chin and ran his finger absently along the rim of the silver bowl. "I saw you at the Thistle."

She angled her head to stare into the fire. A wisp of hair escaped from her meticulous coif and posed along her neck in a sinuous wave. "There is so much you'll never understand."

"Try me."

"We must talk about the cloth."

"Did Adam Becton hire you?"

She added a drowsy smile to her features and settled her head against the chair's high back. "Very well. Aye, Adam did hire me. What of it?"

"He does not seem to approve of your current status."

"Neither do you."

"We weren't talking about me."

"Weren't we?" Her smile brightened enough to cause a frown on Crispin's lips. "No matter. No, he never approved of Nicholas and me. The fool's in love with me."

"That much I reckoned for myself. What I am uncertain of is how *much* he loves you."

She laughed this time. "You think Adam killed Nicholas?"

"It is not beyond the realm of possibility."

"You don't know Adam."

"And you, apparently, do not know what a man is capable of doing for love."

She drank her wine and set the bowl aside. "Can't we discuss the cloth?"

"Life as mistress of this house must have been difficult after being raised from a chambermaid."

Her lids stayed in their languid pose while regarding him. "It was difficult. No one ever gave me a moment's peace."

"The servants?"

"The servants, the vendors, everyone. Until one day I told them all. I *am* mistress here, and if they didn't like it they could shift for themselves. Nicholas did not care if I bought beef from another butcher or corn from a different merchant. He laughed at it. I think he enjoyed raising me to his place. He was not afraid to be unconventional."

"And you rose to the occasion?"

"Oh, aye. I learned to enjoy it, too. Any servant who sneered at me got cuffed right well or dismissed. That's the way in this house."

"And even though your lord and master is dead?"

Her sensuous lips firmed to a tight line. "Aye, it will remain the same. After three years of wedded life, I have learned this business well."

"Do you read, then?"

"Only a little. I do sums, too. Nicholas taught me. But I will learn more."

He smiled into his wine bowl and sipped. He was beginning to like this Philippa Walcote in spite of her morals.

"Enough," she snorted. "The cloth. We must speak of that."

"Yes, and of fees."

She smiled. "So you will take my money now?"

"I am a sensible man."

She rose and reached into the delicate pouch at her embroidered belt. "Sixpence, did you say?"

"A day."

"Aye. Here, take a week's worth, then."

She held out a small pouch too far away for Crispin to reach while sitting. He rose and looked her in the eye. Amusement played on her face, but money never amused him. He finally raised his hand to receive it, and without taking his eyes from hers, he lowered the pouch into his own purse and sat.

"Tell me about this damned cloth."

"The Mandyllon." She said the word and sobered. Sitting rigidly, she curled her free hand into a fist. "It is a veronica—"

"Yes, you said all that. What is this 'curse' you're so afraid of?"

She drew her bottom lip between her teeth. "When in its presence, a person is absolutely incapable of telling a lie. It forces the truth out of you."

Crispin laughed. He set down his bowl before he spilled it. "And that is your curse? Yes, for women it must be so."

"You think it amusing?" she said flatly. "Think of this: What if you were bartering with a wealthy client and must speak the truth? What if you were with your enemy? Your spouse? Or a woman you found appealing?"

Crispin's laughter died.

"Still amusing, is it?"

"You mean to say, you must tell the absolute truth? What you're thinking? What you are . . . feeling?"

"Aye."

They gazed solemnly at one another.

"I concede your point," he said soberly. "Where did your husband acquire such a thing?"

"I don't know. Somewhere in the Holy Land, I think. I am uncertain."

"What does it look like?"

"I only saw it once. So big," she said, gesturing with her arms out. "Square. A simple cloth. But . . . with the face."

"And where did you last see it? Was it in this house? Some other place?"

"In the house. In the solar."

"And where did your husband keep it?"

She snapped to her feet. "If I knew I could find it for myself and destroy it!" Her skirts rippled wildly after her, desperate to keep step as she paced before the fire.

"Destroy such a valuable relic? The face of Christ? Blasphemy."

"God forgive me." She shook her head and crossed herself. "But I believe there is such a thing as too much honesty!"

Crispin rose and joined her by the fire. "Then why all the locks? Were they to keep thieves out, or something in?"

"I don't know. Nicholas was"—she shrugged—"different from other men. Secretive. And wealthy."

"You must have searched the manor yourself, in chests and behind sideboards."

"Of course I have!"

"What of the others? Do they know what it is?"

"The servants? No. Why should they?" She put her hands to her cheeks. Her fingers were long and chapped red, and her nails were bitten short.

He shook his head. "Well, Madam, short of a miracle, I do not know how you expect me to find it."

"That's your job. I've heard many people talk of your deeds, how you found lost objects with so few clues."

"Yes," Crispin said. "I suppose if I had free access to the house, that would make it easier."

"I grant it. Perhaps I will have a key made for you. Adam will not like it," she said with an unladylike smirk. Her accent thickened the angrier she got. "But I am long past worrying over what he likes and what he don't."

"I would also like to examine the solar again."

She hugged herself. Her face shrank into a grimace. "Why must you go there?"

He stood over her not answering, vaguely aware of Jack hovering somewhere in a corner.

"It is just that *he* is there."

"You mean Walcote?"

"Aye. I could not think of any place more suitable."

"I see. Then may I?"

"Aye. And take your servant with you."

The firelight flickered on her rounded cheeks, ambering the pale skin. He wanted to say more, but remembered Jack.

He bowed to her before he could stop himself. Old habits. He led Jack out of the parlor before he fully embarrassed himself.

"She's got her nerve," Jack growled and followed Crispin. "'Can your servant serve wine?' 'Take your servant with you.' Acting like the great lady, and her a chambermaid."

"Strictly speaking, she *is* the lady of this manor and may act accordingly, whether you approve or not."

"*You* don't approve."

"What I think is not your affair. Which reminds me. You are becoming far too familiar with me of late."

"I beg your pardon, Master. But this business has got me befuddled. She was a servant and is now a great lady, and you were a knight but are now little better than a servant. It's getting so I don't know who to bow to no more."

"Do you need to be cuffed to be reminded?" Jack fell silent as Crispin led the way to the solar. The door remained broken but the bits of sharp debris had been removed. Nicholas Walcote lay stretched out on a table covered up to his chest with a linen cloth. He had been cleaned and his hair combed out over his pillow.

Crispin was grateful the merchant had not yet begun to smell.

Jack hovered in the doorway and stared at the candles lit around the body. "I don't much like dead bodies," he whispered.

"You need not come in," said Crispin in the same quiet tone.

"Thank you, Master." Jack crossed his arms over his chest and ducked back into the gallery.

No fire. The room was cold. It kept the body better, he reasoned, and he pulled his cloak over his chest for warmth. The daylight fell gray through the locked window, and it was only this and the meager candlelight that illuminated the now stark room.

He did not know what he was looking for, but he summoned his imagination to feel what the room must have been like that night. He closed his eyes. He remembered how the room smelled of toasted oak and alder from a steady fire in the hearth.

What had Walcote been doing at the time? Did he entertain his murderer? Was he working at the table and taken by surprise? Surely he let the killer in and locked the door behind him. But how did the culprit get out?

Perhaps Walcote worked at the desk. Crispin relaxed and pictured it. Walcote worked and then rose to get a cup of wine. He held it in his hand, and the next thing he knew a knife stabbed his back. He dropped the cup, which spattered wine on the sideboard, and he turned to face his killer, and then—

Crispin's eyes snapped open. "Jack! Secure the door. Alert me if someone comes."

Only Jack's nose appeared at the edge of the jamb. "Aye, Master," he whispered, and the nose disappeared again.

Crispin approached the bier and threw back the sheet. Walcote was wearing a simple linen shift. His skin wore that waxy sheen bereft of color seen only on the dead. Crispin did not hesitate in untying the man's collar. Dead men no longer aroused his discomfort. He opened the shift and pulled the shroud down over his shoulders.

Because the body was clean, he could plainly see the mark of the blade on the upper left shoulder. The blade had pierced the flesh in a smooth tear, but it was a halfhearted stroke. Why such a weak thrust?

Crispin lifted the man's shoulders and turned him on his side to view the wounds on his back. These were more vicious blows, one on top of the other. There were six in all. Jagged tears in the flesh of the back forming a mad herringbone pattern of violence.

Since he did not defend himself, Crispin surmised he was stabbed in the back first. What was Walcote working on at his table? He returned the body like he found it, retying the shift and pulling up the sheet.

He strode to the table, pulled out the high-backed chair, and sat on the soft cushion. He only allowed a momentary feeling of satisfaction with the chair before he settled to his work. Accounting books and journals bound in dark leather sat stacked before him. He picked up the first and thumbed through it, glancing at row upon row of tabulations and names of fabrics. He found the last entry easily. A quill marked the unfinished page. The last tabulation was incomplete. Not unusual. No blood appeared on the page, which reminded him again of the spilled bowl on the floor. Walcote had been surprised while drinking his wine. The second cup remained untouched. Propriety would suggest that that meant there were no visitors.

Crispin thought a bit and turned the accounting book back to the first page and read the date: 1379. Five years ago. He picked up the journal and confirmed his thoughts by checking the first page. Also 1379. Was nothing in this house older than five years?

He picked up another, heavier volume. This did not appear to be a personal accounting, but the expenses of the guild, mostly export taxes. He glanced at it quickly. Eleven hundred fifty-two sacks of raw wool leaving Sandwich. Two hundred bolts of worsted from East Anglia to Calais. The dry pages of commerce. He snorted and snapped the book shut, then stacked all the books together. "Jack!"

The head poked in again.

"Come. Take these books. I don't think Mistress Walcote will mind our borrowing them."

Jack's face squinted. "What do you want them books for?"

"Motive. It wouldn't be the first time a man was killed because of dubious bookkeeping."

Jack looked unconvinced, but he edged through the archway and stared at the covered body before he turned a pale face to Crispin.

Crispin tapped his finger on the topmost book. "Hurry you now. I haven't all day. Walcote won't mind, I assure you."

Jack swallowed hard. "I ain't so sure of that," he whispered. He edged along the cloth-draped wall to the desk. He snatched the books and ran with them back to the door, skidding out into the gallery.

Crispin chuckled. He sat a moment more and stared at the room and the open doorway, his back to the window. He turned and looked, but the window was barred as it had been the first time he entered the room. He looked at the snuffed candle, the blackened curl of a wick, the flat and now frozen pool of wax in its melted hollow.

With a sudden thought, he shot to his feet.

He left the room and stood outside it, looking down the gallery. Below lay the foyer leading south to the dining hall. Trestle tables were stacked against the walls, leaving the expansive floor empty. A few cressets lit a path, but no servants wandered the painted floorboards. Crispin moved to the west of the solar and found an open alcove with a window. Sunlight warmed the white plaster to gold though the alcove was still cold. Tucked in the corner was a small cot with a straw-stuffed mattress. No doubt a maid servant made this her bed. He moved past the alcove and found a door. He knocked first, but without waiting for a reply, tried to open it. Locked. He glanced back at Jack, wondering if he should send him to get a key when he decided not to waste the time. He unbuttoned his coat and he crouched and used his dagger and the sharp aiglet of his shirt's lace to pick the lock. It snapped open, and Jack, straining to watch from his post by the solar, smiled.

Crispin pulled the door open and peered inside. Empty. Perhaps a storeroom.

He shut the door and looked back at Jack. He looked at the door. With wide strides he counted the paces past the storeroom, past the window alcove, and back to the solar. He stared through the open doorway past Walcote's body to the window and paced the steps again back to the storeroom.

He stopped and smiled, rebuttoning his coat.

"Jack," he said, returning to the solar.

"Aye, Master."

"Let's go home. We've done all we can here whilst this body awaits burial."

"Thank you, Master." Jack made a sling with his cloak and slipped the bulky books in under his arm.

Crispin smiled, pleased with himself. They followed the lonely gallery from shadow to light. Crispin decided to skirt Adam and exit by the kitchen outbuildings.

When they entered the kitchens, he cast about until he found the tall figure he sought. "Master Hoode."

John Hoode looked up and smiled on seeing Crispin. He hurried to his side. "Crispin. How did it go?"

"Not badly. I will be here often as I continue my investigations." He wasn't certain if Hoode was up to the challenge, but he needed some- one to do a little spying for him when he wasn't about. "Can you favor me with an errand?" He pulled Hoode aside, and glanced about for any others. "You are new to this household. So it may not necessarily be strange for you to be found in the corridor. You were lost, after all. Yes?"

Hoode studied Crispin's eyes. It took him a few moments but he caught up. "Oh, aye! I get you. Keep me eyes open."

"That's right."

Hoode giggled. "That's all a bit of fun, ain't it? Me spying on the likes of the Walcotes. What a grand jest that is."

Crispin kept his smile in place, though Hoode's fey manner caused a ripple of discomfort sporting up his spine. "Just don't be obvious."

"Oh, no! Course not! Bless my soul. I'll be like a mouse."

"Indeed. I bid you farewell."

He felt Hoode's gaze on him while he tromped through the kitchen courtyard and out the back gate. Crossing the lane, he looked back at the house and its many chimneys and outbuildings. The manor seemed cold to him. Was it merely because of the death within, or was there something inherent in the stones? A house reflected those within its walls. And the Walcote house was not a happy one.

He and Jack wound down arched alleyways and through narrow lanes. They traveled north up Old Cheap, skirting a cluster of noble women riding by on their white and dappled palfreys. He bowed to them as they passed but did not raise his eyes lest he recognize any of them. Or worse, that they recognize him.

Once the horses passed, a goose girl trotted beside Crispin and Jack, moving swiftly ahead of them. She gave them a cursory glance from under her tattered cloak and used a stick to move her charges along. Their gray necks stretched heavenward and they honked the whole way down the road. No doubt they were not happy with their appointment at the poulterer's.

Crispin scarce remembered that Jack was beside him until he spoke suddenly, startling Crispin from his reverie.

"I don't understand."

They turned east at the corner of the Shambles where East Cheap, Paternoster Row, and St. Martin's crossed and had to wait until a cart laden with stacked barrels pulled through the narrow lane. The Shambles, in all its bustle, came into view under a froth of mist rumbling up from the distant Thames.

Crispin glanced down at Jack. "What don't you understand?"

The cart lumbered slowly past them, the wooden wheels straining under the weight of the barrels. The ox pulling the cart lowed and shifted its head in their direction. The long lashes on those dark, liquid eyes blinked at them.

"You're supposed to be this Tracker," said Jack, watching the beast amble away. The cart's wheels splayed the mud beneath it, leaving two long ruts trailing behind. "But all you track are bodies."

Crispin sniffed the desolate air. A chill fell with the twilight. Braziers came to life down the street; vague glowing points amid a rising mist that smelled of seaweed and salt. Shadowy figures huddled near the shopkeeper's glowing fires like lethargic moths. London's underclass. Homeless men. Men and boys much like Jack had been before he insinuated himself into Crispin's life. "If you've no stomach for it you are free to go. I have no hold over you."

"Well—" Jack swiveled his head to take in the cold street with its damp cobblestones, the murky channel down the center of the crooked lane meandering upstream, and lonely men grasping for warmth about the few braziers. "Where would I go?" he answered softly.

"I see. You stay with me out of necessity. Well, I cannot dispute your reasoning."

"It ain't like that." His face grayed from the dimming light. "I like serving you, Master Crispin. I never been treated this good before. You talk to me and ask me things. It's like I was your squire!"

A sigh huffed up from Crispin's chest and settled his mouth into a scowl. Why did the boy have to use *that* word? "Jack." It came out more of a growl than a name.

"You're right good to me," he pressed on, oblivious to Crispin's darkening mood. "That's miraculous!"

"My humiliation is your good fortune. I'm happy for you."

Jack's mouth dropped open. "No, no! Why is everything I say vexing to you?"

"Maybe you talk too much!" He fumbled, removing the key from his scrip, and noticed Jack wore the look of a punished child, chin down, mouth taut. Crispin felt a twinge in his heart that nudged the sourness aside. "I apologize for that," he said soberly. "The truth of it is, I am pleased to have you here. But because I am not a knight, you cannot be a squire. Though were I a knight again—"

Jack's face broke into a broad smile. "Ah now. That's a fine thing you said. Even if you don't mean half of it."

The lane curved and they spied the tinker shop, now washed in closing shadows. Smoke curled from his landlord's chimney and candlelight shone from the seams of their shutters.

But there was a man stamping the ground before the tinker's door. No. Not before the door. Before Crispin's stair. Instinctively, Crispin pushed Jack behind him and rested his hand on his dagger.

The man looked up at their approach, but by then Crispin was close enough to recognize his livery. Crispin's weary shoulders sagged.

"I know, I know," said Crispin. "The sheriff wishes to see me."

5

CRISPIN AND JACK MADE their way under the arch of Newgate prison. The tall stone gate scowled over the Shambles, its two towers like the gateposts of Hell. A portcullis hung over the open maw of the dark archway; fangs waiting to snap. To the south lay the Bailey and Ludgate. To the north Aldersgate and then Cripplegate, guarding the byways in and out of London. But it was in Newgate that men suffered the fates of their masters. Thieves, whores, and traitors all found habitation in the most inhospitable of places. Some paid their debts and were released. These debts could be coin, but more often than not for the simple thief, it was to leave behind a hand or an ear, whatever form the Lord Sheriff thought was mete. Still others made the long journey to Smithfield to meet their Maker.

Crispin never failed to shiver as he crossed beneath the portcullis, ever mindful of his time within these walls as its guest. He, too, thought he was to make the journey to Smithfield. But Fate is an inconstant jester. He never dreamed eight years ago that he would walk free of the prison alive.

As he approached the sheriff's hall, Crispin evened his breathing. The business of crime-solving made strange bedfellows. Crispin's encounters with Wynchecombe had become no easier even after an uncomfortable acquaintance for the last year. Perhaps Simon

Wynchecombe resented a sheriff's responsibilities. Perhaps he envied Crispin's education and former status.

Perhaps he's just a vengeful bastard. Crispin smirked. That one suited best.

Wynchecombe looked up from a parchment and frowned upon seeing the former cutpurse. "What's he doing here?"

Crispin stepped in and moved easily toward Wynchecombe's table. "Jack is my servant, remember?"

The sheriff sat back and laughed. "That's right. You have a thief for a servant. It's fitting."

Crispin stood and endured the sheriff's laughter until Wynchecombe finally invited him to sit. Often, he made Crispin stand throughout the interview just to tweak Crispin's humor. But today, the sheriff seemed to be in a magnanimous mood. Crispin sat while Jack made himself scarce in the shadows. "We haven't seen much of each other lately, have we, Guest? Until yesterday morning, that is."

Crispin said nothing. He rested his hands in his lap in an outward gesture of relaxed calm.

Wynchecombe leaned forward over his desk and smiled. The white teeth seemed whiter under the dark mustache—something like the white scales on the underbelly of a snake. "I haven't any suspects. Have you?"

Crispin looked away. "No, my lord. The case is still fresh."

"But Walcote isn't getting any fresher, is he? And his guild is quite impatient and full of equally rich merchants. I was met by a delegation today demanding—*demanding*, mind you—that I do something about the murder. You know I do not like to be dictated to."

"Yes, my lord."

Wynchecombe studied Crispin's blank expression and scowled. "Nor do I like being patronized."

"If I had pertinent information I would tell you, Lord Sheriff."

"Nonsense! We both know the opposite to be true. Why do you fight me, Guest? You know I will win."

Crispin smiled. "There is always the possibility that you won't."

Wynchecombe slammed the table with his hand. The candle wobbled and its flame sputtered. "I want to know why Walcote hired you, and I want to know now!"

Crispin plucked an imaginary piece of fluff from his coat and flicked it away. Wynchecombe followed each meticulous motion until his eyes narrowed to furious slits.

"The matter is still private, my lord. Were it not—"

Wynchecombe scrambled around the table. Crispin knew it was coming, but before he could steel himself, the sheriff grabbed his coat and hauled him to his feet.

He wondered how the sheriff would start. He didn't wonder long.

Wynchecombe backhanded him hard. And just to make certain Crispin knew it was no mere token, the sheriff did it again to the other cheek.

Crispin's head jerked with each blow, and stars exploded in the back of his eyes. He felt Wynchecombe's ring tear his cheek, felt the warm blood run in a tickling dribble down his face, felt his eye take the brunt of it.

Jack made a small noise from his place in the shadows, like a trapped mouse.

Taking a deep breath, Crispin slowly turned his head to face the sheriff. He ran his tongue in his mouth and tasted the bitter flavor of his own blood.

"I said I want an answer," said Wynchecombe. His voice rumbled like distant thunder.

"And I told you I can't give you one."

Wynchecombe's fist sank into Crispin's belly and he would have dropped to the floor on his knees had the sheriff not been holding him up. Crispin gasped but no sound came from his lips.

"Tell me."

Without voice, Crispin shut his eyes and shook his head.

Wynchecombe dropped Crispin and he tumbled to the floor holding his sore belly. He rolled into a hedgehoglike ball.

The sheriff rubbed his tender knuckles into his palm and walked a slow circuit around Crispin. Wynchecombe leaned down and grabbed his hair, jerking Crispin's head back.

There was no time to feel humiliation at being on his hands and knees. The raw pain of his belly and eye was still too fresh.

"Is it worth taking a beating?"

His eye swelled and shut. Crispin managed a defiant smile. "But you enjoy it so much."

Wynchecombe drew his arm back, and Crispin tensed for the blow. But the sheriff's attention was diverted by a movement in the shadows. He dropped Crispin's hair and stood above him with his legs apart. "It's true. I could easily, and happily, beat you for the rest of the afternoon. But I think I would rather thrash . . . *him*."

Crispin painfully turned his head in the direction the sheriff stared with such glee, and the rebellious smile fell from his bloody lips.

Jack cowered behind the door when the sheriff neared him.

Crispin lurched forward. "No! Wait!"

Wynchecombe closed his enormous hand over Jack's tunic and pulled him from the floor. Walcote's ledgers fell out of his cloak one by one. The sheriff's other hand closed into a red fist and bobbed close to Jack's face.

"Oh please," Wynchecombe oozed, smiling over his shoulder at Crispin. "Just one?"

Crispin's face burned, and his belly felt as if it were folded together and nailed closed. "Release him and I will tell you everything."

"I was just getting started."

"Simon!"

He curled his fist around Jack's tunic even tighter. Jack blanched. His eyes gaped to terrified holes. "It's *Lord Sheriff* to you, remember?"

"My lord . . . please . . ."

Wynchecombe held Jack suspended above the floor for what seemed an interminable time before he grimaced a chuckle and dropped him. Jack scrambled back to his corner like a mouse in search of a hole. He collected the books and scooped them into the safety of his cloak. "Weakness for a servant?" The sheriff tutted. "I am surprised at you, Crispin. It's not a very admirable trait."

Crispin raised his head but could only do so at an odd angle. He squinted with his one good eye. "'You become just by performing just actions.'"

"Not your damned Aristotle again. You seem to hold great store by what that pagan said."

Crispin dragged himself across the floor to the chair but only to lean against it. His head felt close to bursting and his eye felt as if a knife had jabbed it. He put his hand to his head. His hand didn't help the pain, but it reassured him that his head was still in one piece. "There is much wisdom in the writings of antiquity." He said the words mechanically. Perhaps he'd said the same words to Wynchecombe before. Difficult to remember when his head was hammering.

The sheriff moved with deliberate posturing back to his chair and sat, gloating over his beard. "You were about to tell me why Walcote hired you."

Crispin ignored him for the moment and peered as best he could into the dim corner. "Are you well, Jack?"

Mute, Jack nodded vigorously and clasped his cloak up to his chin.

Crispin heaved a sigh, but it sputtered unsuccessfully when a bruised rib twinged his side. "Nicholas Walcote hired me to spy on his wife. He feared she was unfaithful."

Wynchecombe rocked back in his chair and smiled. His mustache bristled. "And was she?"

He took so long deciding what to say that Wynchecombe pulled his dagger and aimed it at Jack. "I'll wager I can get him from here. Pin his shoulder to the wall, maybe."

"Yes!" Crispin hissed with as much scowl as he could muster. "I saw her with her lover."

"Well! Now we're getting somewhere." Wynchecombe sheathed his knife smoothly. "Certainly she must have killed her husband."

"No. There is something odd about that. She's afraid of something. She's more afraid now that he's dead."

"Crispin, I do believe starvation has affected your mind. There are a host of motives for a wife to kill. Or hire someone to do the killing for her." He shook his head. "Could it be you have lost your touch?"

Only my self-worth. He tried to glare at the sheriff but the left side of his head hurt too much, and now he felt dizzy and nauseated.

"The guild has been breathing down my neck for weeks, and now this Walcote business. I tell you, I cannot draw breath without some whining merchant complaining of this shipment and that shipment arriving with less than promised. Now I ask you: what the hell am I supposed to do about a shipment to Calais when I am in London?"

The sheriff droned on. Crispin desperately wanted to hear what he was saying but he found he could no longer understand him, and realized, belatedly, that he was blacking out.

6

CRISPIN AWOKE IN HIS own bed and wondered if he dreamed it, though when he tried to move his head, the pain told him otherwise. Only one eye worked and he hazily recalled why. "Jack?"

"Beside you, Master." Jack put his cool hand on Crispin's forehead. "Are you feeling better, sir?"

"I do not know if 'better' is the word for it. Conscious, perhaps, but little more." He tried to rise, but it felt healthier not to. Jack agreed by pushing him gently back.

"You was thrashed right good. You done it to protect me." He sniffed. His eyes were wet.

"Pull yourself together, Jack."

Jack ran his finger under his wet nose and took it the length of his sleeve. "I'm right grateful, I am. And as for her. You must truly think she's innocent to try to protect her from the sheriff. No one blames you for telling him after all."

Crispin stared up at the ceiling. Jack's words jabbed at a place in his hollow insides. He had to admit that he didn't know what he thought of Philippa Walcote. In fact, he hadn't wished to consider her guilty at all, and that was not like him.

He glanced at Jack's hopeful expression. Since Crispin was incapable by his rank of striking back at the sheriff, though he dearly wanted to and replayed in his head exactly how it would be done, he couldn't allow Wynchecombe to hurt the boy. Not on his account.

"Jack, would you do me a favor?"

Jack knelt by the bed and rested his clasped hands on the straw-stuffed mattress in a prayerful posture. "Anything!"

"I want you to go to the Thistle and see if our friend is still lodged in that room."

"The innkeeper will not say. You heard him."

"And so did you. Did you believe him?"

"Not when I seen the man with me own eyes."

"Then do not ask the innkeeper. Look for yourself. Ask the servants. Perhaps they will be more willing to speak of that room to you."

"I'll need a bribe."

Crispin looked down for his belt but Jack had removed it. He saw it and his purse on the table. "Take a few small coins from my purse. There's a good lad."

Jack turned to stare at the pouch but did not move to fetch it. He pressed his teeth into his lower lip. "You want *me* to get money from *your* purse."

Crispin chuckled through his aching face. "Yes. No stealing this time. I'm actually giving you permission."

Jack licked his lips, swathing his tongue several times over his slick mouth. Finally he rose and approached the purse as if it were a wild animal. He opened the flap with only two fingers and reached in.

"Good heavens, boy!" cried Crispin, laughing. "You're not gutting a fish. Just take it!"

Jack nodded and quickly withdrew a few halpens. He put them in one of the many secret hiding places in his shoulder cape and looked back at Crispin uncertainly.

It was then that Crispin was struck once more by how young the lad was. Jack must have had the devil's own time surviving as long as he did on his own. The boy was resilient. Clever. He reminded Crispin of . . . well, long ago.

He watched Jack shrug on his cloak with a feeling of empathy. A man's life was not easy. And life on the Shambles was harder than most. Was his staying with Crispin only prolonging the inevitable?

Jack looked back at him again and gave him a wary smile. He lifted the latch, yanked on the door ring, and pulled the door open. A misty draft blew in before he slipped out and shut the door behind him.

Alone again, Crispin rose carefully from his cot and swallowed a wave of dizziness. He staggered to the mirror nailed to a timber and stared at his reflection in the small rectangle of polished brass. His left eye looked like two plums pressed together. A gash where Wynchecombe's ring cut him ran unevenly in a rusted brown line down one cheek while the other sported a mottled blue bruise. He knew he could not go out like this even if he could walk. How was he to ask his questions looking like the loser in a cockfight? He took the rag Jack used to wipe the blood from his face and dunked it in the cold water of the bucket and pressed it to the eye. It was going to be a few days before he was presentable again. By then, he hoped to have more answers he could offer to the sheriff and satisfy himself.

THE NEXT MORNING, JACK had not yet returned. Crispin found he could not simply convalesce, so he busied himself poking the fire and eating the rest of the hen Jack had cooked the night before and left for him. He cracked the bones and sucked out the marrow and tossed the waste into the fire, watching it spit while the bones blackened. He leaned out the back courtyard window into the cold, crisp morning, trying to catch a glimpse of the street between two buildings. When that proved futile, he cast his glance instead across the row of courtyards peeking out from an undulating plain of rooftops. Housewives, plagued by children at their feet, hung laundry. Men sat on stools mending the tools of their livelihoods. And always, cats wandered, stalking the family geese.

He turned back to the room, his good eye scanning until it lighted on the stack of Walcote's books. He pulled the chair from the table and sat. Dragging the first book toward him, he opened it. The tangy scent of leather blended with the musty aroma of parchment and ink, recalling to Crispin's mind better days at his own accounting books when he had more than two pence to rub together. Settling down to the business of examining the page, he ran his finger down each column, searching for anything amiss.

For hours he read the entries and tabulations. Only one hand made each entry. He surmised it was that of Nicholas Walcote. No embezzlements, then. No false entries to suggest it, in any event.

He set the book aside and picked up the customs ledger. Many different hands had worked on this book, which dated from two years ago. The entries were full of the minutiae of shipping and exporting; sacks of raw wool and bolts of cloth and the names of ships making for the staple port in France. *The Starling* headed for Calais with 1,152 sacks for the king's export tax of eighty pounds in the early spring of 1382. The *St. George* sailed also to Calais where the taxes were collected for two hundred bolts of dyed cloth. And so it went month after month, entry after entry.

Until a year ago. He read an entry for 1,008 sacks of wool for seventy pounds sailing from the customs port of Sandwich to Calais. Crispin looked at the entry and turned the pages back until he spotted the previous shipments. Clearly they were for 1,152 sacks—eight gross—almost every time for a levied tax of eighty pounds. Page upon page of it.

He studied the new entry. Fewer sacks. And ever after, 1,008 instead of 1,152. Why suddenly were all ships carrying some 144 sacks less? Certainly there would not be less room for them on the ships. He could not tell from the sparse entry, but the same hand seemed to have written only those entries with the 1,008 sacks. He compared it to the entries in Walcote's ledgers. They didn't match. So at least Walcote was not the one recording this customs information, and perhaps he wasn't the one collecting the taxes. Who was it? Only the initials BV were scrawled at the end of the columns. Who was BV? Usually some member of the guild was responsible for such duties, so BV must belong either to the woolman's guild, the weavers, or the mercers.

"Someone is skimming the cream off the milk," he muttered. He had no doubt that the wool suppliers presented eight gross worth of wool in good faith and paid the standard eighty pounds of tax, but someone was making good money collecting the payment, secreting ten pounds of it, and then reporting only seven gross of wool. But who?

Crispin tapped his finger on the hard edge of the leather binding. He was willing to wager that there was another set of books somewhere that showed the proper eight gross sacks for eighty pounds of taxation—just as in the earlier entries. Perhaps Walcote discovered who this knave was. But alas. He would take that information to his grave.

The sun shone weakly from his window and the bells of St. Paul's pealed Terce when there was a knock on his door. Crispin turned. A knock could mean anything: a new client or an old enemy. He crept toward the door and called, "Who goes there?"

"It's me. John Hoode!"

Crispin unbarred the door and opened it. "Master Hoode. How did you find me?"

Hoode ducked his head. "I reckon everyone knows where to find the Tracker."

"I see. What is it?"

When the man lifted his face from his hood he gave a little cry. "Bless my soul! What happened to you?"

Crispin straightened. "The usual encounter with the Lord Sheriff."

"Pardon me for saying, but next time you encounter him, perhaps you should duck."

"Good advice. And so. The reason you are here . . . ?"

"I just thought I should tell you that there was a strange man loitering about outside the Walcote manor last night, just beyond the wall. He didn't do nought. Only stared at the place. The footman at the gatehouse finally shooed him off, but it weren't more than an hour hence that he was back."

"Can you describe him?"

"Naw. It was too dim. But he was about your height and all dark in a cloak. Thought you should know."

Crispin walked to the fire and stared into it. "I thank you for that, John. This is the sort of thing I feared."

"Who is it, Master Crispin? Is it someone who threatens my mistress?"

"Yes. Do continue to watch and alert me as you have done. You are a good man to your new household, John. It will not be forgotten."

"I am glad to hear it. A word from you might put me in good stead. I fear I've gotten on the wrong side of that Becton. He has a hard look in his eye that I do not like."

"Yes. Nor I."

Hoode stood beside Crispin and watched the flames. Crispin turned to him. "Forgive me. May I offer you wine? Or food?"

"Oh, no, Master Crispin. But I thank you. I just wonder . . ." His eyes wandered about the sparse room. "That a man like you must live on the Shambles and do the odd job for the wealthy. It don't seem right."

"I have made my own fate, Master Hoode. And I must live it out until the Final Judgment. God grant that I am better judged then."

"Aye," he answered vaguely, for he surely could not know what Crispin was talking about. "Well then. I must return before I am missed. I will take my leave. God keep you, sir."

"And you."

Hoode opened the door just as Jack returned. They stared at one another and Jack refused to move. Hoode finally took the initiative and decidedly stepped past him, rumbling down the stairs with a mumbled oath.

Jack stayed on the landing and glared after him until his steps had dispersed. It was only then that he turned a warmer expression on Crispin. Under his arm he carried a round loaf of bread with several sausage links dangling precariously from his fingers while the other arm had a small wheel of cheese tucked against a wineskin. A meat pie bulged from his scrip.

"I don't like that fellow. There's a way about him I don't trust."

"He's a good spy. And I must trust him for now." Crispin pushed the candle and books aside and helped Jack with the victuals. "Well? You were gone all night. What of your task?"

Jack placed the food with care on the table and smiled up at Crispin. "Your eye's looking better. Can you see out of it yet?"

"To hell with that. Did you find him?"

"Aye. He was still there, or at least his things were. I did not bother talking to the innkeeper, like you said." He took a long iron fork and skewered two sausages on each prong and propped it over the fire. He withdrew his knife and sliced through the cheese's rind and stacked several thick slivers on the table.

Crispin slammed his hand down over Jack's wrist and glared almost nose to nose with him. *"What did you find?"*

Jack withdrew his hand, shook out the tenderness, and sheathed his dirty knife. "Well now. I went and talked to the chambermaid and she said that the master told her not to speak of the man in the room. She knew nought of the man except that he is a foreigner and keeps odd hours, coming in quite late and leaving early. She said she didn't know why the master would not let anyone speak of him or let on that anyone was in that room." Jack grimaced and blushed. "I didn't have to bribe her. She chucked me chin, told me I was a sweet pup, and to be on me way. I ain't no pup!"

Crispin hid his smile by turning toward the fire. The sausages sizzled over the flames. Their savory aroma filled the room. "Is that why all this bounty?"

"If you mean the food, aye. No pottage tonight! And there's wine here from the Boar's Tusk with a message from Mistress Eleanor. She said she was sorry to have scolded you and hoped you'd be feeling better. She put it on your account."

"You told her."

"Well aye! You saved me from the sheriff. It was a gallant deed."

Crispin sat and dropped his still throbbing head in his hands.

"She said she'd be by tomorrow to see to you."

"Christ!"

"Aye, I know. I told her I was doing the job but she would hear none of it. Women!" He handed Crispin a slice of cheese and stuffed one in his own mouth, chewing noisily.

"Why did this task take you all night?"

Jack swallowed and wiped his mouth with his sleeve. "I wanted to keep a sharp eye on the knave's room. I stayed in the inn's hall as long as they would let me before they sent me away and barred the door. I stood by a brazier all night and watched the window." And as if to prove the point, he did not bother to stifle a yawn as wide as Newgate's archway.

Crispin poured himself some wine and drank it all in one swallow. He poured more and dug his fingers into the meat pie, scooping out a ragged chunk. He chewed and stopped when his aching jaw told him to slow down. Jack tended to the sausages.

"So this man lives in the Thistle without anyone's knowing who he is. Curious."

Jack gestured with his knife. Pieces of meat pie flew from the blade's tip. "I thought so, too. 'Who is this knave?' I thought to m'self. So at dawn when he left his lodgings, I went up to his room and had another little look round."

Crispin leaned forward and slowly bit into the greasy sausage that Jack handed him. A dribble of grease ran down his chin but he wiped it neatly with his hand. "Indeed. What did you find?"

Jack stared at the ceiling and chewed as if picturing the room before him. "A right strange arrangement it was, I don't mind saying," he said, mouth full. "He had all manner of papers lying about. They looked like the same writing we saw before. I would have taken one for you, but you said before you couldn't read it and he might have missed it. In his trunk he had all sorts of strange foreign clothes. Smelled funny, too."

"How do you mean 'strange'?"

"Robes all in silk. Sashes. No coat or houppelande. Only them robes. They all smelled like a mince pie."

"Robes, eh? Like something in a church window?"

"Aye. That's clever, that." He smiled at Crispin's description. "Aye. Like them three kings going off to Bethlehem."

And smelling like spices. Exotic spices. What was such a man doing with Philippa Walcote? It was time to find out.

7

AGAINST JACK'S ADMONISHMENT, CRISPIN rose early the next morning. He shaved quickly and carefully over his bruised chin, and examined his eye in the brass mirror. It wasn't as bad as yesterday. At least he could open it fully now, but the bruise was still dark and puffy. If he could have afforded it, he would have called in a barber to leech the bruising from his eye. But as it was, cold compresses would have to suffice.

Crispin left his lodgings and plunged into London's weather. Rain fell in indiscriminate sheets, pelting some streets and ignoring others. Huddled in his hood, Crispin trotted along the muddy avenue, grateful when the Thistle arose from the persistent drizzle. He ducked in the door and shook out his cloak, using the opportunity to scan the smoky room.

He saw the innkeeper and approached him in a swift, sure gait.

The man turned, and Crispin thought he detected the merest hint of recognition on his face.

"My good sir," said the innkeeper. "How can I serve you?"

Crispin's right hand toyed with his dagger's hilt while he clutched the man's arm with the left. "You can serve me right well," he said in low tones. The man alternated between staring at Crispin's hand as it tightened on his arm and his face. "You can tell me the name of the man in that corner room upstairs."

"I-I told you before. There ain't no one in that—"

"Then let us go now. If what you say is true, there will be no chest of clothes, no papers, no hearth embers—"

"No!" He pulled back from Crispin, yanking them both away from the stairs. "He'll kill me!" he whispered.

Crispin let him go and stood back. He patted his dagger. "Either him or me."

The man scanned the room and motioned for Crispin to come into the kitchens.

A short man sat beside a huge kettle hanging from an iron rod swung over the fire. The aroma of savory meat and spices bubbled from the steamy cauldron's depths. Two assistants argued while they clattered iron pans and wooden bowls in a wide washtub, scrubbing the pans with large bristle brushes.

The noisy room seemed to convince the innkeeper he would not be overheard. In fact, Crispin found it difficult to hear the man.

"He paid me a right good sum to tell folk he weren't there," said the innkeeper, mouthing his words in exaggerated motions. "And he threatened me, too, I don't mind saying."

"Who is he?"

"He calls himself Smith."

" 'Calls himself'?"

"Can't be his true name. He's a foreigner."

"From where?"

"Can't rightly say. Maybe he's a Moor. He's dark enough."

"Maybe." Crispin took a halpens from his pouch and gave it to the man. "It isn't gold, but perhaps you will hold your tongue about my asking."

The man nodded and clutched the coin in a whitening fist. "There's no need to tell the gentleman aught."

* * *

CRISPIN SPENT ALL DAY in the Thistle's raucous tavern, drinking wine from a chipped horn cup and picking periodically from several pullet carcasses before him, now cold, their grease congealing on a wooden plank.

He sat in a far corner against the wall, watching patrons come and go while the frantic innkeeper moved nervously between the tables trying not to look at him.

Sitting low on his bench, Crispin spotted a hunched figure entering the tavern and trying to lose himself in the crowd. The man glanced once at Crispin then darted forward with all intentions of escape, until Crispin stuck out his foot. The man tumbled to the floor amid the laughter of those seated nearby and looked back over his shoulder from his place in the filthy straw.

Crispin looked down at him, his lips twisted in a smile. "Master Lenny. I thought it was you. Up to your old tricks?"

"Why it's Master Crispin!" Lenny rose and shook the straw from his tattered cloak. "I didn't notice it was you, sir." He started to sit beside Crispin, seemed to think better of it, then gingerly took a place beside him after all. He cringed but managed a weak smile when Crispin put his arm around him.

"Skulking in a tavern," said Crispin. "You can't be up to any good."

"Well, I could say the same of you"—he glanced up at Crispin's face; his smile fell—"but I won't."

"How long has it been, Lenny, since I last sent you to gaol?"

"Oh, nigh on eight months, Master Crispin. The sheriff released me two months ago. I ain't been arrested since. And look." He raised his hand and wiggled the fingers. "I ain't lost a hand or ear yet. Thanks to you, I hear tell."

Crispin looked away. "What would the sheriff want with your grimy hand?"

Lenny laughed. He ran his hand over the stubble on his pointed chin. His hair receded, leaving a wide dome atop and stringy dark hair dangling down around it. His neck was thin and crooked like a buzzard's. "I reckon you're right there, m'lord."

"Not a lord, Lenny." He patted Lenny's shoulder and released him. It had been many a year since he was "Lord" anything.

He cast his thoughts back to the present and gazed at Lenny. "I don't think I'll tell the sheriff I saw you," said Crispin.

"Ah now! Master Crispin, that's right Christian of you. Anything you want, anything you need, you just call on old Lenny."

"I might need you at that, Lenny. Where do you call home these days?"

"Oh, here and there."

"You don't seem to understand. I may have a job for you. I know this inn is one of your favorite spots to cut a purse."

"Ah now, Master Crispin! Such lies to tell about old Lenny. I think me feelings are hurt."

"Put your feelings aside. I want information."

"It's that way, is it? Well then." He sidled closer and spoke in low tones so that Crispin bent over. Lenny's harsh, foul breath hissed in Crispin's ear. "What's that you're looking for? Old Lenny knows, he does. He knows him what comes and him what goes."

Crispin smiled. "I'd like you to keep an eye on the place for a few days. If anything unusual happens, let me know. I'm particularly looking for a foreign man. Looks like a Saracen."

"A tall man? Swarthy? Bit of a mystery?" Lenny turned his head and Crispin followed his gaze. A man in a pointed oversized hood trudged through the door.

"In fact . . . *that* man," Crispin said quietly. The man's cloak reached the floor and seemed to cover him from front to back. Crispin caught the innkeeper's eye but the man quickly turned away and scurried into the kitchens, pushing a befuddled servant out into the tavern in his place.

"You know my lodgings, don't you? If you see him come or go, or discover his destinations, inform me." Crispin managed to find a farthing in his scrip and pressed it into Lenny's hand. "Get my meaning?"

Lenny's face broke into a wide, toothless grin. "Thank you, Master Crispin! I've always said what a fine gentleman you are!" Lenny scooted off the bench and bowed, stepping backward toward the hearth. His gray clothes blended into the shadows and smoke.

Over his cup, Crispin hid his face behind his upraised hand and watched the hooded man make his way up the stairs. The man stood at the landing, glanced down with a shadowed face at the bustling patrons, and stepped quickly into his room.

Crispin set his cup down, belched, and rose. He looked around the tavern but no one was paying him any heed when he stepped lightly up the stairs. He knocked on the door. No reply, but the thin strip of flickering light below the door vanished. Crispin smiled grimly. He knocked again, and again received only quiet. He drew near the door, and in a harsh whisper said, "Smith! I know you are there. Best let me in before I call the hue and cry."

For a moment nothing happened. Crispin waited, poised to knock again, when the latch lifted. The door opened to a thin slit. Crispin could just see the slim outline of half a face through the narrow opening. "What do you want?" said the voice behind the door. His accent reminded Crispin of his days in the Holy Land with the duke of Lancaster's retinue. The followers of Muhammad were swarthy and dark-haired and spoke in a tongue like this man. Smith indeed!

"I would talk with you."

"I will cut the tongue out of that dog of an innkeeper."

"You needn't. I can be quite persuasive in my own way."

The single brown eye that studied Crispin blinked once. The voice grunted, "I do not care to talk to you or anyone."

The door began to close, but Crispin leaned heavily against it. "I wish to speak of Philippa Walcote."

The pressure on the door ceased. "Who?"

"She is a client of mine. I wish to ask some questions regarding your relationship with her."

The man gave a lecherous chuckle behind the door and suddenly slammed it, throwing the bolt.

Crispin clenched his teeth and stared impotently at the closed door for a long moment. He flicked his gaze to a nearby rushlight and thought of setting the door on fire before a better plan occurred to him.

Hurrying down the steps, Crispin trotted out the door to the court-yard and found the same ladder from before leaning against the stable wall. He grabbed it and gently placed it under the window. The shutters were slightly ajar and he smiled as he climbed.

Once at the top rung he peered into the room through the cracked shutters and saw the man sitting before the fire. Crispin girded himself and leaped, shoulder first.

He crashed through the shutters and rolled across the floor before regaining his feet, pulling his dagger.

The man was up, his chair thrown down. He reached for his own dagger, but Crispin shook his head. "Too late for that. Sit down."

The man scowled. Keeping his gaze glued to Crispin, he bent, righted the chair, and gingerly sat.

"Keep your hands where I can see them," Crispin ordered, and the man complied. His face was round and flat, mouth wide like a frog's with bulging amphibian eyes sitting below the dark crests of black, bushy brows. Bronzed skin tones told of sunny places. "Now then, Master Smith. What is your real name?"

"Does it matter?"

"I'm not a patient man. I begin by slapping, move quickly to my fists, and then to my knife. You won't find it pleasant."

The man registered no emotion except for a fleeting look of admiration. "Are you skilled enough to slice thin strips of flesh from the muscle? This is very excruciating and very effective."

Crispin tightened his grip on the dagger. "Does knowledge of your name require such extremes?"

"Abid Assad Mahmoud. It is easier for you English to pronounce 'Smith.'" When he said "Smith" his wide mouth stretched, revealing uneven, serrated teeth.

Crispin nodded. "You're a Saracen."

"I am of the fortunate race of the Prophet Muhammad, infidel. But who I am is of no importance."

"What have you to do with Philippa Walcote?"

"That whore?"

Before he knew what he was doing, Crispin backhanded Mahmoud hard. He was satisfied to see blood on the man's mouth. But Mahmoud seemed satisfied, too, and a smile grew on his features before he spat the blood onto the floor.

Crispin straightened, keeping the dagger at the ready. "I prefer a more civilized description."

"Is there a more civilized description for her kind? A woman who would lay with a man for a price?"

How good it would feel, thought Crispin, to plunge his knife into the man's eye. After thrashing about a bit, he would die as the blade slowly bored into his brain.

Crispin gritted his teeth again and sheathed the blade to remove the temptation. "She is a wealthy woman," he replied more calmly than he felt. "She has no need to sell herself."

"Did I say it was for money? Does not everyone have a price?"

Crispin drew aim down his sharp nose at Mahmoud. "You extorted her for sex? What kind of man are you?"

"The kind who gets what he wants."

The door flung open. Two figures silhouetted against the bright doorway rushed forward. Crispin tried to draw his dagger, but one man closed enormous hands over his throat. The hands pressed tighter until Crispin could not take another breath. The already dark room sank to blackness and then nothing.

8

COLD WATER LAPPED OVER Crispin's nose and mouth, and he
jerked awake, choking and spitting. He blinked, trying to make sense
of his surroundings. He shivered from the cold and wet. Dark. He
seemed to be moving, floating.

Slowly, he realized his hands were lashed behind his back and his
ankles tied together. He bobbed in the water against something hard
and jagged.

Now wide-eyed and fully awake, Crispin measured his predicament. Dead of night, floating in the Thames, and bound. His feet
were tied to something. A weight? But if they were, shouldn't he be in
the bottom of the river by now?

He jerked his legs but they were caught on something. Whatever
they had used hadn't worked and his own natural buoyancy had kept
him alive. At least for now. He had obviously drifted with the current
and was deposited under a wharf.

A swell thrashed him against the crusty pier and washed over his
face. He spat the brackish water and lifted his chin. If he did not
drown with the tide, he would certainly be battered to death.

Night still hung above the lapping water in dense, bloated clouds
of fog. To call for help was useless. No one would hear. He struggled

with his bonds, but the water made the rough rope tight. His clothes added more weight. His belt cinched the wet garments to his waist.

The belt. His knife! Still there?

With cold-deadened hands, he felt with the tips of his fingers for the belt. Index and middle fingers grasped it. He pulled in his gut and managed to inch the belt slowly around his waist. Another swell made him rise and washed another brackish swallow of water in his mouth. He shivered but willed himself to stop, to calm his racked body. In such a state, the work would take longer, and he knew he didn't have much time left. His whole body felt numb and heavy as if it had soaked up the entire Thames.

Laboriously, he continued to drag the belt, but it pulled his coat into bulging gathers.

His fingers touched something. The scabbard? He walked his fingers along the leather until he felt the dagger's metal guard. He pulled the belt further—difficult for the soaking coat—and managed to wrap his fingers around the hilt.

A disorienting wave lifted him and he hit the pier. Barnacles cut into his shoulder, exciting a wave of pain. He spat water, forgetting the ache and numbness, and concentrated on the dagger's hilt.

Slowly, he edged the knife from the sheath. The hilt danced on the tips of his deadened fingers. Then the knife slipped. He clenched his hands. They were so cold he wasn't sure if he had it. He squeezed with all his might and detected something there. *Not the coat*, he prayed. Something hard between his fingers.

The knife hilt.

He forced his lungs to breathe fully and evenly against his shivering. He inched the blade from its sheath, using his heartbeat as a measuring guide. Slowly . . . slowly. He felt the tip linger on the edge of the sheath and teeter once free. The knife hung for a moment in his hands. He blew out a breath just as a swell covered his mouth and his breath came out as bubbles. He crashed against the pier again, numbing the scratched shoulder. He tightened his grip on the knife, thankful to have a hold of it.

Though he could no longer feel his knees, he bent them so his knife could reach the tether at his ankles. The action rolled his back and pulled his face below the water. He held his breath for as long as he could and sawed at the wet rope.

Flexing his knees again, he popped his face above the water, took a deep breath, and plunged again, straining his shoulders to saw his feet free from behind his back. Back and forth he bent and flexed and then rested. It seemed to take hours. Was it taking hours? Crispin's mind unfocused, and he shook out his head to sharpen his concentration again. If he let his mind go he would certainly die.

The rope snapped and his numb feet floated free. He rested a moment before he pulled his knees to his chest and rolled in the water. With a grunt, he yanked his bound hands up from under his feet to the front. One hand hung on his boot. The effort tired him and he bobbed in the water for a span, spine curled, one leg straight with the other gathered to his chest. He breathed, gazed for a moment at the stars, and wondered, only briefly, if it was the last time he would see them.

With waning strength he pulled his hand free. Both legs were now straight and his arms hung forward. With hands still bound, he swam to shore, unsure where along the Thames he was, and crawled up the bank. He lay on the rocky beach, shivering and panting. Gathering what was left of his strength, he drew the knife blade down with his fingers and sawed at the bonds at his wrist while lying prone, the waves lapping at his boots. And then . . .

Free.

Crispin sprawled on his back, arms splayed like a damp crucifix, the stones of the shore digging into his spine. But he did not care. He was alive. Finally he turned over and rose on his hands and knees, spitting out the last of the Thames. Unsteadily he regained his feet and wrapped his sodden cloak about him, though its icy dampness did little to protect from the cold. *I must go home* pulsed through his mind. Between the strangulation by Mahmoud's henchmen and the near drowning, Crispin's head was good for nothing but the one thought.

He staggered up the bank and glanced up the road, recognizing Thames Street at the mouth of the Walbrook. At least he landed on the correct side of the river, though he had a long way to go to the Shambles.

Crispin gathered his cloak and hugged himself, dragging his numb feet one in front of the other. Vaguely, he thought of seeking shelter in a tavern, but those establishments were surely barred at this time of night. He saw no lights in any windows.

The wind gave no quarter and whipped about his wet clothes, encasing him in an icy cocoon.

Somehow he managed to get to the Shambles, to ascend the stairs of Martin Kemp's tinker shop. But when he reached the landing he was unable to uncurl his claw of a hand to open his own door. Out of the wind but far from warm, Crispin collapsed at his threshold just as Jack Tucker opened the door.

CRISPIN DREAMED OF THE giant hearths at Lancaster's palace. Sheathed in a large fur robe, he settled on a cushion before the blazing fire. A pot of mulled wine warmed soothingly near the flames and its aroma of spices and cinnamon melted his humor into a mellow mood.

Someone nudged his shoulder. "Master," he said. "Master Crispin."

Crispin opened his sticky eyes and slowly recognized Jack. The robes wound round him were not fur but woolens, and the spiced aroma from the fire was little more than his steaming clothes drying before the hearth.

"My lord," said Jack, kneeling by the bed and ignoring Crispin's admonitions not to use the latent title. "What happened to you, sir?"

Crispin pulled the warm, dry blanket under his chin. He looked down at his wrist and the raw weal encircling the bone where the ropes had been. "Our friend at the Thistle," he began, in a raspy whisper, "has even bigger friends. I do not think I was meant to survive."

He recounted to Jack all he knew, from the first moments of his encounter with Mahmoud to his struggle in the freezing Thames.

Jack did not close his mouth throughout the telling, shaking his head and muttering prayers. When Crispin finished, Jack frowned. "So Philippa Walcote sold her body to this pagan—not for money, but because . . . because why?"

"An interesting question. One I shall put to her the moment I am able to stand."

Jack rubbed his mouth and squinted. "But Master. Might she be in danger now that this man has told you their doings?"

"They think I am dead. But she needs to be warned that perhaps Mahmoud's intentions have changed. You'd better give her a message."

Jack nodded, his hand on his knife hilt.

Crispin thought of asking Jack to get his writing things, but he worried at Philippa's reading skills. "Get her alone, Jack. Tell her that the man at the Thistle has told me all and her life may be in jeopardy." He lay back and licked his lips. They tasted of fear. "Go quickly, Jack."

9

CRISPIN AWOKE THE NEXT morning. No sign of Jack, and the fire dimmed to a few halfhearted flames. Crispin wrapped the woolens about him and staggered toward the hearth. He grasped the poker and broke up the slabs of peat mingled with bundled sticks, renewing the fire's fervor. He stood unsteadily and stared into the hearth, hoping Jack's message was made plain enough to Philippa. His heart buffeted his chest when he thought of her. Why was she giving herself to this man? Was she mad? What did she need to protect so badly that she was willing to subject herself to Mahmoud's lust? Was it the Mandyllon?

He straightened. He still felt shaky but wanted to get to Philippa himself and talk with her. She must not go back to Mahmoud . . . or did she already know that? Better yet, he'd rather pay a visit to Mahmoud and find out what the man was hiding. If it was something about the Mandyllon, perhaps he could bargain.

After all, Crispin knew where it was.

He threw off the blankets and carefully dressed. The clothes were dry but still smelled of the Thames, though with a smoky tinge.

He descended the steps unsteadily, resting halfway. He supported himself with a hand to the wall and continued down until he reached the bottom.

He lifted his head and stared down the avenue. He hadn't felt this weak in a long time and wondered if this were the best time to face Mahmoud. But then the scene of Philippa in Mahmoud's room filled his mind. Damn her and her secrecy! If only she would say. How he hated secrets.

The Thistle had never seemed farther.

He trudged down lane after lane, hugging his cloak against the shrill wind that snaked through the twisting streets. It brought with it a cascade of whirling brown leaves plucked from autumn-dead trees. They rambled about his feet like playful pups, darting unpredictably before and behind. Their playfulness would turn soon enough once the earnestness of winter hit—not with a patter but more like the sound of rattling bones.

His steps echoed. *His* steps? He took a brief glance behind and saw, distantly, a man in livery, head bent forward out of the wind. The man trudged diligently though not as quickly as Crispin.

Crispin turned a few corners, just to see, and looked back again.

The man was gone.

Suspicious. Every footfall was now filled with portent. His mouth felt dry even though he'd almost swallowed all the Thames. It wasn't water he wanted. It was wine, and plenty of it.

Crispin reached the Thistle and spied Lenny trying to blend into the street's shadows. Crispin glanced at him and Lenny gave him an acknowledging nod.

Entering the inn's warm interior, Crispin sighed. The smoky fire partially obscured the nameless men beside the hearth, and the others at farther tables were too absorbed by their drink and food to bother with him.

He stood for a moment and scanned the room, trying to locate the men who guarded Mahmoud, but he did not recognize anyone. The men who had tried to kill him seemed enormous, but he never really got a good look at them. They could be any of a number of these men in the room, laughing over their beakers of ale.

It didn't matter. He strode across the room, licking his lips at the many jugs of wine, and caught sight of the innkeeper. The man blanched when he spied Crispin and tried to escape through the kitchens.

Crispin lunged for the kitchen curtain and grabbed the innkeeper by the long tail of his hood. "Leaving?" he growled and drew him into a corner of the warm kitchen. Crispin pulled him close till he almost cradled the man against him.

The innkeeper turned a bruised face to Crispin. "Now good Master, you've done me ill. See what he's done!"

"Give me the key."

He shook his head furiously. "He'll kill me! He said so."

"How much gold did they give you to look the other way as they dragged me bound and bleeding into the night?"

"But—" the tavernkeeper sputtered.

Crispin's fist silenced the man. When he crumpled to the floor, Crispin farmed the key ring from his belt. He offered a warning sneer to the petrified kitchen servants and made for the stairs. When he reached the landing, he used the key and flung wide the door. Mahmoud sat hunched over his plate of roasted meat and pickled cucumbers. When he saw Crispin, he tossed the entire table aside.

"You!" Mahmoud reached for the curved dagger at his belt, but he was far too slow. Crispin threw a sloppy punch. Instead of a smooth uppercut, it was a ragged sideways swipe, but it did the trick as neatly as a clear shot. His knuckles connected with the jaw, slamming the teeth together. Blood spurted between Mahmoud's suddenly flaccid lips. A fan of red sprayed across his chest. He staggered backward, giving Crispin the opportunity to drop his fist in Mahmoud's belly. Mahmoud bent double and struggled for breath and footing. Crispin closed and locked the door. No more interruptions.

He returned to Mahmoud, watched him gasp for a moment bent as he was, and with a smile of satisfaction, reared back and kicked him in the face with the heel of his boot.

Mahmoud fell to the floor unconscious. A patch of blood and spittle pooled under his cheek.

Crispin rubbed his hand and unsheathed Mahmoud's dagger. He examined its curved blade and admired its sharpness before tossing it into the fire.

Crispin righted the table and looked for a wine jug but remembered that Saracens were disposed against spirits. "Uncivilized," he muttered and picked up the chair and sat. He watched Mahmoud's immobile form gurgle. Each breath made red, bloody bubbles at his nostrils.

The sunlight in the room soon changed. Crispin decided he could wait no longer. He took a nearby jug of water and poured it on the man's head.

Mahmoud sputtered and blinked. He scrambled to a sitting position and glared at Crispin. He ran his hand over his face, wincing at the newly formed bruises. "You are most difficult to kill," he sneered.

"So I've been told." Crispin crouched close before him and Mahmoud darted a glance down for his own blade, but Crispin nodded toward the fire. Mahmoud looked, gasped, and turned a burning countenance to Crispin.

"There'll be no games this time," said Crispin. "Why did you and your men try to kill me?"

Mahmoud repositioned himself as if he were used to sitting on the floor. He looked at his unbound wrists.

"No, I didn't bind you, though perhaps I should have done. I also did not call the sheriff. I thought to discuss this man to man." He smiled grimly. "I still may bind you or call the sheriff. It all depends on you."

Mahmoud ran the back of his hand under his chin and wiped away the blood. He chuckled. "I like men who are hard to kill. It is more satisfactory when the task is finally done."

Crispin stood, smiled at Mahmoud, even chuckled along with him, and kicked him in the face again.

The Saracen fell back, his smile gone. Groggily, he righted himself. His dark eyes, crinkled to mere slashes, followed Crispin's every move.

Crispin sat again. His smile never faded from his face. "You are in no position to talk of killing. Shall we get on with it?"

Mahmoud's expression turned dour. His cheek swelled from Crispin's boot. He shrugged. "Why not?" He glanced at the other chair by the hearth. "May I rise?"

Crispin's crooked smile remained. "No."

The Saracen touched his bleeding forehead with a trembling hand. Crispin knew it was not from fear. "I am a member of a . . . how shall I call it? A syndicate."

"Of Saracens?"

"No. Italians. Their interests are my interests."

"Why is that?"

He smiled. There was blood on his teeth. "Because they pay me."

"What is this syndicate?"

Mahmoud rolled his tongue in his mouth and spat out a tooth. "Merchants. Men with a great deal to gain by combining forces."

"A guild, you mean?"

"No, not a guild. Something far more powerful. Guilds do not have as members—" He stopped himself. He pointed a scolding uncle's finger at Crispin with a laugh. "I mustn't tell, must I? Too much loose information could make my employers very unhappy. And that could be lethal."

"Very well. The members of this syndicate are secret and powerful. I assume their activities are far from legal."

"They operate somewhat outside the law and also within it. They fix prices for goods, create demand, strangle the supply to raise prices. Even piracy."

Crispin nodded. "I see. Criminals operating a cartel."

"Criminals? Oh no. Men such as these are never called criminals. They are called sir."

"Even a lord can be a criminal," he said, examining his nails. "I used to be both." His smile broadened, but it wasn't pleasant. He leaned to-ward Mahmoud. "Why are they operating in England? Should I not go to court with this information, these aliens working their wiles on English soil?"

"Do what you wish. The authorities will never find them. Or me. We are like smoke. Dispersed with a whisper."

Crispin eyed the door. "Smoke, eh? Even smoke has a source that can be located."

"But only once the fire is long gone."

Crispin considered. This cartel sounded like an ambitious enter-prise. Mahmoud hinted at the high status of its masters. If they were Italians then this implicated dukes and princes. The Italians were famed for such treachery among their courtiers. This was a great deal more to worry over than he thought.

He studied Mahmoud's bruised and swelling face. This was the face he saw mauling Philippa in this room. "What has any of this to do with Philippa Walcote?"

Mahmoud sat back and made a noise of disgust in the back of his throat. "This again? Let us just say . . . it was a bonus."

Crispin rose.

Mahmoud raised his hand in defense. "If you kick me again, I fear I shall have no more teeth left to tell you what you wish to know."

Crispin deliberated and took his time. Was Mahmoud's informa-tion more important than Crispin's desire to batter him to death? In the end, he decided he'd at least listen first. There would always be more time later for violence.

He sat and pulled the chair closer and rested a taut fist against his thigh. "I'm all ears."

Mahmoud licked his lips before spitting another tooth into his hand. He looked at it, sneered at Crispin, and threw it over his shoul-der. "It is best you do not know too much. What these men did to you—what they tried to do to you—is nothing compared to what they might attempt this time."

"Are you trying to warn me off?"

"It is for your own good. You are obviously a very clever man. You must know that staying alive is the best trick of all."

"What makes you believe you can frighten me?"

"Frighten?" He shrugged. "Very well. What is your price, then?"

"There is something called honor, you bastard. I do not have a price."

"I understand your price is sixpence a day."

Crispin's grin returned. "That is my fee. As for my price, there is none high enough."

"So I am told."

"So you know me."

"I know of you. And so I tell you truly, man to man, you must not pursue this."

Crispin rose but only to pace. Mahmoud kept a nervous eye on him.

Crispin glanced at the light from under the door and saw no shadows of men lying in wait. Neither did he see anything at the shattered window. "Pursue what?"

Mahmoud's frog's mouth slid open, the widely spaced teeth now wider. "I will give you nothing more."

Crispin looked down at the blood on his boots. "My foot is not in the least tired."

"Do with me what you will. I am trained to withstand it."

Crispin appraised the man, certain he was telling the truth. "A pagan bedding a Christian woman. Give me a reason why I should not kill you now."

"If I die, so does the woman."

A chill vibrated down Crispin's spine and radiated to the back of his knees. Now more than ever he wanted to kill him. He did everything he could to control that urge, including putting the chair and table between them.

"So you see," continued Mahmoud, "there is nothing more to

discuss. My associates will be surprised to hear of your recovery, but I will tell them, if you make no more provocative moves, to let you be. Should it appear that you are uncooperative, then your resurrection will be short-lived."

"*You*, threatening *me*? You, who have my boot marks upon your face?"

"It is a small price to pay. And my associates are many. My employers have long arms."

Crispin chuffed a laugh. "Italian syndicate indeed! What nonsense. A mob of Venetian merchants!"

"Lombardy."

"Lombardy, is it?"

Mahmoud's smile dimmed. "Perhaps." He shrugged, a little nervously, Crispin thought. Had he given away too much? "If you don't believe me, well then. You must certainly kill me."

Crispin's lip curled. He approached Mahmoud with steady steps. His naked hand curled into a fist.

"Yet I see in your eyes that kernel of doubt," said Mahmoud quickly. "Do I speak the truth? If she died it would be your fault. And you are the kind of man who possesses the luxury of guilt. Whereas I am not."

Crispin did not stop his advance. He grabbed the man's hair, yanked, and pulled his dagger, close to sliding its sharp edge over his throat. Mahmoud never took his gaze from Crispin's.

The blade poised at Mahmoud's throat a long time. Crispin watched the play of firelight undulate on the knife's shiny face.

But as much as he desired to spill the Saracen's blood, to let it run hot and fast across the floor, he worried Mahmoud might have spoken the truth. He could not let harm come to Philippa. The thought curdled his blood.

He withdrew his blade and backed away. "You will have no more congress with her."

"Perhaps."

Crispin decided to play his hand. "Is it the cloth you want?"

Mahmoud blinked slowly but betrayed nothing, neither recognition of the cloth nor puzzlement.

"Did you hear me?"

"Quite well, Lord Crispin. I simply have no reply."

Mahmoud's loosened tongue had fallen silent and there was nothing more Crispin could do. But there was one thing he could make certain of. "Nevertheless, you will have nothing more to do with Philippa Walcote."

Mahmoud smiled.

"There is worse I can do to you than kill." To emphasize the point, Crispin crouched beside Mahmoud, picked up a cucumber from the floor, and beheaded the tip with the sharp knife.

Mahmoud's smile faded.

"We have an understanding," said Crispin through his teeth. He tossed the cucumber aside and rose to his full height. Crispin wiped the knife, sheathed it, and strode with deliberate indolence to the exit, slamming the door behind him.

HIS ONLY THOUGHT WAS to get to Philippa as quickly as possible, but the rain was rasping harder, making the heavily trodden street a slurry.

Crispin finally arrived at the Walcote manor and made his way to the kitchen entrance. He felt relief at seeing a friendly face.

"John Hoode!" he called and the man stopped.

"Crispin! Tut! Your face will never heal if you keep getting into fights."

Crispin touched his swollen cheek. In his confrontation with Mahmoud, he'd forgotten it. He took Hoode aside and spoke in low tones. "Never mind that. I know you are here in the kitchens, but I want you to do your best to keep an eye on your mistress."

Hoode's tone dropped to match Crispin's. "Whatever for?"

"Her life may be in danger. Since you are here in this house when I am not, I ask that you be vigilant."

"Bless me!" he whispered in an irritatingly high tenor. "I won't have to fight anyone, will I? I don't mind saying that I'm not made for that."

Crispin eyed his long hands and tapered fingers. "I hope it will not come to that. Just make certain to send a message to me if any foreigners come to call."

"What sort of foreigners?"

"Saracens. Or Italians. Both are dangerous."

"Can you tell me what this is about? I'll feel a bit of a fool jumping at the merest shadow, thinking the worst."

He eyed Hoode and forced his lips into a tight line. "Perhaps it is best not to speak of it. Only inform me if these strangers intrude."

"I don't know how I'm to do that, unless you let your man stay."

"Is Jack here now?"

"Oh aye. I thought you knew."

"Where?"

Hoode led Crispin into a storeroom. Jack sat on a firkin, his face bulging with food and a half-eaten pasty in his hand.

"Master!" he sputtered. Food dribbled down his shirt when he shot to his feet. He swallowed hastily and wiped his mouth with his hand. He looked down at the pasty and stuffed it in his scrip. "I thought I'd find you here anon. I've been looking for you. I've got something from the sheriff."

Crispin watched Jack wipe his hands down his tunic. It did not bode well that the sheriff was sending him written messages.

With relatively clean hands, Jack pulled the missive free from his belt and handed the folded paper to Crispin. Crispin raised a brow at the wax seal and turned the parcel in his hands. The thick parchment was rough under his fingers and it made a soft crackling sound as he turned it again.

He bent the parchment at the seal and snapped it, pushing the rest open with a fingernail and cursing when some of the wax embedded under the nail. Carefully, he unfolded the missive and flattened it against his thigh. He lifted it to the light and read.

"He sealed it and everything," said Jack excitedly. "What's it mean?"

Crispin lowered the parchment again, the formal words on the missive running through his mind. "It is a summons, a formal command to attend him."

Jack scratched his chin. "He's called you before with messengers. Why so proper this time?"

"Indeed. That's what worries me." The note was plain enough; the language uninspired and vague. He folded it again and put it in his purse. "Did you give your message to Mistress Walcote?"

"Aye. But she pretended she didn't know what I was talking about."

"Damn the woman!" His hand slapped the scabbard, trying to find comfort in the hard solidity of the weapon. He had no time for her now. "I must answer this summons. Stay here. Tell Mistress Walcote that you will escort her to the Boar's Tusk in an hour's time. Do not take 'no' for an answer. Hoode here will explain. He'll send you to me if it is necessary."

10

WHEN CRISPIN REACHED WYNCHECOMBE'S hall he stood in the doorway a long time before the sheriff acknowledged him. With a curt nod, Wynchecombe motioned for Crispin to enter and he walked cautiously forward under the arch. Piled with writs, Wynchecombe's table stood beside the roaring hearth. Crispin stood as close as he could to the fire, though it was hard to feel real warmth in such a place.

The sheriff took a swig of his wine without looking up and signed a document before reaching for another. He read it, his head tracking from side to side.

Crispin had known Simon Wynchecombe long enough to realize he was being played with. The man delayed the inevitable—whatever that was and for whatever reason. Was it the seriousness of the summons that gave Wynchecombe pause? The thought certainly pitched the butterflies in Crispin's stomach into a blizzard.

The fire cast a bright and deceptively comforting glow into the room, and a fat candle on his desk did its best to illumine the papers. The oiled animal skin stretched taut in the window frame allowed the sunlight, such as it was, to filter through its golden aura. A rushlight torch in a sconce brightened a corner, but this, too, could only do so much for the gloom that frowned across the tower room. Crispin wasn't certain whether Wynchecombe preferred it dark or didn't know any better.

The sheriff poised his quill over the document and lingered. The tip dripped a blob of black ink onto the page but it didn't distract the sheriff. Finally, he tossed the paper aside unsigned with an exhaled, "Bah!"

Raising his head at last, he glared at Crispin through his black brows. His mouth turned down in a gargoyle's exaggerated grimace when he looked him over. "By the mass! What happened to you?"

Crispin did not touch his face this time. The dull throb of leftover bruises reminded him enough of what his face looked like. His neck still felt the marks of the henchman's fingers. "Some of it is your work and some the work of others."

"You continue to be popular," the sheriff said with a smirk.

"As always, my Lord Sheriff." Crispin thought it mete to add a bow, but it appeared more patronizing than appeasing. "Prior to this you sent messengers and 'escorts.'" He pulled the missive from his scrip and held it up before letting it glide to the table. "Why this time a summons?"

"A summons is official. It is a record that you were called to this place at this time." Wynchecombe picked up the document and called for his clerk in the outer room. The burly man entered, took the parchment from Wynchecombe's hand, and left the room, raising his head only once to glare at Crispin. "Sometimes," said the sheriff, "it's important to have a record."

"I ask again. Why?"

Wynchecombe glared at him, paused for some sort of emphasis—that he was among the elect and Crispin was not. But it did no good. "Dammit Crispin. Must you be privy to everything?" He lifted his papers halfheartedly and let them fall again. "We have an informal relationship, you and I. Perhaps too informal."

"Is that *your* complaint? Or the complaint of others?"

"I will not discuss this with you. I called you here and it is enough that I did so. This is the office of the Lord Sheriff. That explanation should be satisfactory enough for you. Now I want to know if you have discovered the murderer yet?"

"No. Have you?"

Wynchecombe made a disgusted snort and sat back, allowing informality to creep back into their parley. "You have no idea the trouble this work is. Sheriffing. I tried to refuse it when the 'honor' came my way, but the king's laws make certain one's obedience."

"Heavy fines?"

"'Heavy' is not the word. I have my own business to run, you know. But when the king commands . . ."

"Yes, I know well."

Wynchecombe seemed to forget his own troubles for a moment and smiled at Crispin's. "So you do."

"Simon, my patience is sorely tried. Did you bring me here to tell me new evidence or to acquire some from me?"

"Do you have new evidence?"

Crispin's crooked smile returned. "No."

"Liar." Wynchecombe rose and leaned over his desk. "And don't call me Simon."

"Of course, my lord." He raised a hand to his aching head. He wished Wynchecombe would let him sit before he fell over.

Wynchecombe lowered back into his chair and waved Crispin to one as well. Crispin eased down.

The sheriff gnarled his hands into frustrated fists. His features darkened in the dim light of his chamber.

"This business of Nicholas Walcote," said the sheriff. "I think you best leave it to the authorities."

"Oh? Why?"

The sheriff slammed his fist against the table. He gritted his teeth. "Because I said so!"

"Oh well then. That is settled."

"Don't be flippant, Guest. I do not think you would fare well if I decided to take my fists to you again."

"I've had enough of fists for the moment," he admitted and rubbed his jaw.

"I heard some strange tidings about you. Something about getting tossed into the Thames?"

Crispin chuckled. "There's nothing to tell. As you say. I am still popular."

"If you will not say, then there is nothing I can do. Content yourself and forget about Walcote."

"And why should I care to do that? The man owes me money."

"The man is dead."

"Yes. And I admit that makes it harder to collect."

"What did he owe you?" Wynchecombe reached for his scrip and brought out some coins from a pouch.

Crispin rose. His lips parted with disbelief. "What . . . what are you doing?"

"I'm paying the debt so that you can put this aside."

"What goes on here? You? Paying my fee?"

"Crispin, just take these coins and content you."

None of it made sense. A syndicate. Saracens. Italians. A dead merchant and a holy relic. And now Wynchecombe paying his fee? "Who told you to warn me off this case? You said the guild was pressuring you to make a conclusion. Did they force you to write this summons? What do they have to do with the king's justice?" Crispin's mind lighted on the accounting ledgers and especially the customs book back in his lodgings. It also made him think of the man in livery following him. Was it a guild's livery?

Wynchecombe screwed up his lips but said nothing. "Mark me," he said at last. "Bad things can happen to disobedient servants. So why don't you be an obedient fellow and forget about the murder and simply take these coins!"

"To hell with your coins!"

"Don't pursue this. You will regret it if you do."

Almost the same words Mahmoud used. Crispin studied the

sheriff's tightened face, and though its expression appeared strained, it revealed nothing more.

"Just do as I bid, Crispin. For your own good, stay out of this."

The wet wood on the fire hissed its steam, and a rat scurried somewhere along the wall; a counterpoint to the silence and to Crispin's undigested thoughts.

"I see. May I go, Lord Sheriff?"

Wynchecombe sighed. "Are you going to leave it alone?"

He blinked slowly. "May I go?"

The sheriff rolled back in his thronelike chair and curled his fingers around the carved arms. He raised one hand to gnaw at a knuckle. An oval stone on his ring reflected the disinterested light. He stroked his mustache with the ring until he dropped his hand to his lap. "Go, then. But if you do not heed me, no one but God can help you."

Crispin bowed low, the way he used to at court, and swept quickly from the chamber.

HE WALKED BRUSQUELY TOWARD the Boar's Tusk wondering what had just transpired. Obviously Wynchecombe was hiding something. He'd never told Crispin to stay away from an investigation before. If anything, the opposite was true. *Was* the mercer's guild pressuring the sheriff? And if so, what did they hold over Wynchecombe that they could twist him to their will?

Crispin turned his head, glancing up Newgate's high walls before they disappeared beyond the roof peaks and spires of London's clustered streets. The only thing that made him feel better at all was the prospect of wine at the Boar's Tusk and of seeing Philippa, though not necessarily in that order.

He crossed the lane and only glanced to the side to make certain no carts would run him down when he noticed two men a stone's throw away. They wouldn't have been particularly noticeable had the one not had extremely broad shoulders and a head of black, curly hair. His well-shaped but large nose overshadowed dark, thick lips. The other man was small-boned and stood shorter, only making it as far as the larger one's shoulder. His face, sharp and pointed, was more like a rat's. They wore decent clothes but not English garb. And they were staring at him.

Crispin walked a long time, but he couldn't be certain they weren't following him until he ducked down an alley and out into another avenue. A surreptitious glance back told him he had company.

He wove through alleys that were little more than a tight gap, and stepped quickly down familiar streets. *Stay with me, gentlemen. It's only a little farther.*

He found the dead-end alley he wanted and climbed some barrels to the roof. He laid himself flat on the rain-slick tiles, loosened two slates—one for each hand—and waited.

II

THE THUD OF THE men's footsteps approached, and Crispin heard them enter the dead-end alley and stop. Crispin resisted the urge to look over the edge of the eave, knowing they would probably be looking up.

"*Joseph Santo!*" swore one of them. "*Porcoddio!*"

"*Siamo nella merda!*" said the other one.

By their voices he knew their exact location. He hurled the slates over the roof. They landed with a pop on each head.

Crispin heard the men swear and go down. He slipped over the edge to look. The smaller one raised his hand to his head and Crispin noticed he was missing two fingers down to the first knuckles.

Crispin leaped down and blocked the alley's mouth. He drew his dagger. "Who are you?"

The smaller one glared at Crispin and drew his own long, thin dagger. "Devil take you, *bastardo!*"

"Wait," said the other, holding the smaller one back. The wide-shouldered one straightened, still grimacing at the ache in his head. "We're only here to talk to this *stronzo*, remember?"

The small one made a disgusted snort and slammed his dagger in its sheath.

"I ask again," said Crispin. "Who are you?"

"I'm Sclavo," said the large man. "And this," he motioned to his companion, "is Two-Fingers."

"Interesting. Here in England we only give our animals such appellations."

Two-Fingers lunged, but Sclavo held him back again. "I may not stop him next time, *Signore* Guest. After all, he's the one who tied your hands and feet good and tight, did he not?"

"*Sì.* You do not forget your midnight swim, eh?" asked Two-Fingers.

Crispin frowned. "No, I recall it very well."

Sclavo chuckled. "Not many have escaped us. You embarrassed us in front of our master."

"Indeed. Forgive me for surviving. Such bad manners."

"No matter," said Sclavo. "We have much to discuss. Shall we go elsewhere? This alley is damp."

Not the Boar's Tusk. Philippa was there. "Yes, after you, gentlemen." He motioned with the dagger and stepped aside out of their reach.

With the two walking in front of him, Crispin directed them to the Dog and Bone, a tavern south of his lodgings and situated on Carter Lane, huddled in the shadow of St. Paul's. They entered first and sat at a table close to the entrance. Should they turn on him, he'd need a quick escape, so he broke his usual custom and kept his back to the door.

The Dog and Bone was smaller than the Boar's Tusk and much grimier. The great room always smelled as if something had died in one of its corners.

"Our master wishes to make negotiation with you," said Sclavo. He rested his arm on the sticky table and hunched his massive shoulders. "He knows who you are."

"I'm enchanted. But I have nothing more to say to Mahmoud."

Sclavo looked at Two-Fingers and laughed. "Mahmoud? He is not our master. We merely do occasional tasks for him. On orders from our master."

"Then who is your master?"

Sclavo chuckled. Two-Fingers made a sound like a laugh, but it was a noise more like a cat coughing up a hairball. "We do not speak his name," said Sclavo.

"I won't negotiate with men I don't know."

"Don't refuse so quickly, *Signore* Guest. If you do not like our offer, you can go on your way."

"Am I expected to believe that?"

Sclavo shrugged. "We have no orders to kill you. If we had . . ." He shrugged again. Two-Fingers giggled. "We would not be having this conversation."

Crispin smiled. "Like the last time, eh?"

Two-Fingers stopped. He reached for his dagger, but Sclavo shook his head. "You are so hot-headed, *il mio amico*."

Two-Fingers gestured with the two fingers of his other hand and spat at Crispin.

Sclavo smiled. "What would you say to bags of coins?"

Crispin lowered his brows. "Italian?"

Sclavo smiled. His thick, dark lips made a clownish show of it. "Italian, English. Whichever you prefer. Eight hundred pounds is easy to come by."

Crispin leaned back and rubbed his mouth. "I am afraid, Master Sclavo, I do not understand you."

Sclavo looked at Two-Fingers. "'Pounds' is the right word, no?" He turned to Crispin. "Our master offers you eight hundred pounds. It is an enormous sum, no? Eight hundred pounds would make you a great man of property. I understand your king's laws allow for a man who owns eighty pounds worth of land to become a knight."

Crispin scowled.

"But perhaps," Sclavo went on, "he does not mean *any* man."

"Where would your master get so many English coins?" Crispin snapped.

Sclavo only smiled.

Crispin had not seen such a fortune since his days as a lord. But more astonishing was Sclavo's master willing to offer it—and in pounds. Crispin put a few thoughts together and didn't like the implications.

He relaxed his face, made it as neutral as he could. "Indeed. And what are the other conditions?"

"No conditions. No percentages. An outright gift. It is my master's way of an apology for trying to kill you. We thought, well, does it matter? It was a mistake. Our master wishes to make amends."

"It matters to me. What 'mistake'?"

Sclavo's fingers intertwined and then opened. He did this several times in a row. Finally he leaned forward. "It was thought," he said quietly, "*you* killed Walcote, and my master did not yet want him dead. Such an offense is punishable by death." He smiled broadly and sat back. "Fortunately, you did not die."

"Fortunately. Judge, jury, and executioner, eh? Your master must be quite a fellow. I should like to meet him."

"Trust me. You do not."

Crispin tapped his fingers on his scabbard. "Then what about this generous gift? Surely there is something your master desires in return other than my undying respect."

"There is one thing. He would very much like the return of a particular piece of cloth he was promised."

"I see. Eight hundred pounds is an amazing show of confidence in my abilities."

Sclavo shrugged. "As I said, he knows of you."

"Will you grant me time to consider?"

Sclavo sat back and opened his large hands generously. "Of course. We will give you a day."

"A day?"

"Surely a man in your circumstances can decide in a day whether or not to become a wealthy man. When you've decided, send a message." He looked around him and smiled. "To the Dog and Bone."

"Not the Thistle?"

Sclavo smiled. "The Dog and Bone." He rose. Two-Fingers stood beside him. He grinned insincerely and bobbed his head.

Crispin, too, rose. He nodded to them, slipped out of the bench, and left.

They thought he killed Walcote. Why did they even suspect him? And more important, why should they care?

He stepped out onto the muddy lane. Careful to skirt puddles edged in frost that the vague sun did little to thaw, he grimaced when his foot dipped into an icy rut. A hole in his boot saw to it that his toes quickly chilled.

He stepped up under an eave and looked behind him, shaking out his boot. They didn't follow. He breathed a little easier and watched a cloud of breath swirl from his nose. Interesting. They were not Mahmoud's henchmen, even though they had acted as such. Who was their true master then? There were a score of possibilities, but the bigger picture was becoming more intriguing. "What a tapestry is woven from a single piece of cloth!"

Ideas flitted through his mind as he strode down the lane toward the Boar's Tusk and Philippa, when Crispin stopped in the middle of the street. A dreadful thought suddenly occurred to him. He pivoted away from the tavern and turned toward his lodgings instead. He had to have another look at those ledgers first.

He hustled down the Shambles and trotted up the stairs to his lodgings. When he opened the door his glance took in the table where he had left the books and he stopped dead in the threshold.

Gone.

He rushed in and looked under the table, under the bed, on the pantry shelves, at the window and finally stood with fists at his hips.

"Well," he said to the vacant room. "That answers that question."

CRISPIN TROTTED TOWARD GUTTER Lane and swore the whole way. He suspected the thieves were too clever to let themselves be seen.

He even worried that Sclavo and the taciturn Two-Fingers were sent as a ruse to keep him out of the way.

No, there was too much sincerity, too much information in their directives. And they simply could have coshed Crispin on the head again. They were sincere, right enough. But what was the game?

He ducked his head into the drizzly weather, tossing his hood over his damp hair.

The Mandyllon. This most holy of relics was the prize to the man with the most ruthless agenda. That such treachery could be associated with something so opposed to evil! Walcote was murdered . . . but maybe it wasn't for the cloth. Maybe it was for information he had. Maybe it was for what he discovered in those books. *Those damned books that are now missing!* There was corruption among the customs officers, or at least one who dealt in England's fabric market. How far did the corruption reach? And what did this ultimately have to do with these Italians?

Crispin tried to remember back to when he was a player in the politics of court. Eight years ago—longer—the Lombardy region was ruled by Milan, and the duke of Milan was—

"Bernabò Visconti," he murmured. He remembered him. He'd met him once while sent on a mission to Milan for Lancaster. Crispin was supposed to negotiate a port for trade.

Crispin recalled his arrival to Milan. He was treated well and there was a woman of the court he was particularly friendly with. He smiled. She was blue-eyed and golden-haired but was certainly no angel. The thought made him smile broader until his grin fell. The court of Visconti was not a place to let one's guard down as Crispin had. The treacherous duke agreed to all Crispin laid out to him, but later Crispin was drugged and the tables turned.

Lancaster was angry but not at Crispin, and vowed revenge though he never quite got it.

Visconti would most certainly be behind this bid for the Mandyllon. He dabbled in acquiring territory and riches as other men played at chess, and all his minions and competitors were the pawns. Poisoning, torture, extortion, abduction—these were the rates of exchange to him. He thought nothing of conniving a war between his neighbors and, like the opportunistic rook, would take over the unguarded nest.

Visconti wanted the Mandyllon, but this export scandal also smacked of his doing. Visconti must have men placed in the controller's office, possibly even the guilds themselves, and was stealing these taxes. Crispin knew the taxes were collected to fund King Richard's war chest, but what if Visconti wanted to interfere with that? There was only one person to ask.

Lancaster.

12

LANCASTER ONCE OWNED THE Savoy, a palace overlooking the Thames, but three years ago a peasant rabble burned it to the ground. Even with his many other residences in England and France, he usually stayed at court at Westminster Palace. Since King Richard was currently in residence, so was the rest of the court.

Crispin looked out across the palace courtyard. Westminster Palace was situated in the city of Westminster—close enough to London for the court to keep an eye skinned on its capital, but far enough away to avoid the rabble when necessary. It was a large set of rambling buildings, a grand edifice of sandy stone and arched windows, chapels, apartments. Its exterior was certainly not as grand as its interiors of painted floors, sumptuous tapestries, seeming miles of passageways and corridors, and the immense great hall as large as any cathedral space.

But it was still a formidable structure. It did not sit on some promontory, unapproachable by the common citizen, but seemed to revel in its central accessibility. The king, when in residence, made certain to meet with the burgesses and aldermen of London and Westminster weekly, making decisions as mundane as how many chickens could be traded for how many slabs of pork. Even young Richard with his favorites and cronies could not alter what had been for centuries.

Crispin recalled fondly the dinners in the great hall, the quiet alcoves for trysts, and even the masses celebrated with the other courtiers and hangers-on in St. Mary Undercroft. But more often than not he was in the company of Lancaster even at mass in the ornate Chapel of St. Stephen, the twin of the grand Sainte-Chapelle in Paris. Lancaster liked to keep Crispin at his side like a lapdog, but Crispin had not minded. He had been privy to many of the machinations of court, and enjoyed the status for which he was being groomed.

Until it all fell apart.

Crispin had only been to court once in the last eight years. Raised in Lancaster's household like many other noble-born boys fostered by wealthy men, Crispin began as a page, and at eighteen, Lancaster knighted him. And just as Jack served Crispin, Crispin, too, attended the man well and became Lancaster's protégé. He had enjoyed living in familiar society with Lancaster's son, Henry of Bolingbroke. Crispin's shoulders had served as "horse" many a time for young Henry. He could scarcely believe the boy he'd helped to raise was now a man of seventeen—the same age as his cousin the king.

Approaching the place forbidden him knotted his gut, but he preferred to remember the good memories in Lancaster's company than dwell on that dreadful course of events that sent him spinning away from court like a falling star.

He crossed St. Margaret's, reached the top step to the Great Gateway, and rested his fingers on the damp granite. Raising his head, he stared at one of the guards standing stiffly under the gatehouse arch. With a face stern in its tight conical helm, silvery camail surrounding his cheeks and chin, the guard's gaze took in Crispin and then dismissed him.

Crispin edged closer. His feet disrupted the gravel path.

The guard looked his way again. "Your business?"

Crispin looked the man up and down. He threw back his shoulders and raised his chin. "I wish to speak to his grace the duke of Lancaster. Tell him Crispin Guest is at the gate."

The guard's immovable face showed surprise at Crispin's manner of speech, which did not conform to the shabbiness of his clothes.

Crispin urged him to his task with a practiced tilt of the head before he turned his back on the guard. The guard left to fetch a page and Crispin waited, tapping his fingers on his scabbard, pacing and watching riders and carts travel along St. Margaret's Street.

He looked down at his shabby cotehardie. Clean, but there was no doubt of the coat's age. His stockings, too, could use some repair, but he never seemed to have the time, though Jack made certain to sew up the holes when he found them, much as Crispin had done for Lancaster's surcote after a battle when Crispin was Jack's age.

After a long spell, the page returned with what looked like a steward in tow and Crispin snapped to attention. The steward's long face sported a prominent chin and small eyes. He wore long robes trimmed in fur. A chatelaine of keys clinked importantly from his belt. He wore the badge of Gaunt on his breast.

Crispin did not recognize him, but by the scowl on the man's face, he certainly seemed to know Crispin.

The steward scrambled forward and took Crispin's arm, but Crispin wasn't fond of such familiarities and firmly removed it.

"Master Guest," said the steward. He rubbed his sore hand, the one Crispin removed from his sleeve. "If you have come for alms, I suggest you try the kitchens."

Crispin's face warmed. "I have *not* come for charity! I have vital information to impart to his grace the duke."

"His grace does not wish to receive missives from you, Master Guest." He scanned the courtyard with nervous eyes. "Of this you must certainly be aware. I must ask you to leave. His grace the duke is not at home to you."

Crispin's features stiffened. "Did he tell you so?"

"Yes, he did. Do yourself a courtesy and do not return. You do not wish to endanger my lord of Gaunt by your presence, do you?"

Crispin clenched his jaw. His molars crunched in his head. He opened his mouth to protest but didn't know what to say.

"Please, Master Guest," said the steward quietly. "The king has spies everywhere. Should they report that you were here—"

"Say no more." Crispin stared at the busy ward. Londoners walked stiffly in the wind, wrapping their cloaks tightly over their breasts. The courtyard's shrill wind was not as cold as the frost that struck his heart.

He turned back briefly to the steward, gave him a courtly bow, and noticed a growing look of pity before he jerked away from his gaze.

His heavy steps snapped over the gravel in the courtyard to the street. It was a long walk, as long as the lists, before he reached an ornate stone archway that marked the edge of the king's palace grounds.

He should have expected the rejection. In a small place in the back of his head he did expect it, but this knowledge did not make the hurt any less stinging. It was as if a father had disowned his son.

He passed under the arched gateway and came upon a wide avenue. He turned right and ducked between the shadows of spacious houses boasting large gardens and walked a long way along walled courtyards, at least a bowshot, until he reached the end of the lane, where the Thames cut the city in half. He leaned over the sea wall and stared down into its brown depths. This river nearly swallowed him up only two days ago. The men who tried to kill him were now willing to offer a king's ransom to possess the Mandyllon. Yet even if Crispin earned such bounty, it could not buy him an audience with Lancaster. That avenue was closed. How he hated the circumstances that kept him from the place he belonged!

His nails dug into the stone wall. Didn't Lancaster realize that Crispin had done it for *him*, risked all for *him*?

"But treason is treason," he murmured. The river didn't care if he poured his heart into it, told it his tales of woe. The Thames kept flowing regardless. Kept winding its way through London, carving a division between the best and the worst of the old city. That's why Crispin had stayed on the north side. No Southwark for him. No dreary low speech such as came through Jack's lips. Or Philippa Walcote's.

Yet he was still a man between. Like the river. Between the rich and the lowly and belonging to neither. He, too, would simply flow on.

He loosened a pebble with his fingers and tossed it down into the water. It sank below the surface, never to be seen again. He slammed the wall with his fists. "Damn the king to the lowest level of hell!" he hissed.

"Is it Crispin? Crispin Guest?"

He spun. The female voice startled him, but he could not mistake the soft Spanish dialect where his name sounded more like "Creespin."

Costanza of Castile gazed down on him from her carriage.

"Your grace," he said with a deep bow.

Her maid beside her rolled up the curtain for the duchess. The duchess of Lancaster rested her arm on the sill of the canvas-covered cart and leaned out. "It has been so long." Her smile was gentle and offered him all the regret, all the kindness his sore heart yearned for.

"But you have not changed, my lady."

She laughed. "So full of flattery. It was always so with you. In truth, I miss it."

Her lips clamped down on that last and they stared at each other in silence. She broke their stalemate by waving her hand. "But here you are. Have you come to court at last to see us? Our prodigal son."

He turned a glance down the long avenue toward the unyielding gates just around the corner. "I think it best I do not. The king—"

She dismissed the king with an angry gesture. He knew she did not fear the boy king of England. Not when her father had been king of Castile and her husband, Lancaster, ruled the king's own council. "I think my lord would be happy to see you again."

"My lady, his grace does not share that sentiment."

"Then why are you here?"

A lie eluded him. "I . . . had hoped to speak with him. But it is better—"

"Nonsense. Come with me. Lewis, help him in."

The coachman eyed Crispin. Crispin backed away. "My lady, no. The duke already refused my admittance."

"Are you disobeying a command from your better, Master Guest? I said, get in!"

Grateful, he nevertheless feared her misplaced loyalty would do them both ill. But she was right. He could not naysay her, especially in front of her servants.

Lewis lowered the coach's gate, which also served as a step. Crispin ducked as he entered the arched compartment and sat opposite her along the pillowed bench.

"Let us hope John is in an agreeable mood today," she said.

Crispin hoped so, too, and he tried to sit back and relax. The unwieldy carriage bumped along the avenue, rattling those within and making it an uncomfortable ride, even with pillows beneath them.

The maid did her best not to stare at Crispin. He did not know where to look either, and gazed out the small window while holding fast to the bench for dear life.

The carriage passed through the gates and stopped before the massive arched portico. The door opened, and Lancaster's steward rushed forward to greet the duchess. She emerged first, and the man bowed.

Crispin stepped down from the carriage, and the steward's face went white.

"My lady—" the steward tried to interject, but Costanza only raised her chin.

"Where is my lord husband?"

"His grace is in his apartments, my lady. In the parlor, but—"

"Very well. Come, Crispin."

Crispin looked back at the sputtering steward. There was nothing for Crispin to say to him, and he only shrugged at the man and followed the duchess inside. The familiar corridors and halls settled him in a place somewhere between comfort and misgiving. This was home to him, yet he did not belong here anymore.

Shadows parted for rushlights, and they walked a long way, first through the massive great hall, through a close, through a chapel, and down a long corridor until they turned a corner and entered the warm apartments of the duke. Crispin recalled the parlor well with its carved oak beams and wood-paneled ceiling, heavy tapestries, carved pillars, ornate sideboards, and lush chairs. The fireplace stood as tall as a man and as wide as five of them. Made of carved stone, it boasted the badges of Gaunt impaled by Castile. A great log within burned with a rolling golden fire, casting an aroma of toasted pine and spicy ash into the chamber. A corona filled with blazing candles stood nearly in the center of the room. Not far from the hearth sat the man himself at his desk, enthroned in his chair, nose immersed in his books. The quill, poised like a dagger, stood straight up in his hand.

He looked up and smiled upon seeing his wife. The smile fell away when Crispin stepped from behind her.

Lancaster stood so abruptly the heavy chair fell back. "God's blood!"

Crispin bowed and opened his hands. "Your grace, forgive me—"

Lancaster drew his sword and lunged forward, two, three strides. "By God, when I give an order I expect it to be obeyed!"

Crispin waited. The sword would either strike him or not. Either way suited.

"My lord husband! Is this the courtesy you extend to my guests?"

Lancaster stared at her. His scowl hid amid the dark beard and mustache. The sword lowered and his shoulders with it. "You did this," he said to her. "You brought him here."

"In all fairness," she said, moving forward and laying a gentle, white hand on Lancaster's sword arm, "he protested. I forced him to it."

With a huff that gusted his mustache, Lancaster slid the blade back in its sheath. Without a word, he made a slow circlet of his overturned chair and finally stood behind it. "You take liberties, Madam," he said gently to his wife. "You do not understand the seriousness—"

"I understand when an old friend is neglected. And I understand when it is politically expedient. But I also understand that our friend Crispin does not take such a visitation lightly, and therefore it must be of some import." She angled her head at Crispin. The gold cages cupping the rolled braids at her ears sparkled when she turned. "It is of some import, is it not?" she whispered to him. "Do not make a liar out of me."

"Yes, my lady." He bowed to her and looked up hopefully at Lancaster. "It is."

The duke closed his eyes for a moment. The dark lids rose slowly and he sighed. He leaned down, righted his chair, and sat heavily. "Will you leave us?" he asked her.

She curtseyed, pressed her hand a moment on Crispin's, and left.

Crispin stood alone waiting for Lancaster to speak. The roaring fire diminished under Lancaster's presence and even the wooden floor feared to creak lest his eye be directed there.

It was one of the longest silences of Crispin's life.

At length, the duke cleared his throat, closed his books one by one, and set his quill aside. "When the king asks me why you were here," he said, raising his face, "I hope to answer him with substance. For he *will* ask me, and I must make it known that no new conspiracies are afoot."

Crispin looked at the scuffed toes of his boots. "I needed to come—"

"Rashness, Crispin. Always your downfall. You do not spend enough time reasoning it out."

"Your grace—"

"Is it another one of your criminal inquiries? Why you cannot leave it to the law I will never understand."

"Because the law founders on its own ineptness . . . your grace."

By the look on Lancaster's face, he didn't exactly agree. The duke rose from his chair and took his time approaching. Lancaster studied

\

Crispin's threadbare coat, its patches, and the careless stitching that repaired his stockings.

Crispin felt each blink of the man's lash, each snort of disdain in his throat. To appear before his lord in something little better than rags . . . Crispin felt his face flush with heat.

Finally, Lancaster stopped and looked Crispin in the eye. "I thought I made it clear that I did all I could for you. Wasn't saving your life good enough?"

The words smarted. "And I thanked you for it. But there is information only you can provide. No one else in the council will have anything to do with me. I hoped you would have the courage to admit me."

Lancaster's hand slapped his sword hilt. "How dare you!"

Crispin eyed the sword and slowly raised his gaze. "What more can be done to me?"

Lancaster's brows were perfect black arches. His lower lip jutted slightly forward. "I can think of a thing or two," he said in a deadly voice.

Crispin's blood chilled, but he would not stand down. "I would not be here if I did not think England's welfare was at stake."

Lancaster's hand fell away from his sword. "So"—he snorted—"your *loyalty* brings you?"

"I am London born and raised, your grace. I am as much England as the king."

Lancaster huffed a sound somewhere between a laugh and a grunt. "His Majesty would not be particularly pleased to hear that." He glared at Crispin before retreating to the sideboard. He poured himself wine from a silver flagon but offered none to Crispin. He stood with his back to him and drank.

Crispin studied Lancaster's wide shoulders. Being at home, the duke wore no armor, but Crispin was almost more used to him in the black armor he was so fond of. Today he wore a velvet houppelande whose sleeve points surpassed the gown's knee-length hem and nearly touched the floor. The coat's face was quartered by the colorful arms of Gaunt and Castile. Only ten years Crispin's senior, he seemed so much older, so much stronger and heroic. Here was a man with claims to the throne of Castile and Leon. He was unafraid of any power in Europe. And though he warned Crispin of the king's wrath, Crispin suspected he did not fear Richard himself.

"What worries you so about England's welfare," Lancaster asked, his back still to Crispin, "that only the Tracker could salvage it?"

He did not know Lancaster knew his new title. He felt uncomfortable hearing him utter it. "I know of a scheme that has our enemies embezzling England's export taxes."

Lancaster spun and stared at him openmouthed.

Crispin's solemn lips curved up at one edge. "Is that important enough to concern you?"

"Who? Who is stealing the king's money?"

"I have reason to believe it is the duke of Milan, Bernabò Visconti."

Lancaster set down the bowl and grabbed Crispin's arm to steer him toward two chairs at the fire. He pushed Crispin into one and sat in the other. "Tell me what you know."

Crispin's heart panged. This was too much like the old days. "I do not know much. Only that there is an Italian syndicate working its plots in England. I suspect they have on their payroll a guild member who performs creative bookkeeping at the staple ports."

"Do you have proof?"

Crispin leaned forward and rested his fist on his thigh. "Alas, no. The ledgers were stolen from my lodgings. I think a man was murdered because he knew the truth."

"Who was this murdered man?"

"A mercer. A rich one. Nicholas Walcote. I suspect those particular funds are stolen to prevent Richard from lining his war chest. Does he plan on marching to France any time soon?"

Lancaster sat back and pinched his lower lip between his thumb and finger. "Yes. That is . . . he did. Before Parliament advised him there were insufficient funds for such a venture. Now I know why."

"Why would Visconti wish to interfere with our war with France? What's to be gained?"

Lancaster sat as he was for a long time. He lowered his hand at last and let his arm drape over the chair arm. "Do you remember Geoffrey Chaucer?"

The name sent a warmth of memories through Crispin's mind. "Of course. He served in your household. We were the best of friends. But it has been years since I have seen him." Another ache of longing tightened his chest. Naturally he was forbidden from seeing his former friends for fear that the king's vengeance would rain down upon them. They had been like brothers and never would he risk that.

He cleared his thickened throat. "I hear of his works from time to time."

"Yes. I am his patron, as you know. But he is also a customs controller . . . and a sometimes spy for the crown."

"*Geoffrey?*"

"Do you recall when I sent you to Visconti's court?"

"Yes. I still smart from my stupidity."

"You are not the only one. It pleased Visconti to make fools of the king's emissaries. Chaucer was sent some years ago and also quite recently."

"Can you tell me what he discovered?"

"Only that your fears are true. Visconti has been negotiating with France for months, perhaps longer. We believe his intentions are to prevent our troops from invading France, and in return, he will receive control of Calais and the route to Flanders."

"He wants to control the wool market."

"Yes. And if he does, it will bankrupt England."

Crispin's gaze never left Lancaster's. "You don't mean that."

"I do. If Visconti controls the major ports to Europe, he will control what and where we sell our goods. That cannot stand. I have operatives in Italy now." He cast a hand irritably skyward. "My grandfather and his Italian bankers! If King Edward Longshanks had not aligned himself with these Italian Jews in the first place—"

"Yet it was your grandfather who established the collection of export taxes on wool. Almost one hundred years of successful taxation."

"Still, I never trusted these foreigners. And now they forestall our goods, commit piracy, and steal our taxes."

"Perhaps not all can be blamed on these Italians. Parliament froze wages but did not freeze prices. Wat Tyler—"

"Burned down my house!" Lancaster rose to the edge of his chair. "Do you traffic with his like now?"

"No, your grace. I merely point out that he and his ilk were angry at the state of commerce. The ills of the market may well have been ripe for the picking."

Lancaster scowled and sat back. His tensed shoulders dropped again. "We did it to ourselves?"

"The door was left open. Now the rats have come in."

Lancaster's hand curled into a fist. "I should strike you for such insolence."

Crispin blinked. "As you will, my lord."

Crispin eyed his former mentor, awaiting a clout. Lancaster had done it many times before when Crispin was a much younger man. But this time the duke did not move. Instead he leaned back in his chair and studied Crispin. Lancaster raised his hand, but not to strike. He gestured at Crispin's face. "Who did that to you?"

Crispin raised his hand to his face, partially obscuring it from view. Damn. He'd forgotten how he looked. "It is part and parcel of the job."

"Is it?" Lancaster put a thumb to his mouth and ran it across the upper lip and then down his dark mustache.

This felt far too comfortable, recalled too many nights similar to this. *I want to come home,* Crispin longed to cry. *Here, where I belong!* His gaze slid upward toward the duke's and met his dark eyes. They regarded Crispin with sudden gentleness. Crispin could almost imagine him saying, as he had said so often, "Crispin, my lad."

Feeling a sting at his eyes, Crispin sprang to his feet, turning his face away from the man. "There is much for me to do," said Crispin, rubbing his hands together. They couldn't seem to get warm. "Forgive me for intruding upon your privacy."

"It is not an intrusion," the duke said softly. "It is more . . ." He shook his head, his face contorted with warring emotions. "More like a breath of fresh air."

"Don't." Crispin stared into the fire until his eyes had a reason to burn.

Lancaster sighed and didn't speak again for several heartbeats. But when he did speak, it was as if reluctant to let Crispin go so soon. "The king's guards can be put at your disposal."

"Oh?" Crispin chuckled guardedly. "So quickly my fortunes turn."

"I can make the king understand—"

"Do not trouble yourself. It is dangerous to speak of him and me in the same sentence, remember? And I work alone."

"Crispin, do not let your stubborn streak undo you again. There is too much at stake for your pride to get in the way."

Crispin rolled his shoulders and straightened. "I work best alone. I find it difficult to trust others." Lancaster nodded but still looked concerned. To mollify, Crispin added, "Should I need the court's help, I shall work through the Lord Sheriff's office."

Lancaster snapped his head in a nod. "Better." He rose and stood toe to toe with Crispin. "It seems you did have information of great import. I must thank the intelligence of my wife."

"The duchess is always to be highly praised."

Lancaster looked Crispin over again and even smiled. "Until we meet again, Crispin." He turned, but over his shoulder he added, "But not too soon, eh?"

* * *

LEAVING COURT, CRISPIN FELT satisfied relief. Vindication sometimes came at a price. At least this time he had not paid too dearly. And it had been good to be in the man's presence again.

So Visconti wanted to maneuver the English market not by armed invasion but by backroom conspiracies. If he and his men killed Nicholas Walcote, it wasn't for the Mandyllon. Whoever has the books must be Walcote's killer. But what about the locked door to Walcote's solar?

Whoever killed him had a key or plotted with someone who had a key. And whoever killed him either altered the guild's ledgers or conspired with those who did. Perhaps the killer did not care about the holy cloth. And yet it was all about cloth in one way or another.

Crispin looked up and measured the sky. Noon. And a rendezvous with Philippa was long overdue. He had to risk her anger and make one more stop.

13

CRISPIN WAITED ACROSS THE street from the Dog and Bone. He leaned against a wall under an eave and out of the stinging damp of an icy rain. He withdrew his knife and cleaned his nails.

Two familiar figures lumbered out of the distance and stood at the corner, a wide-shouldered man and his shorter companion.

Crispin let them stand a moment in the rain before he sheathed his knife and pushed off from the wall.

"Gentlemen," he said, striding toward them.

They flinched. "We did not expect to see you so soon, *Signore* Guest," said Sclavo.

"I am here to answer your master about his generous offer."

"And? What is your answer?"

"I know where the Mandyllon is."

"Then you will get it for us?"

"Not so fast. There's a little something that needs cleaning up first."

"And what is that?"

"I know that Bernabò Visconti is behind this scheme."

The two fell silent. Two-Fingers mumbled something in Italian to his companion and touched his knife. Sclavo silenced him with a gesture of his hand. He looked up at Crispin and smiled. "A very interesting supposition. I wonder how you came by it."

"I haven't always lived at the Shambles, Master Sclavo. I have met your master before."

"I did not say his grace the duke was my master."

"You didn't have to. I want to meet with him."

Sclavo laughed. His wide square teeth were visible in his open mouth, like horse's teeth. "Oh *Signore*. It isn't healthy to know too much."

"I have seen the Thames up close, gentlemen."

"You are like the cat with nine lives," said Two-Fingers. His teeth bit down on each word, snapping them like a rat snaps at a flea. "But even a cat has only so many."

"Well? Do I meet with him? It is only directly to him that I will hand over the Mandyllon for my exorbitant fee."

Sclavo kept his smile. "Our master does not bargain with peasants."

The last word dug a blade into Crispin's gut. He resisted the urge to pull his dagger and gritted his teeth not quite into a smile. "Then I would speak to your head man in England."

Sclavo darted a glance at Two-Fingers. "How did you know there is a man in England?"

"Because you just answered it. Well?"

Sclavo frowned. It pleased Crispin to finally cut through the Italian's armored façade. "That might be possible," said Sclavo. "Give us a day to arrange a meeting."

"A few hours. I'm not a patient man." He bowed to the silent men and left them on the street. It was good to feel in charge again, if only to a few henchmen. He lifted his leather hood over his head and hurried through the rain to the Boar's Tusk. Crispin turned the corner of Gutter Lane and spied the tavern. Jack stood outside patting his arms to keep warm. His shabby hood only partially covered his curls of ginger hair.

Crispin frowned. "Jack! Why aren't you inside safeguarding Mistress Walcote?"

"I wanted to keep my eyes skinned for you. Besides, she don't want that kind of fussing. She told me so herself."

"That doesn't mean she doesn't need it." Crispin pushed through the door and stood on the threshold, craning his neck to see. His gaze skimmed over the heads of the patrons—mostly men and travelers who chatted and laughed noisily over the clatter of cups and music from a man playing a bagpipe and a boy keeping the beat with a drum.

Jack pointed. "She's there, sir. Right where I left her."

Crispin saw her. She tried to be the dainty lady, but her nature would not allow it. She leaned over her beaker of ale with her elbow on the table like any kitchen wench. Her fist propped up her chin, and her other hand beat the rhythm of the piper's music. Her shoulders followed suit, and if the table hadn't been in her way, Crispin was certain she would be dancing.

The leering man beside her, eyeing her fine clothes, did not seem to concern her, but he troubled Crispin.

"Go along back to our lodgings, Jack. By the way, you did not move those books I had on the table, did you?"

"No, Master."

"Very well. Go on back to the Shambles, then."

He heard Jack mumble something about "not so much as a 'thank you,'" but he was too distracted to pay the boy much mind.

Crispin strode forward and stood behind her. The man beside her on the bench leaned toward her, no doubt close to offering an inappropriate remark when he spied Crispin glowering down at him, hand on hilt. The man flinched and stealthily slid away, leaving a space on the bench for Crispin to fill.

Philippa turned and her merry expression soured. "Christ's toes! Where the hell have you been? I've been sitting here for two hours!"

Crispin said nothing and sat.

"You think because you are this *Tracker* you can keep a body waiting as long as you like?" She pushed her beaker forward and stood.

"Sit down."

"I will not."

He grabbed her wrist and yanked her down to the bench. Her rump met the seat with a smack. "I've experienced quite a lot this morning, and I've no time for your ill humor. I need facts, not tantrums."

"Very well," she said grudgingly and settled herself. "What happened at the sheriff's that took so long? Why did he summon you? Has it to do with the cloth?"

Crispin smiled without the flecks of humor. "Jack talks too much," he grumbled. "But since you asked, I will be plain with you if you will do the same for me."

She blinked, and her expression fell into practiced indifference. "I will be as plain as I can."

Crispin leaned in conspiratorially and she did likewise. Her scent of spiced perfume reached out for him, wrapped sinuous arms of aroma about his senses, and drew him even closer.

She detected his subtle gesture and angled her face upward toward his. He felt her breath against his face and even on his own parted lips. If he moved two inches more, their lips would touch. The thought flushed his face, and he cursed his pounding heart. He tried to remind himself brusquely who she was, but it only made him tick off the obvious: a widow, a rich merchant, a sensuous woman. The adulteress and the chambermaid now seemed distant.

He used his own words to splash cold water on his thoughts. "I met with your acquaintance Abid Assad Mahmoud."

He waited for a reaction from her, but she didn't so much as flick an eyelash.

"He admitted to me," he said, his voice growing quieter, "that he extorted certain services from you."

Still she said nothing.

Crispin dropped his gaze. His voice took on a gentle quality. "Philippa, why did you do it? Who are you protecting? If it was for Nicholas Walcote's sake there is no longer a reason to protect him."

He wasn't surprised that she did not answer him. He surprised himself, however, for the next words coming from his own mouth. "For what it's worth, I believe you must have had a very good reason."

He recoiled slightly when her hand touched his face. He hadn't expected it, hadn't anticipated the gentle touch, how the fingers delicately stroked over the many bruises. But still she said nothing and finally let her hand fall away.

"Dammit, woman. Don't you want my help?"

"I want you to find that cloth."

Crispin opened his mouth to impart an indelicate phrase when Eleanor arrived with a leather flagon of wine and a bowl. Eleanor had the sense to say nothing, but she made an approving nod toward Philippa before she left them. Crispin frowned, poured the wine, and took up his bowl without waiting for Philippa. He drank deeply, emptied it, and poured another. Sliding his arm across the table, he leaned on it and looked into the wine. "I nearly got myself killed for you," he hissed. "The least you could do is cooperate."

"Is that what happened to your face?"

He snorted, almost a laugh. "You should see the other fellow." His face dipped into the wine again. He licked his lips. "Tell me about this Italian syndicate."

His words finally provoked a reaction. Philippa's fingers clawed into his arm. "What do you know about *them*?"

"Only as much as our friend Mahmoud would say, which was not much."

"Mahmoud? *He* told you?"

"Come, come. Surely you knew he was involved."

The horror on her face proved she did not. "They tried to kill you?"

"Yes, but I escaped. Barely. I wouldn't mind knowing what I risked my neck for."

She had no breath with which to say it, but her lips formed the words nonetheless: *the cloth.*

"This syndicate wants the Mandyllon?"

She nodded.

"If you wish to be rid of it, then why not give it to them?"

"But I don't know where it is!"

Crispin took another drink. He licked the wine from his lips and set the bowl aside. "I do."

"*What?*"

He stood and pulled at his coat to straighten it. "I know where it is. Shall we go and retrieve it?"

Philippa shot to her feet. "How long have you known?"

"A few days."

Crispin stepped over the bench and headed for the door, not waiting to see if the woman followed.

Hastily, Philippa yanked her hood over her head and scrambled after him. The rain gusted at them as he opened the tavern door and she paused to adjust her cloak. When she stepped over the threshold, he closed the door behind her and stood on the granite step. A misty rain sprayed their faces, leaving tiny pearls of raindrops on her lashes. "You couldn't have told me?"

He turned a smile toward her. "It wouldn't have done you any good." He stepped out into the mud and forged up the road.

She caught up to him again. "So they killed Nicholas for it?"

"Perhaps. But I don't think it likely."

"Why not?"

"Because they wanted to know where the Mandyllon is, and killing him made that impossible. Except for you."

"Me?"

"They might think *you* know where it is."

She put a hand to her throat and shook her head. Her feet worked quickly to keep pace with him.

"So I ask again: tell me about this syndicate."

She glanced behind her into the gray mist. Crispin thought that was a good idea and did the same. Soggy Londoners traveled down the lanes, some with baskets tucked under their arms. Others milled near shop fronts and smoky braziers, but even though they wore blues and reds, the rain made all equal in waterlogged gray.

No sign of Sclavo or Two-Fingers or even men in livery.

"I don't know much about the syndicate. Nicholas mentioned them only once. He hadn't meant to. I think it was the power of the Mandyllon that forced it from him, though he was the only one I knew who could lie in front of it."

"Don't be a fool," he muttered.

She tossed her head at him. "I do believe I am paying *you*. You do remember that, don't you?"

"I recall something like it."

"Then I suggest you act more polite to her what pays you."

She made no more pretense of a cultivated accent. The sound of her plain Southwark speech caused an ache of revulsion in his chest. He tightened his jaw. At that moment, it was easier to visualize the chambermaid in her.

At last, they reached the Walcote gatehouse, but when they stood before the doors of the manor itself, Philippa hesitated. She stood rigidly under the comfort of the vestibule while the rain picked up momentum and hammered the gravel courtyard. Her features lay hidden by the drenched hood until she raised her head. Her face, flushed with youthful sincerity and just a touch of ingenuousness, caught his full attention. The cold kissed each rounded cheek with a red spot, contrasting the milkiness of her skin. Her lips were rosy and swollen from chewing them.

"I'm frightened," she said.

Her words snuffed Crispin's anger as cleanly as fingers suffocating a wick. He drew his hand over his dagger's hilt and rested it there. "I will let no harm come to you." She continued looking at him with a renewal of something he had no time to explore. That look caused him to blush. He hid it by advancing on the door. "Let us get it done quickly, then," he said.

14

CRISPIN AND PHILIPPA APPROACHED the solar and she dropped her stride, slowing as they neared it. "The solar?" she asked.

"Yes."

"But he is still there."

"Walcote? When will you bury the man?"

"The funeral is tomorrow. The guild, the servants—there was so much to be done. I-I had to do it all myself and I wasn't certain of— Believe me, I wanted it much sooner!"

"I do believe you." Crispin entered the room and grimaced at the smell. All the rosemary and spices in the world could not mask the odor of decay. Only two candles were lit and the sheet was drawn up over the shrunken features of the dead merchant. Burial tomorrow would not come soon enough.

Crispin turned toward the wall. Movement. A figure lurking in the shadows. Crispin pulled his dagger and regretted for the thousandth time that he no longer carried a sword.

"You there! I see you! Make yourself known!"

Candlelight cast a wan glow on the man's features.

"Put your weapon away, friend Crispin," said John Hoode, his voice trembling. He put his hand back up to his face, covering nose and mouth from the smell.

Crispin's heart started again and he slammed the blade in its sheath. "You frightened the wits out of me," he said and wiped the sweat away from his upper lip. "What are you doing here?"

"There's the burial tomorrow. I thought—"

Crispin's agitation melted and he reached out and patted Hoode's shoulder. Crispin nodded and glanced back toward Philippa in the doorway. He leaned in toward Hoode and asked softly, "What's the news from the kitchens?"

"The kitchens? That's not my—"

Hoode stopped and stared at Crispin. His gaze made a quick circuit of the room, caught Philippa in the doorway, and finally lit on Crispin again. His lips turned up in a frightened smile. "I must go."

Crispin followed him out past Philippa and caught up with him on the gallery. Hoode glanced at his mistress's back nervously.

"What is it, John? Anything to report to me?"

Hoode looked again at Philippa and Crispin edged him further away from her. "I did not wish to speak before her," he said. "But it's that Adam Becton again. Verily, he can get himself into a rage."

"I think that Becton is"—he glanced once at Philippa—"preoccupied."

"I think he is unstable. Mark me. He's going to hurt someone. I hope it won't be me." He raised his smooth fingers to his lips.

"Don't worry. Stay out of his way. I hope to conclude this soon." He patted Hoode's shoulder again, and sent him on his way. He made an apologetic lilt to his shoulders to Philippa and steered her back toward the solar.

"Who was that peculiar fellow?" she asked.

"He's one of your servants. I asked him to keep an eye on things."

"*He's* going to protect me?"

"He's my sentinel only. I was to be called immediately."

She vaguely nodded and made no move to enter the room.

"Philippa, you must come in."

"Must I?"

He glanced at Walcote on his bier. "He is covered."

She breathed a trembling sigh and crossed the threshold, averting her gaze from the body. "It can't be in here. I searched it myself."

"Yet it is."

"Where?"

He walked to the far wall adjacent to the window. Dark blue drapery hung from mid-height along the walls of the entire room, covering the lime-washed plaster. He slipped his hand beneath the cloth, pushing it aside as best he could, and ran his hands along the plaster surface. "Fetch me a candle."

Philippa pressed her lips together and grasped enough courage to take one of the fat candles at Walcote's head. She brought it to Crispin and held it for him. "What are you looking for?"

"A way in."

"What do you mean 'a way in'?"

"There is a secret door to a secret room."

She stared at him. The candlelight warmed her face, beautiful even in its perplexity. "How do you know?"

"Have you ever been to the Tower of London?"

"Of course not."

"If you had, you would know that there is a level of false windows in the White Tower."

"False windows? Why?"

"To confuse the enemy. An attacking force would believe there is another level. More men, more defenses."

"What has this to do with—"

"I noticed a window on the outside wall quite close to this one. Too close. When I investigated inside and paced it off, the windows I saw inside did not correspond to the windows I saw outside. Thicker walls where there should not be. Ergo, secret room."

She shook her head. "If this wall opens, I shall pay you twice what I owe you."

"When this wall opens I will have earned it."

Crispin's fingers searched along the way under the heavy blue cloth. But the drapery was proving to be an impediment to his progress and he almost tore it down in his frustration. Instead, he carefully unhooked it from the pegs set in the wall and laid it down upon the wooden floor, fold on fold. He stepped over the bunched cloth and continued his slow examination of the solar's north wall. Philippa followed as he inched along, holding the candle for him with trembling fingers. The yellow glow cast a slanted halo across the smooth plane.

Crispin knocked on the wall with his knuckles, cocking his head to listen for a change in tone. He had been at it a long time. What if he were wrong? He certainly didn't relish appearing the fool in front of the woman, especially after his bravado about knowing where the damned cloth was.

He slid his fingers toward the corner and felt nothing but the same even plaster. His disappointment was almost keener than his embarrassment. If this secret door was not so, then he had no idea where this cloth could be. And he hated to be wrong, particularly where his fee was concerned.

Just as he was about to give up, his fingertips encountered a seam by the corner timber. "Ah!" Relief and a renewed wave of confidence made him chuckle. He drew his dagger and worked it into the crack. It widened. What appeared to be an ordinary plaster wall, was instead a clever door.

A click and creaking wood. A portion of the wall eased aside. A dark, narrow gap appeared at the corner nearest the window and the smell of mold and mildew tumbled out with a sighing puff of air. The door opened only a shoulder's width, but it was enough for a man to squeeze through.

"The candle." He put out his hand. Philippa's excited breath gusted on his neck. His hand closed over the thick column of wax as she thrust the candle into his palm. The flame wavered from his own excitement and he gingerly pushed the candle through the opening.

Immediately the small space jumped into view. He was surprised by what he saw. Certainly he had seen similar passages in palaces and castles, but nothing like this in a manor house. It made him wonder if his own long-lost manor had such spaces.

A thick layer of dust covered the walls and floor. His eyes ran over the textures of stone alcoves and carved pillars. No hasty room this. This was created when the house was built. God only knew why.

Crispin lowered the candle, dripping some wax on his boot as he tilted the wax pillar for better light. A set of scrambled footprints on the floor mingled with drops of dried blood. He knelt on one knee and studied the scene.

"Did you find the cloth?" Philippa's hushed voice came from the doorway.

"Not yet. But I did find how the murderer entered and exited the solar."

Her head appeared at the edge and she strained to look. He pointed to the footprints and the dark drops among them. When he lifted the candle, the light illumined a small area, but he saw that the passage went farther. "This is not a room only. It is a passage."

"Nicholas never mentioned this."

"No, I don't imagine he would have done." Crispin walked down the narrow corridor, moving the candle above and below. A stone staircase trailing downward fell away in the gloom.

"Don't go!" Philippa's whispered echo skipped along the narrow walls.

He turned. She was lit by the sliver of the doorway where the candlelight and a rushlight outside the solar cast her in a ghostly glow. "Will you not have me search?"

"I don't know."

"I will be gone for only a few moments. This passage may not go very far."

Maneuvering carefully down the steps, he made certain to keep one hand on the wall. Should the flame go out, his touch with the wall might be his only hope of finding his way back through the suf-focating darkness.

The steps curved in a long, easy spiral, descending for what seemed like a long time. The walls muffled the sounds of servants, and he smelled vague odors. The kitchens?

Other than the ethereal resonances behind the thick timbers and daub, Crispin's footsteps were his only company save for the secret noises of a rat close by gnawing on its dinner.

Crispin continued until his echoing steps changed to flat splashes. He lowered the candle's light toward the floor and it reflected back at him.

Water. And rising. It smelled stagnant of mildew. By the echoing sound of his steps, he sensed a wall blocking his progress. When he neared, the candle's light confirmed it. Ahead he saw the faint outline of a door.

He set the candle down in the ankle-deep water and used both hands to feel along the wall's edges. He pushed and pried but nothing budged. "Open, dammit!" and he slammed the corner with his fist. The stone groaned and opened. Cold, wet air whooshed in, snuffing the candle.

The soft outside light more than filled the small space—until the door jammed, open only a cubit wide.

Crispin looked at the candle with its wisp of evaporating smoke and then back up the blackened passage. He sighed. He did not savor feeling his way blindly back to the solar. He turned to the opening and decided to go that way. Wherever that led. He only hoped he could fit through the crack.

He shoved his shoulder in, closed his eyes, and tried to relax. Eas-ing forward, he scraped both sides of his body squeezing through. *Now I know what wheat feels like ground between millstones.* He winced. His dagger hilt screeched along the rock. The door never budged, and he breathed evenly, trying not to think about getting stuck. And just as the thought lifted into the ether, he could move no further.

Damn. His head aimed toward the opening. No chance to look behind him for any kind of assistance. He tried to ease back. No good. Just as stuck that way, too.

His predicament was much like this investigation. Caught between two opposing forces, he moved blindly. Either way could stop him in his tracks.

He pulled in his gut and pushed as hard as he could, grunting with the effort, but he was stuck fast. Philippa knew where he was, but it might be some time before she sent someone to look for him. He pushed again with a great exhaled groan and his body suddenly slipped. He could move again!

Inching forward, he felt cold ahead. His hand touched something wet but he dared not yank the hand back. The shoulder freed and he popped his head out. Green and brown stippled light cascaded around him, and then he realized he stood along a wall of dead ivy. He pulled himself out the rest of the way and stood on the gravel path, feeling a bit as if he were birthed from the wall.

The garden. The hidden passage meandered around and down again toward the back courtyard garden. He looked up at the solar's window some fifteen feet up and then at the false one beside it. Looking down at his coat, he straightened his belt that was wrenched halfway around him and then wiped away the granite dust from his chest. He walked to the part of the garden wall he had scaled before with Jack, and climbed.

He lighted on the other side and strode around the wall to the front entrance. Adam Becton answered his knock and opened the door. The steward looked surprised but said nothing, and stepped aside to let Crispin through. Crispin took the stairs two at a time, crossed the solar's threshold, and stood noiselessly behind Philippa whose head and shoulders were lost within the passage's gloom.

"Lose something?"

It was worth it to see her jump. She spun so quickly she nearly lost her balance.

"What are you doing there!"

"The passage lets out in the garden. Since my candle went out, I thought it safer to come round."

She tried to retrieve her tattered dignity by lifting her chin. "What about the Mandyllon?"

"I quite lost track of that," he mumbled sheepishly and stepped back into the passage. "Candle." He held out his hand again.

"It's the only one left." She slapped it into his palm.

Before the footprints and blood had distracted him, he remembered seeing an alcove near the passage's doorway cut into the inner wall with a lancet arch and carved pillars on either side. There, on a shelf, sat a carved wooden box as long and as wide as the length of a man's arm. Chip-carved geometric designs with a center rosette decorated the lid. The box had no dust on it.

Crispin motioned Philippa forward. She hesitated before plunging into the passage. He handed her the candle and lifted the box. He carried it out of the passage and set it on Walcote's desk. She followed him, her hand at her throat.

Crispin felt a tingle of excitement trill through his gut. It was a bit like finding a fairy's legendary cache of gold. Perhaps it would all disappear with the daylight.

He ran his hands over the carved designs. "Moorish," he announced.

His thumbs pressed the front of the lid and raised it.

The gray light from the window flowed over the shadows within the box and revealed a folded yellowed cloth. Crispin dipped his fingers in the box and lifted the material into the light. He laid it on the table and unfolded it. At first, it merely looked like a discolored and very old piece of linen, about the size of a baby's swaddling. He ran the fabric between his fingers, feeling its smoothness, its tight weave. He lifted it and turned it toward the window, bathing the cloth in the last rays of the dreary day.

Then he saw it.

Faint, as if rubbed and touched by countless fingers for centuries, the dim, brown image of a face.

"Blessed *Jesu*." The skeptic in Crispin fled to the corner and cowered. The face on the cloth was that of a man with a beard, someone about Crispin's age or older. An ordinary face, as if the maker smeared his skin with some sort of pigment and carefully transferred his features to the cloth. Except that the eyes were open and the brown stains did not appear to be pigment. The image almost looked . . . burned on.

Crispin tried to breathe and when he successfully inhaled once, he chided himself. *Don't be a fool, Crispin. You know such things do not exist.*

The cloth felt very light in weight and smelled slightly musty with a wisp of the scent of balsam. His fingers tingled where he touched it, or was it merely his imagination?

"That's it, isn't it?" Philippa's voice constricted to a gasp.

Crispin folded the cloth. "Yes, it looks like it. Would you like to get a better look?"

She shook her head vigorously. "Just take it away."

Instead of replacing it into the box, Crispin unbuttoned his coat and stuffed it in. He closed the box and carried it back to the alcove. He scanned the hidden passage one last time and stepped back over its threshold. With both hands, he pushed on the door, which obliged by moving back into place and clicking closed. The innocuous seam disappeared into the shadows and out of detection. He pulled the folds of drapery from the floor and replaced them artfully on their pegs.

When he turned, Philippa held out a pouch with the full length of her arm. She shook the little bag, and he heard the jangle of coins. "Take it. You've earned it."

Should he hold out his hand like a beggar? It was especially galling from the likes of Philippa, but just then, his confused emotions could not sort out exactly why this simple transaction disturbed him. He swallowed his pride and snatched the pouch, dispatching it in his purse.

"There is no doubt," he said, buttoning his coat, "that the murderer left this room through that portal. Possibly he even entered by it."

"Why didn't he take the cloth then?"

"Perhaps he was frightened off by a servant and thought to come back later. Or he had no time to search for it."

"Very well," she said, her tone clipped. "You have found your killer's secret and that cloth. And you've been paid. Now, please, take it away."

He bowed. "Yes, Madam."

Crispin moved toward the threshold. He didn't yet know what he would do with the cloth, or what he would tell the sheriff. Or who killed Walcote, for that matter. Or what to do about the foreigners.

When Philippa spoke, her words stopped his thoughts altogether. "Is this the last I see of you?"

He turned and saw the sinuous undulation of woman lit by the glittering flattery of candlelight. His senses warmed.

Crispin took strange delight in saying, "There is still a murder to investigate. I believe you will see me again."

He wasn't certain if he detected a mote of triumph in her face. She was on the cusp of saying more when there was a scrambling on the stairs. Adam Becton stumbled in, nearly knocking Crispin aside.

He bowed to Philippa. "Mistress," he panted. "There are— There is—" He stared at Crispin.

She clucked her tongue at Adam and raised her chin. "What is it, Adam? Tell me."

"Well," he glanced at Crispin, "they've just arrived. They are in the parlor."

Philippa tightened her shoulders. Crispin imagined all the mourners and how tiresome they could become. "Who?" she asked, exasperated.

"Master Walcote's *brothers*," he breathed.

Philippa's flushed cheeks suddenly drained of color. "*Brothers?* Merciful Jesus!"

15

PHILIPPA'S HAND WENT TO her throat. She hurried out the door with Adam at her heels.

Crispin stood alone in the solar with the ripe body of Nicholas Walcote for company. He looked at the corpse but knew he'd get better answers downstairs.

Adam scrambled to precede Philippa to the parlor and he unlocked the door and entered. Crispin made it to the shadow of the doorway in time to observe three people—two men and one woman—stand and turn their heads. Adam bowed and announced, "Madam Philippa Walcote," and stepped aside.

One of the men marched forward. His frowning dark brows matched dark greasy hair that was cut across his forehead and was covered by a green rondelle hat, which sported a shell pin from Santiago de Compostela. His green houppelande sleeves boasted two more pilgrim badges, but it was the gown's design Crispin took special note of. The sleeves were cut long as was the fashion, but they didn't quite touch the floor as he expected from a man in a wealthy cloth merchant family. Nor did the toes of his shoes stretch out in exaggerated points.

"Why were we locked in this room?" the man demanded.

"My apologies," said Philippa, employing her best cultivated speech, though it riffled along the edge of hysteria. "It was Nicholas's custom to lock the doors. He insisted on it."

The man's face reddened, set to erupt. Crispin decided to intrude and nodded to Adam as he entered.

The servant licked his lips and announced, "Crispin Guest—the . . . Tracker."

They all turned toward him. The first man in green approached Crispin and eyed his threadbare clothes. "'Tracker'? What by God is that?"

"I explore crimes. The murder of your brother, for instance."

"Are you the sheriff, then?"

"No, but I often work with him."

"This is all nonsense!" cried the man. "Not so much as a messenger was sent to us about Nicholas! We had to hear about it from common talk. And this wife of his. This is the first we've heard of that!"

"Talk travels quicker than any messenger," said Crispin, but he absorbed the brother's other words with curiosity.

The man huffed and muttered under his breath, fingering the tiny gold monstrance hanging from a chain around his neck.

"Please, Lionel," said the woman. She glided toward him and slipped her arm in his. The nap of her scarlet velvet gown did not shine like Crispin remembered from similar fabrics he used to call his own, but it was trimmed richly in fur. But not fox. Squirrel perhaps? "You're frightening the girl," she went on. The woman's face was long and pinched and looked as if she were sniffing something unpleasant. "Let our dear sister-in-law speak. She has such a delightful accent. I myself am curious as to when exactly they were married."

Philippa paled and pressed her lips together. Without missing a beat, she spoke in the most refined accent she could muster, pronouncing her words with assiduous accuracy. "We have been married for three years. This is the first I heard that Nicholas had brothers."

"This is really too much!" bellowed Lionel.

The woman's wan smile reminded Crispin of the serpent of Eden.

"Nicholas was always wont to keep to himself, husband. This is just one more example—"

"Keep your opinions to yourself, Maude," said the other man. Though husky, the breadth of his bright red shoulder cape made his head look small. Nose reminiscent of Lionel's, his other features, including his coloring, were more like Nicholas's. His face, not as broad as the other brother, angled down to a cleft chin covered with the shadow of a latent beard.

"I beg your pardon, *dear* Clarence," said his sister-in-law. She swept her skirt aside to walk deliberately in front of him.

The beefy Clarence lifted his nose at Maude and turned to pour himself wine from a flagon on a nearby sideboard.

Lionel bobbed his head in emphasis. "It is like Nicholas to do exactly what he liked."

"Was it like him to get murdered?" said Crispin. Curious to see their reaction, Crispin wasn't disappointed.

"Now see here!" Lionel advanced on Crispin. "Sheriff or not, you've no right—"

"He *isn't* the sheriff," reminded his brother Clarence into his wine bowl.

Crispin gazed down his nose at Lionel, deflecting the man's scathing look. "I am curious. Nicholas Walcote was an enigma in London. Did he always live in this house?"

Lionel calmed and he glanced at Clarence, but it seemed Clarence was used to deferring to Lionel. "We all lived here. We were raised in this house."

"It was the family business, then?"

"Yes. And when Father died we thought to continue on here, all of us. It was not to be."

"Why?"

"Nicholas was impossible to work with! He insisted on his own way, his rules, his decisions."

"So you left."

"Yes. Clarence left first."

Crispin turned to the other brother. Clarence seemed surprised to be addressed and raised his brows. "Yes, I went to Whittlesey and started my own business there."

"I joined him soon after," said Lionel.

Clarence drank the contents of the bowl and poured more. "Yes, lucky me."

"So the two of you entered into business together."

Clarence laughed but there was no mirth in the sound. "As if I would be caught dead—"

The others held their collective breaths. In the silence, everyone remembered the body in the solar. Clarence shrugged and took a drink. "Dear Lionel tried to take it over and I was forced to retreat to St. Neot to start on my own. Again."

"You'd have run it into the ground," said Lionel.

"Be still, old man, or you may find yourself on a bier."

Lionel growled, fisted his hand, and rushed his brother, but Crispin got between them and held up his hands. "Masters! This is a house in mourning!"

Clarence shook out his shoulders. Without any show of embarrassment, he scanned the room and retreated to the sideboard to pour more wine.

Red-faced, Lionel calmed and turned his back on his brother.

"Why don't we all sit down," Crispin suggested, and brought a chair for the tight-lipped Philippa, then pulled another forward for Clarence. Lionel and Maude had their chairs and they looked at each other. As if on cue, they both sat at the same time. Crispin stood above them. "Differences there may have been," he went on, "but this is the end of a life. Perhaps it is time to set old hurts aside."

"In this family," said Maude, "old hurts are never set aside. They are simply stored for future use."

"This is absurd," muttered Clarence, knocking back another drink of wine. "I want to know who killed Nick . . . and I want to congratulate the killer."

Philippa stared at him aghast.

"No one knows who killed him," said Crispin. "Not yet."

Clarence and Lionel brooded from their separate places in the room: Clarence by the sideboard and Lionel sitting by his wife and glowering at Philippa.

Crispin turned to Lionel. "It has been a long time, I take it, since you set foot in this house."

"Little has changed."

"Quite true," said Maude, running her finger along the imaginary dust on her chair's arm. "And yet *we* have been doing all the talking. Nicholas has a wife. Apparently." They all looked at Philippa. "We had quite given up hope of his ever acquiring one."

"Is that a jab at me?" said Clarence over his shoulder.

"No, dear Clarence," she said. "I suppose there is hope someday of your finding a wife. The world is full of God's great miracles, after all."

"Tell that harridan of yours to mind her own damn business," he said into his bowl.

Lionel's face flushed, but before he could bellow again, Maude interrupted. "Pay him no heed." She waved a hand devoid of ornament. "We must find out about our dear sister." Maude turned to her. "Phyllida—"

"*Philippa.*"

"Of course. Such a delightful name. Tell us of your family? Are they mercers?"

Philippa glanced at Crispin with such raw desperation that his mind frantically worked on a distraction. Before he could conjure anything, Philippa blurted out what surely should have been suppressed.

"No, we were never merchants. My family were servants. I was my master's— I was Nicholas's chambermaid."

Maude screeched like a cat hurled from a rooftop and slumped in her chair. Lionel bellowed something unintelligible, and Clarence burst out laughing. "By my Lady!" he crowed. "That's the best Nick's done yet! Damn me! I wish I could shake his hand!"

"Be still, you idiot!" cried Lionel. "Someone get my wife some wine! You!" he pointed to Adam, face as white as the walls.

The steward ran to comply and Crispin watched the room dissolve into chaos. Why did Philippa do it? Surely she must have known what turmoil such an announcement would cause. He stared at her, tried to discern her expression, but all he could reckon was confusion and fear.

Adam returned and handed Lionel a cup of wine, which he gave to his wife. She held the back of her hand to her forehead and took several sips between moans.

"So," said Lionel over his shoulder. "You're only just a chambermaid."

Philippa's hands closed into tight fists. They trembled at her sides. "I am Nicholas's wife. I have been for three years!" She dropped all pretense of a cultivated accent, releasing the thickness of her speech. "It ain't my fault I was a servant or that he didn't tell me nought about you! He didn't tell me a lot of things."

"Masters," placated Crispin, "is this truly necessary? The man has been murdered. The culprit must be found. This is more important than rank."

Crispin surprised himself when the words came out of his mouth. He always believed rank was paramount. All his past experience and his long years of resentment told him so. But with a dead man rotting upstairs, the murderer free and seeking the object hidden on Crispin's person, it was obvious, even to him, that the greater danger lay in the unknown.

Maude propped herself up and glared at Crispin, her pinched face contracting even more. "Nothing is more important than rank," she hissed. "There is the family name to consider. And children. Good God!" Her hands flew to her breast. "Are there any children?"

"Sadly, no," said Philippa, regaining something of her old self. She raised her chin. "I think this is quite enough for one day. The funeral is tomorrow. Nicholas will be buried, then you can all return to your precious estates and trouble us no more. I, for one, can't wait!"

"Is she tossing us out?" asked Clarence, face suddenly serious.

Crispin repressed a smile. "It would seem so."

Lionel postured to his full height. "Not before I see my brother and bid him—"

Clarence chuckled into his cup. "Good riddance? Must make sure he's dead, after all."

Lionel sneered at his brother. "Be still, or you'll find a knife in *your* back."

Crispin maneuvered next to Lionel. "How did you know Nicholas was stabbed in the back?"

Lionel stared at Crispin with eyes bulging. Clarence gestured with his cup and splashed some of the wine on the floor between Crispin and Lionel. "Everyone knows that," said Clarence. "We all heard about it."

Lionel turned his attention toward Philippa. Her bravado faded under the onslaught of his dark expression. "Where is he?" Lionel asked.

"In the solar," she sputtered with a look of horror. "But—"

"Let's go and make an end to this, then." He stalked from the room, his shadow stretching ominously behind him. Clarence put down his bowl and sneered over his shoulder at Crispin. Maude lifted herself from her seat, and seeing no one left but Crispin and Adam to view her performance, abruptly shook herself free of it and stomped after her husband.

Philippa ran after them up the stairs.

Crispin shook his head in disgust and took the stairs two at a time, passing over the solar's threshold just as Philippa took her place behind her kinsmen.

Lionel held his nose and stood at Nicholas's covered head. Clarence merely grimaced at the smell but Maude looked no different. "This is our farewell, Nicholas," Lionel pronounced. "Whether you are in Heaven or Hell, well, that is between you and your Maker, for I shall not pray for you." He grabbed the sheet and threw it back.

Philippa held her hand to her mouth. Whether or not it was to suppress a scream, Crispin did not know.

All the others were silent for a moment. But then Lionel looked at his wife and then his brother. As one, the three turned accusatory faces toward Philippa.

"This is not Nicholas Walcote!" Lionel declared. "Where is my brother?"

16

CRISPIN MOVED FORWARD AS if in a dream. *She knew.* A moat of anger welled around that thought.

He raised his voice above the angry chatter of the others. "If this man is not your brother, then who is he?"

"I don't know. But I do know he is not Nicholas!" Lionel trumpeted.

"It's been years since you've seen him. How can you be sure?"

"We know our own brother!" said Clarence.

Crispin angled toward Philippa. Her face collapsed into horrified fear. Tears ran in double streams down both cheeks and flowed to her jaw where they stayed in paralyzed drips, too afraid to drop away. "Philippa," he said, perhaps more gently than she deserved. "Tell me."

Gallows fear. That's what Crispin called the expression she wore. He saw it on many a prisoner's face before they were led to the gallows, and then as the rope dropped over their heads; that desperate realization that it wasn't a nightmare, that it was real and happening now.

"I meant no harm," she whispered. She twisted her red fingers together, and sucked the spilled tears at the edges of her mouth. "I meant no harm."

"Well, Sheriff. This is certainly a strange set of circumstances—"

"He isn't the sarding sheriff, you jackass!" cried Clarence.

Lionel scowled at his brother.

"But maybe he will oblige us by calling the sheriff," said Maude. "There is a great deal that needs explanation."

Crispin gritted his teeth. There was nothing he could do. This situation had grown far beyond his ability to influence or control, and he wasn't about to put his own head in a noose for her. Tautly he moved toward the passageway and spotted the steward. "Adam, you will have to send for the sheriff," he said.

SIMON WYNCHECOMBE MET THEM in the parlor and scanned their faces. He frowned darkest when passing his gaze over Crispin. "Couldn't do what I told you," his expression seemed to say. But Crispin lost all patience with him. He desperately wanted to get Philippa alone to ask her what was on her mind, but there was no opportunity.

The others sat in a rough half circle while Philippa stood in the center like a trapped animal. She trembled, and Crispin did not know whether he longed more to comfort her or to throttle her.

"Well, Madam," said the sheriff, his voice rumbling deep in his throat. "You have been living a lie, calling yourself the wife of Nicholas Walcote when in fact the man in question is *not* Nicholas Walcote. Several questions come to mind: Why did you two perpetrate this deception? Why was he murdered? Where is the real Nicholas Walcote, and is that unfortunate also murdered?"

Philippa stared at the floor.

"Madam? I asked you a question."

Her voice was unnaturally thin. It seared Crispin's gut to hear such surrender. "You won't believe me."

Wynchecombe smiled. The white teeth under the dark mustache reminded Crispin of the carved gargoyles projecting from the eaves of churches. *He is only fulfilling his obligation.* But Crispin still wanted to lash out at him. A fist to those teeth would do nicely for a start.

"Speak, Madam," Wynchecombe urged. "It will go better for you."

She wiped her face sloppily and swallowed. Her chin trembled when she opened her mouth. "When I was hired to this household five years ago, I thought he was Nicholas Walcote. We all did. What reason had we to think otherwise? Everything seemed normal. I served as a chambermaid, and I did my job well. I was a good girl. Honest and hardworking, and not a soul had a complaint against me. Nicholas took a fancy to me. He'd come across me while I was at me work, accidental at first. Then I realized he sought me out. Two years later he married me. We put up the banns and everything. We were married lawfully!"

"That isn't quite true," said Wynchecombe with too much enjoyment for Crispin's ears. "You see, you married a man under an alias. I am no man of law, but that is surely not a valid marriage."

She looked from one unsympathetic face to another. "But the priest was there! We made our vows—"

"Under a name that was not his to give. But this matter is for an ecclesiastical court. Go on."

Philippa took a moment to absorb this news. She ran a dry tongue over her pale lips. "A year ago he returned from traveling. On business, I thought. But something frightened him. He put locks on all the inner doors and instructed the steward to keep them locked. That was when he told me he wasn't Nicholas Walcote."

Maude made a shrill sound that startled everyone. Wynchecombe stared at her with irritation. "Who did he say he was?"

"He didn't."

"Then where is Nicholas Walcote?"

Her tears flowed again and she hugged herself. "He's dead. Nicholas said he met the real Master Walcote some years ago while traveling. He said they looked alike but that Walcote was killed."

"Where?"

"In Rome. He got the idea to pretend to be him. It worked so well that he just assumed his life. He only left the house to travel abroad and so no one questioned it."

"What did you do once you discovered his secret?"

"What could I do? I knew we was in trouble. I couldn't say nought to nobody!"

"You knew it was unlawful. Why did you not come to me?" asked the sheriff.

"I didn't want to think of what would happen—"

"You didn't want to lose your position, you mean."

"That's right!" she screamed, throwing back her head and staring at each tight-lipped Walcote in the circle. "Why should I? I'd given up enough, haven't I? Peace of mind. Me soul. Which of you would go back to being a servant? I'd a done anything to stay where I was!"

Almost too eager, Wynchecombe asked, "Even murder?"

She plunged her knuckle between her lips in a vain attempt to take back her words. "No, I never killed nobody. I don't know who killed my Nicholas—"

"Make her stop calling him that!" Maude shouted.

Philippa tossed back her head. A braid unwound from its careful coiffure and dangled at her shoulder. "I don't know what else to call him."

"He's a criminal," said Lionel. "Call him that."

"He's dead." Crispin spoke from behind them. "At least have mercy on that. And he was murdered."

"Yes, and she did it!" Clarence stood and pointed an accusing finger at Philippa.

"To what gain?" asked Crispin. "This very inquisition?"

"Ah, you think you're clever," said Lionel. "But she did not know that Nicholas had brothers and that we could identify him. She thought to be sole heir."

Crispin's sneer vanished. The man was right. Was the secret too much for her to bear? That was a better motive for murder than some fabled Italian syndicate.

Then he remembered. Why didn't she mention the cloth?

"*We* are the heirs," said Lionel. He threw his shoulders back triumphantly.

"At least you said 'we,' " grumbled Clarence.

Maude stood to rest her hands on her husband's shoulders. "That is so. Lionel and Clarence are the heirs. She has no rights at all. And I daresay, she wasn't even lawfully married to the man she lived with for three years."

"What's to be done with her?" Clarence asked.

"Throw her out!" roared Maude. "We certainly don't need that kind of chambermaid in this household. She'd stir up more trouble, I'll wager."

"Well, woman," said Wynchecombe. "You heard your mistress."

Lionel lurched toward the sheriff, but Wynchecombe's glare stymied his progress. "You're not going to arrest her?" he asked. "She stole Nicholas's money!"

"And surely she killed that man upstairs," Maude added.

Wynchecombe's glance slid toward Crispin. Only the corner of his mouth drew up in a smile. "Shall I arrest her?"

"Possibly, my lord." Crispin rested his hands behind his back, the only way to keep from wrapping them around Wynchecombe's throat. "But I would wait. There is more here than meets the eye. I make a solemn promise to you, Lord Sheriff, to keep an eye on her and report to you her whereabouts. She can't go far."

"Indeed," the sheriff chuckled. "Very well, Guest. She is your responsibility. If I decide to arrest her and she can't be found, then I suppose you shall hang in her stead. It looks like everyone wins." He clapped his hand on his sword hilt. "I will, of course, require a surety to allow her into your custody."

She shook her head at Crispin. He knew it would be a rich sum. He also knew she recently paid him with a full pouch and probably had nothing left on her person.

With reluctance, Crispin reached into his purse and pulled out the coin pouch. *Easily gotten, easily gone.* "Will this be sufficient?"

The sheriff took it and measured it in his palm. He smiled. "Why Crispin. You are full of surprises today." The sheriff's smile took in everyone before he pocketed the money pouch, turned, and swept out of the room.

Once the sheriff left, the Walcotes moved collectively to one side of the room opposite Philippa; an army taking its defensive position.

"I think it time the wench leaves," said Maude.

"I will help her collect her baggage," said Crispin, but Lionel harrumphed himself forward and waved his hand in the air.

"No, no, no. None of it belongs to her, after all, now does it?"

"I suppose you'd like me to go off naked!"

Both Lionel and Clarence raised their brows but Maude slapped her husband's shoulder and offered an insincere smile. "She may take what she is wearing and return it when she can."

"Very charitable," muttered Crispin. Philippa looked up at him defiantly, and he motioned for her to go. "Masters, mistress," he said in parting. "I trust you do not mind seeing me again. I am still investigating a murder."

"So you say," said Maude, staring meaningfully at Philippa. "But it seems to me that you put yourself to far more trouble than necessary."

17

CRISPIN REACHED THE FRESH cold air of the courtyard and his shoulders finally relaxed. He led the silent Philippa beyond the gatehouse and they stood undecidedly at the muddy crossroads in front of the Walcote manor.

Crispin tried to speak several times, but he did not think he could manage his anger.

Abruptly she turned to him. "Say it all. You want to. You probably even think I killed him."

"Did you?"

"You already asked me that. Didn't you believe my answer?"

"That was then."

"And now? Not just a chambermaid and an adulteress, but a liar, a thief, and a murderer. Is that it? Or maybe I left out whore."

Crispin eyed the street peripherally. Perhaps this wasn't the best place for this discussion. He longed for a drink. "I don't like being lied to."

"I didn't lie to you. I, well, I tried not to. There were just some things I couldn't tell you. Can't you understand why? Everything that happened in that room was all that I feared. That is my home, Crispin." Teardrops beaded her lashes. "I can't even be a servant there no more.

I haven't two pence to rub together. Even these clothes— That bitch wants them back, and I'll send them, mark my words!"

Crispin's throat felt thick. He wanted nothing more than to leave her in the street and get himself drunk at the Boar's Tusk, but with his name on a surety he had no recourse but to keep an eye on her. "Where does your family dwell? I will take you there."

"I ain't got a family. I got nowhere to go."

"Nowhere? No one?"

She stood red-faced and tearstained, but still striking, still unashamed and defiant.

God help me.

She wiped her face with her hand. "I don't need no one."

"I suppose . . . you may stay with me. Temporarily. I have nothing but the floor to offer you."

"I've had worse."

THE SUN LAY FAR below the horizon by the time they neared the Shambles. Crispin noted a man in livery following them, but when Crispin stopped on the pretense of taking a pebble from his boot, the man vanished.

Long shadows blended with the darkness, crossing over one another in a thatching of dismal contours. Philippa had stopped weeping a long time ago, and they hadn't spoken since leaving the manor. When he looked past her, a hunched figure emerged from the dark.

"Wait here," he said to her before he joined the short man.

Lenny's bulging eyes winced furtively up and down the street.

"What's the news, Lenny?"

"Good ev'n, Master Crispin," he said with an abbreviated bow. He gestured toward Philippa rubbing her arms in the cold. "Don't mean to interrupt your doings." He added a wink.

Crispin scowled. "Just tell me what you have for me."

"Well, I seen that Moor leave his lodgings and I followed him."

"Indeed. Where did he go?"

"Hired himself a messenger. Gave him a paper and sent him off."

"And where did this messenger go?"

"Ah! I thought you'd want to know that. So I followed him to the Walcote manor. That big stone house? Didn't see nought else after that."

"Interesting. And when did all these mysterious doings take place?"

"Last night around dusk. Then I went back to the Thistle to see if that Moor was still there."

"And was he?"

"All at ease in his room, he was. The knave."

"Much thanks, Lenny." Crispin managed to find a farthing in the corner of his purse and handed it over.

"Oh, indeed!" said Lenny, saluting with the coin. "Right you are, Master Crispin. Any time, good sir. Am I to keep an eye peeled still for this Moor?"

"If you would. Off with you now."

"Fare you well. And good luck with the lady."

Why would Mahmoud send a messenger to the Walcote manor? Sending a missive to Philippa? Crispin glanced at her. She seemed small and lost in the pall of her cloak. It covered all of her. Only her sheltered head and shoulders marked her shape.

By the time he looked back, Lenny had vanished.

"Who was that?"

Her pale skin looked blue in the cloud-veiled moonlight. She composed herself but without the sparkle he knew before.

He pulled his hood forward and sniffed at the cold. "An associate." He strode forward and she followed.

"You deal with many questionable characters."

He hurried his pace. "Yes—cutthroats, cutpurses, and the like. That is the scope of my universe," he said tightly.

"And now I am one of them."

He said nothing to that. The resignation in her voice might have been justified, but it rang inharmoniously on his ear.

They reached the Shambles, which gave up its particular fragrance even in the darkness. No mistaking the odor of death and butchering. Even when the wind changed direction, the street was not spared. Tallow vats billowed their perfume skyward, clouds of it roaming lazily.

Ahead lay the tinker's shop, and Crispin directed Philippa and took out his key. They climbed the stairs, reached for the room's lock, and the door flung open. "It's about time, Master! I was worried—"

Jack Tucker froze in place and stared at Philippa, her face streaked with old tears, one braid draped limply over a shoulder.

Crispin leaned toward Jack. "Jack, would you do me the favor of finding other lodgings tonight? Mistress Wal . . . Philippa is going to be my guest."

Jack blushed and straightened. "Oh, right then. As you will." He recovered quickly, licked his lips, and scratched his head. Freckles that took on a merry life of their own in the sunlight disappeared in the darkness of the landing. He thumbed behind him into the shadows. "I'll just be going now, will I?"

He backed out the door and Crispin closed it on him, but not before jutting his face between the slash of door and jamb. "I'll make it up to you, Jack."

Jack winked, found a place in the corner of the landing, and curled up under his cloak.

When Crispin turned back, he saw Philippa warming herself halfheartedly by the fire. He detected very little of the spirited woman she had been, but it was hardly unexpected.

He realized he tended to her as if she were a highborn lady. Servants were accustomed to sleeping several in a bed, sometimes male and female together. Surely Philippa had done so. No need, then, to send Jack out, yet he made no move to call him back.

He sat on the bed, pulled off his boots, and rubbed his feet. "Jack usually sleeps in that corner where the straw is. You'll find it comfortable enough."

She nodded. Skirt folding beneath her, she sank down before the fire and unbraided her hair.

Crispin tried not to watch and got up in his stocking feet to rummage among the jars and sacks on his pantry shelf. Finding a hard-crusted pasty leaning against a crock of pickled onions, he grabbed it, sniffed its slightly stale crust, and broke it in two. He laid one half on the table and pushed it toward her. He returned to the bed, laid down on his back, and tore into the stale meat pie.

He chewed in silence for an uncomfortable moment before he glanced her way.

The fire glazed her brassy hair, and the newly unbound tresses frizzed about her face in a golden halo. She raked her fingers through it, trying to comb out the curls. The action only served to soften her features. Her white face, fragile and alluring, shimmered in the firelight.

The dry dough stuck in his throat. He sat up, hoping wine would help. "That one on the table is for you."

He reached for the wine jug and made a prayer of thanks when he lifted and found it full. He poured a bowl for himself and one for her. He scooted the chair to the table.

Philippa held the pasty but did not eat.

"You'd better eat that. That surety money was to pay for food. There isn't any more."

"I'm so sorry."

Crispin sighed. "Don't vex yourself."

"You must hate me."

"No. I'm angry, but I don't hate you."

"Surely you see how I couldn't tell you. You're honest. You would have had to report to the sheriff that my husband was not Nicholas Walcote. That's why when Mahmoud threatened to tell—"

She pressed her lips closed, frowned, and gingerly put the pasty to her trembling mouth.

Crispin froze. He felt like a fool. Worse. "I'm an idiot," he told the rafters.

"I lay with that vile man as much to protect Nicholas as me. It was nothing to me," she said, eyes closed over damp lashes. "I was *not* there with Mahmoud. I was anywhere but there." She opened her eyes again and fixed them on Crispin. "Whatever else he was, Nicholas was good to me. I won't forget him for that. I did it for him. I owed him. He would've understood that, wouldn't he?"

He shook his head. "I know not. This is a very sad affair."

"Do you think those Italians killed Nicholas? He was afraid they had followed him. He said as much."

When he'd dispatched the pasty he wiped his hands down his coat. Mahmoud's missive recently sent to the Walcote Manor rose up in his mind. "Well, one thing is certain: Mahmoud will no longer extort you."

She sighed, her first sound of relief. She looked up at him from her place by the fire.

Mahmoud. A vile man with vile habits. A Saracen. He glowered at her, wanting to know, yet not wanting to ask. "How could you do it?" he blurted. "Give yourself to a stranger. To a *Saracen*! What of your virtue—"

"Virtue? Do you think I was a maiden when I met Nicholas, or whatever the poor bastard's name was?" She pulled a piece of the crust away with her fingers and stuffed it in her mouth. "Life's hard in the scullery," she said, cheek bulging. "You do a lot for an extra scrap of bread."

"You said you were a chambermaid."

"I was at the Walcote manor, but I didn't start that way. Me mum was a scullion. I worked alongside her. Don't remember when I didn't. One day, she was stirring a cauldron when the chain holding it above the fire broke. I remember water and steam everywhere. And I remember her screaming. It scalded her to death." She chewed thoughtfully. "When I buried her, I vowed I'd get m'self out of the kitchens, and I did. I'd never thought to reach so high." She sighed with her entire body. "Maybe it was only a dream. You can take the girl out of the scullery, perhaps, but you can't take the scullery out of the girl."

Crispin tried hard to remember his own servants and could not recall if he had ever set eyes on a scullion in his manor in Sheen. He felt ashamed.

He leaned on his arm and studied her. "You rose from the very bottom. You can even read. Remarkable."

"I'm a fair remarkable wench," she said, smiling briefly. She finished the rest of her food in silence. She collected her wine bowl, pulled a stool to the table, and sat opposite him. "You're fair remarkable yourself. So why'd *you* do it? Take me in, I mean."

"You remind me of someone."

"Oh? Who?"

He smiled. "Me."

Her eyes brightened and she reached her hand across the table to touch his. Before she could, Crispin shot from his chair and moved away. She rose and edged toward him.

"It don't matter why."

"Philippa . . ."

"What matters is you did. 'Cause you're decent and true." She stood toe to toe with him and looked up unafraid. He recognized that confidence, and it twisted a knot in his gut. Her hair, like fleece, curly and wild, was edged with gold from the firelight raging behind her. Her lips glistened with wine, but it wasn't just the liquor that gave them their rosy hue.

He stared at her for a long moment. Before he had time to question the sanity of it, he took a step toward her and dipped his face and kissed her soft lips, drawing on them until nothing remained but the taste of her. Hands found her back and he lifted her toward him, pressing her warm body against his, savoring the length of her, each dip and valley. The kiss grew harder, almost cruel. But she gave as good as she got and used her teeth and tongue like weapons. His hands slid about her waist.

Her soft body melded to his like a tight-fitting garment and he smothered himself in her, rejoicing in that brassy fleece cascading about his cheeks. He grasped her head with one hand, allowing the tresses to tickle his wrist. He sealed his mouth to hers and feasted, nose inhaling sweat and sweetness and woman.

He released her head and waist to run his hands along her shoulders to the back of her neck, fingers working at the laces of her gown.

"What are you doing?" she asked drowsily to his moist cheek.

"I'm undressing you," he rasped. "Any objections?"

She gave a breathy laugh. "No."

The word barely left her lips when the gown slipped to her feet.

18

CRISPIN LAY FOR THE second time that night with his face under Philippa's chin. His cheek rested comfortably on the softness of her bosom and he inhaled the muskiness of bedded woman.

"Tell me who you are, Crispin," she said again. He silenced her the first time with kisses that turned to more. Now he was weak and drowsy and all he could do was angle his face upward and kiss her jaw. It tasted of him.

"Must we speak of such things?" His voice mumbled against her skin. "Are there not better topics of conversation when lovers are abed?"

She smiled. He could tell because the shadows and angles of her jaw changed. "Are we lovers now?"

"If you would have it so."

"Does that mean," she said with a false coquette in her voice, "that you would lie with me again?"

"And again and again. When a job is worth doing—" He nuzzled her until she pulled away.

"Then you should tell me."

"Hmm?" He found a better spot to nuzzle, flicking his tongue.

She squirmed away and gathered the bedclothes over her breasts. "About your past. You don't belong on the Shambles. Why are you here, Crispin?"

He stopped. *Women!* Sighing, he rolled off of her and lay on his back to stare up at the cobwebbed rafters. "Why is my history so important?"

She rolled onto her belly. Propped up on her elbows, she gazed down at him. Her locks fell softly over one eye. "Because it makes you so secretive and mistrusting. And I would know and share your pain as you shared mine."

"No one can share this."

"Yet I would still know."

He looked at her. "Stubborn."

She frowned playfully. "Determined."

Her face was, in fact, determined, and he shook his head at it. "'I was shipwrecked before I got aboard,'" he sighed.

"What?"

"It's a quotation. From a philosopher I favor." He hoped it would distract her, but he saw from the corner of his eye that she was not deterred.

"Very well." He settled his interlaced hands on his bare chest and stared upward. "Eight years ago, I was a knight."

"A knight! You?"

He nodded, his head sliding on the rough cloth of the pillow. "I fought great battles, I warred in France, in Germany, fought the Turk, and went on a crusading pilgrimage in the Holy Land. I owned fields, flocks, woodlands, villeins. I dressed in the finest clothes, drank the finest wines, ate course after course in my great hall at my barony in Sheen not far from the king's own residence. I served and was served in the great hall in Westminster Palace—when Edward of Windsor was king."

"What happened?"

"I did a stupid, foolish thing. I wagered on the wrong horse."

She cocked her head charmingly. He took her hand and stroked it. "You see, I was the duke of Lancaster's man. He fostered me in his household. Made me a knight. But that gratitude blinded me to my duty. I felt that he should have been heir when his brother Edward of

Woodstock died. I could not imagine this great realm ruled by Edward's son Richard when the duke lived and breathed."

"Hush, Crispin." She looked to the shuttered window in fear, but he had long since stopped worrying over speaking treason.

"There were others who did not share my view of Lancaster," he went on. "They wanted to bring him and his men down. They hatched a plot, intimating that Lancaster was ready to move against Richard and take the throne for himself." He shook his head, still amazed he believed it. "It was not true, of course, but I—brash, young fool that I was—thought it was so, and I joined my name to the conspirators."

She said nothing. Her hand went to her lips.

"The treasonous plot was soon unmasked and many were executed. I should have been among them, but my liege lord Lancaster pleaded for my life. By then, Richard was crowned and he only ten years old. Though he did not yet have the rule of the country, he had a say in my fate." He nodded ruefully. "I remember the day well. Richard called his court and I stood before them all. He announced in his clear, young voice that I was a knight no more. And further, that all my lands and my wealth were forfeit to the crown, and that my title was abolished. I was stripped of my armor, my shield, and my sword, and left with nothing but the clothes on my back." He smiled at her sadly. "Sound familiar?"

"Oh, Crispin."

"He told the court that any lord who succored me would see the same fate or worse, and I was set loose on the road as I was."

"But what of your kinsmen?"

"The male line had died out. I have some female cousins in the Marches, but after I was degraded, well. I'm certain they prayed I would disown them. I was utterly alone. But I managed to survive as you see me now."

She glanced about the small room she once called a stable. "It's very cozy here."

He kissed her hand before releasing it. "It's dismal, but it's all I can afford."

Philippa glanced away before rolling on her back to join Crispin in contemplating the ceiling. She pulled the covers lightly over her and turned to smile at him. "Poor dear. Me? Well, I can be a chambermaid again, maybe even a chatelaine. But you—"

He frowned, realizing how much he had revealed. "Don't worry over me," he said brusquely.

"Doesn't anyone worry over you?"

"Jack does."

He felt her stare at him before she said, "Is there no *woman* to care about you?"

He closed his eyes. "Once or twice. Briefly."

She turned over onto her belly again, rolling herself in the sheet. She ran her fingers lightly over his sable chest hair. "If I had been a chambermaid in your manor in Sheen and I had caught your eye, would you have married me?"

Crispin opened one eye to look at her and just as quickly shut it.

Only a few short moments ago he felt drowsy with languor, but now he was wide awake. He knew he should answer her, but the time stretched so long that she squirmed beside him.

"It's a simple question," she said. "Or is it?"

He snapped open his eyes. He shuffled himself up to a sitting position and lay his hands on his thighs over the covers. His head rested against the plaster wall. The wall felt cold. "You want the truth?" Her only acknowledgment was her intensely concentrated stare down her nose. He suspected that the truth she said she wanted wasn't the one he was about to give her. "The answer is 'no.' Does that surprise you? It shouldn't. I was a lord of the court. A knight. I would never have married my chambermaid. No such man would have done."

She folded her arms over her ample chest and pouted. "I see. Well then, you answered that right well."

Women! Their pouts were such sharp weapons. And they wielded them well. Her hurt look was almost as good as its equally quick change to a pixie smile. He couldn't trust that kind of smile. Especially when it hid behind that sleepy way of hers, drooped lids that so easily enticed him to her will. "You aren't a lord now," she purred.

He studied her, somehow able to resist her allure. "It's in the blood." He chuckled at the memory of his conversation with Eleanor. "This is my 'true image' you see before you. But I was betrothed once."

"What happened?"

He rolled his eyes and closed them again. "You can guess."

"She broke the betrothal because you were no longer a knight? And yet, if it is 'in the blood' as you say, what should it matter?"

He opened his eyes and fixed them on her. It wasn't hard to do. The sheet wound tightly about her chest and hid her charms, but only tantalized by creating depth and darkness between her breasts. Her hair teased her white shoulders and caressed her face in soft curls and shadow. He was surprised by the regret tingeing his words. "This is no fit place to bring a wife."

She looked at him a long time. A sigh eased over her pert lips before she snuggled against him and cast her arm across his chest. In spite of himself, he liked the feel of it.

"It's no good, you know," she said softly. He felt her breath tickle the hair on his chest. "I'm falling in love with you."

Crispin felt a stab in his heart. A not entirely unfamiliar feeling, but not a welcomed one. He thought to keep silent and drift off to sleep again, but instead his lips unaccountably parted. "I think I love you, too."

He searched the rafters. Maybe something heavy would fall on him. "Funny," he said. "I never intended to say that aloud."

Philippa's warm body rested against his for another pleasant moment. But suddenly, as if the house were afire, she scrambled out of bed. *"It's here, ain't it!"*

Her naked body gleamed in the waning firelight but she clutched her breast as if enduring chest pains. His heartbeat thrummed before he understood what she was talking about.

"The Mandyllon? Don't be a fool. Of course it is, but—"

She rummaged for her clothes and drew on her shift. "You must get it out of here! I won't spend one more moment in its presence. It made you say all those things. Don't you remember? It made *me tell the truth to the sheriff*!"

Crispin dismissed it. Hysteria. And confession was good for the soul. Although he, too, had acknowledged love for her he had no intention of voicing. But he owed that to his sleepiness and a certain amount of shared vulnerability. All easily explained.

Wasn't it?

"Philippa, it is the middle of the"—he glanced toward the shuttered window and noted light creeping through—"morning," he finished lamely. "Come back to bed."

She cowered near the opposite wall looking down at her feet. Nothing could convince her, so he dragged himself from the tangle of bedsheets and stood naked on the cold floor. His stockings, lying across the floorboards like a skinned snake, were still tied to his under braies, so he pulled on each one and slipped the braies up. He shrugged into his shirt and when he grabbed his cotehardie, the Mandyllon fell out of it onto the floor. She gave a little screech and he quickly tucked it beneath his cote as he pulled it on, snorting at himself at the freshly torn-off buttons.

"Put yourself at ease," he said, buckling his belt. He patted the lump the Mandyllon made inside his coat. "I will find a suitable hiding place until I can decide what's to be done with it." He leaned toward her to kiss, but she backed away, pointing to his chest. He scowled instead and pulled open the door.

Jack stood on the landing wearing an expectant smile.

Crispin closed Philippa in the room behind him and rubbed his unshaven jaw. He didn't know why he felt embarrassed. "Look Jack, this was all unexpected."

"Course."

"Stop looking at me like that. Do you need to be cuffed to remind you who is master here?"

"Oh, I know right well who the master is here. She is."

Crispin's anger drained away and he leaned limply against the closed door. "I fear you are right. I suppose I must tell you what transpired."

The boy tucked his hands behind his back and shuffled his feet. Under his breath he said, "I know what transpired—"

Crispin cuffed him lightly. "Not *that*! I mean yesterday. Walcote's brothers came calling, and they declared that the dead man is not Nicholas Walcote."

"'Slud! Who is he, then?"

"No one seems to know. But Philippa knew he was an imposter. She tried to suppress it. Then the sheriff interceded and, well, it was determined that she should be cast out. It wasn't even a lawful marriage, and so she is left with nothing."

"Oh, Master! It's just like what happened to you!"

"Yes, and perhaps that is why I'm sympathetic. Or—" He turned toward the door as if he could spy her through the wood. "I, uh . . ." Taking in Jack's expression, he decided he didn't have to share all his thoughts and suspicions with the boy. "I have an errand to run. Watch over her while I am out."

"Aye, Master. With pleasure, sir."

Crispin rambled down the stairs and swore into the wind. He glanced up the Shambles one way and down the other. Animal carcasses hung from great metal hooks near the shop fronts, hallowed, skinned, and bereft of head and forelimbs. He felt a little like that himself.

What was he going to do about these foreign villains; what about the cloth? And what, by all the saints, was he to do about Philippa? The sheriff still thought her guilty of murder but Crispin believed otherwise. Or was it merely his feelings getting in the way?

A pleasant ache suffused his chest when he thought about her desirable softness, her eager compliance. He looked up to the window. A cold sweat dampened his chemise when he also thought about his admission to her.

He lightly touched the Mandyllon under his coat. He didn't believe in the power of such things. He knew about profitable traffic in relics, and how easily faked they were. Wasn't this just one more of those? Still, it was provable. All he had to do was deliberately lie in its presence.

A lie was easy to conjure. He'd made many as a means to his ends. A lie was only another tool, like a dagger or a sword.

He strolled down the lane, trying to think of a lie. A butcher called out to him. "Come sir! This is the finest flesh in all of London, except of course for the stews in Southwark." He laughed at his own bawdy jest and Crispin turned to him. "Oh! Master Crispin. I did not see it was you."

"Master Dickon," Crispin responded. "I know how it is in Southwark," he said with a crooked smile. "How is the meat in your own establishment today?"

Dickon lay his hand on a haunch swinging from an overhead hook. "Truth to tell, it ain't as fine as it could be. Lots of gristle in this one. Better for stewing than roasting, but I will still try to get the best price. And a good price I will offer to you, of course."

Crispin eyed him. "Did you truly mean to tell me that?" he asked in a hushed tone. "About the gristle."

The butcher thought a moment. "Well now, I doubt I would tell another man such, but I have always tried to be honest with you, sir."

"Are you certain? Did you not just get a sudden urge to tell me the truth?"

Dickon smiled awkwardly. "I don't rightly know, sir. I don't know until the moment strikes me, do I?"

Crispin nodded, dissatisfied. He thanked the butcher and proceeded on his way, heading up the small incline of the Shambles, which inevitably led him to Newgate and its prison.

He hadn't meant to arrive there, but as he looked up its fortress walls and thought of its guards and many cells, an idea occurred to him.

19

CRISPIN SAUNTERED DOWN THE dim corridors, the guards nodding to him in recognition of his uneasy relationship with Simon Wynchecombe. That alone allowed him free rein in Newgate, though it wasn't his favorite haunt. Usually he headed directly for Wynchecombe's hall in the corner tower, but today he swallowed his own revulsion of the place and strolled among the few cells, each arched portal closed up tight. Black iron hinges, double, triple strength, bolted tightly to the heavy oaken doors. Some doors had smaller, barred spy-holes, yet still others had none, making them dark and lonely places of despair.

He traveled down the passage lit only by an occasional pitch torch or cresset. All the doors seemed to be closed until he reached the end of the passage. One cell stood open. The straw that served as bedding and toilet sat in an unattended dung cart. Crispin darted a glance down both sides of the empty passage before slipping into the cell, cold with its open arrow-slit window. Embedded grillwork in the stone sill made certain the prisoner could not escape even if it were possible to squeeze through the tight window. If he managed even this feat, he would plunge four stories down, though a death in freedom was often preferable to the uncertain future of prison walls.

Crispin knew the feeling.

He ran his hands along the stone walls, looking for crumbling mortar. Reaching above his head, his fingers caught on a loose stone and he used his nails to pry it free. A hole barely big enough for his purposes, he nevertheless took out the folded cloth and did his best to stuff it in the hole. "If this is your face on this cloth, Lord, then I beg your mercy," he grunted, pushing the stone block back into place. It teetered, trying to fit. Crispin withdrew his dagger and used the pommel to pound it in the rest of the way. He craned his neck to look at it and decided it needed mortar.

Under the window, a permanent mud hole collected from streaks of dribbling rain running down the discolored wall. He used his dagger again to scrape some with his blade and pasted it between the joints. He worked at it for a few minutes and then stood back to admire his effort. *I'm no mason, but if no one is looking for it, then I have nothing to fear.*

He wiped his blade on his coat, sheathed it, and clapped the mud from his hands.

"Miss the place?"

Crispin stepped back, his hand on his dagger. He looked up at a squint-faced guard with a three-day beard and a leather cap slightly askew on his head. Ginger hair peeked from a tear in the cap, sticking out straight from his head like a sentinel.

"I am only looking around, Malvyn."

Malvyn tapped his knife on the side of his face, scratching his unshaven chin. The blade was nicked and stained. Crispin wondered if he ever cleaned it.

"And here is his lord, standing in a cell again. What do we make of that? Shouldn't you be in the sheriff's hall?"

"I am not seeking out the sheriff today." Crispin crossed the threshold and stood upwind of the gaoler before he turned his back on him.

"Now, Crispin. I thought we had become friends while you was here."

Crispin chuckled with bared teeth. "We were never friends. I loathed the air you breathed." He waved his hand before his own sharp nose. "I still do."

"Now, now. Rudeness? That was never tolerated when you was a prisoner here." He grabbed Crispin's arm.

The cold feel of the man's fingers closing over his skin flooded Crispin's mind with memories he had no desire to revisit. He stiffened and spun. With a much stronger grip than Malvyn's, he captured the man's wrist and twisted until he sank down on one knee with a yowl.

"I am no longer a prisoner here!" Crispin growled. "And I will thank you not to touch me." Crispin twisted the arm once more simply because he enjoyed it. With a feral grunt he released him, tossing the captured hand aside.

Clumsily, the man rose and found his footing. He scowled, face reddening as he wobbled toward Crispin to spear him with his finger. "You'll come to regret this," he snarled.

Crispin straightened his coat and turned on his heel. He didn't look back as he strode down the passage. "That I doubt."

CRISPIN TOOK THE STAIRS to his lodgings two at a time. He was anxious to see Philippa and tell her . . . tell her what? That he loved her? He'd said it once and didn't know how it could be true. But didn't he feel his heart leap when he looked at her? Didn't he admire how she had lifted herself from her hardships? He wouldn't speak of it again. Maybe she wouldn't either. He chuckled at that. Wishful thinking. At least she would be relieved the Mandyllon was gone.

He opened his door carelessly, expecting to find both Philippa and Jack.

He did not expect the man across the room or the one behind the door.

2 0

DARK-HAIRED AND DARK-SKINNED, THE men wore livery. Crispin thought he recognized them.

But more notably, they both carried crossbows, and the weapons were cocked and aimed at him.

"Gentlemen," said Crispin. "If I knew you were coming I would have prepared better hospitality."

"You are to please come with us," said the one across the room. His accent was thick with the sunshine and olive oil of the southern part of the continent.

Crispin slowly shook his head. "I do not think I would profit from that."

"It is not a matter of what you think. It is a matter of who is better armed, no?"

Both foreign men smiled and raised their weapons higher. Crispin smiled, too, and nodded, all the while wondering where the hell Philippa and Jack could be. He decided he wouldn't fancy ending up at the bottom of the Thames with two quarrels in him. That would help no one.

The closest man made a move toward him. With blood pumping madly through his every fiber, Crispin tensed and before the man could grab him, Crispin darted his hand forward and closed it around the wrist with the crossbow. With all his strength, he slammed it hard against the wall—once, twice. The man protested in Italian and was wrenched off balance by Crispin's unrelenting blows. He nearly fell into Crispin, still holding tight to the weapon.

With an inarticulate shout, the man across the room lifted his crossbow and aimed.

Crispin spied him over the struggling man's shoulder. With widened eyes, he yanked his attacker in front of him.

A whoosh and a thud told Crispin the bolt struck true—and hit square in the back of the man he pinned. The man cried out, twisting, clawing at the bolt in his back. But his thrashing grew weaker. Blood darkened the back of his coat.

The face of the other man parched white in horror and he lowered his weapon for only a moment before he snapped to and struggled to reload.

With a groan, Crispin's attacker slumped to his knees, but without missing a beat, Crispin snatched the weapon from the man's limp hand, aimed the crossbow, and pulled the trigger.

Both bodies hit the floor at the same time.

The room suddenly fell to silence. One of the men was whimpering. Crispin could not tell which one.

Panting, Crispin stepped back and stared at the bodies now littering his floor. Blood was seeping over the floorboards. And urine. He could smell it. At least one of them was already dead and the other soon would be.

He hefted the crossbow in his hand and studied the compact weapon with a sense of giddiness at having escaped the sharp scythe of Death once more. The gears and windlass of the crossbow interested him for only a moment. A fool's weapon. Give him a dagger or a hunting bow any day.

He dropped the crossbow on top of the closest man.

The hard stillness was broken by the sound of slow, deliberate clapping, one hand striking the other. Crispin jerked toward the doorway, his hand on his dagger.

Abid Assad Mahmoud leaned in the jamb as if he had been there a long time. Perhaps he had. He stopped clapping when Crispin glared at him.

"My compliments," said the man. "Well played."

"Your crossbowmen, I presume?"

"Yes, but"—he looked them over and tutted—"mine no more."

"Have you come to finish the task?" Crispin's hand had not left his dagger.

"No. Only to tell you how disappointed I am. The girl was a special bonus. And now, well, there is nothing left with which to extort her."

"No, your game is done."

"Not quite. There is still the matter of the cloth."

"And so. You admit it at last."

"Yet you knew all along." The Saracen walked into the room and looked about with a sneer on his bruised face. "So what do we have left to bargain with?"

"I do not wish to bargain with your like."

"You do not know my like. I am a very valuable man in my country. But you are an infidel. All you see is the color of my skin. I must be pasty-white like the rest of you English in order to be trusted. What a small people you are."

"I was in the Holy Land, Mahmoud. I saw followers of Muhammad treat us 'pasty' English and French with inhumanity."

"As did your crusaders to our people. The sword cuts both ways."

Crispin closed his hands into fists. He hoped he could use them. "What do you want, Mahmoud? I tire of this. Others want this cloth. What is your claim on it? Does it belong to you?"

"The Mandyllon? In a sense."

"In what sense?"

He blinked slowly. His wide mouth spread in a crocodile's smile.

There was still swelling and bruising about his cheek and eye. It pleased Crispin to see it. "We commissioned it," said Mahmoud.

"What do you mean you commissioned it? How is that possible?"

"Not the original one, of course." He touched the back of Crispin's chair. "Will you invite me to sit?"

"No."

Mahmoud sat anyway. He eased back in the chair with an air of indifference, but all his muscles appeared taut and ready for any move from Crispin. "The man you know as Nicholas Walcote was paid to make a copy of the Mandyllon," he said. "He was a clever thief, though. He made his copy, and when it was time for us to collect the true one, he made a substitution. It seems he left with the real cloth and we were left with the copy. This made our masters very unhappy. And when they are unhappy, people die."

"You never met the real Walcote?"

"Alas, no."

Crispin mulled the information, staring blindly at the nearest dead man. Blood stained the shirt around the arrow. *Masters?* "Then the missing cloth is the real one?"

"Missing?" Mahmoud laughed. "Crispin, you play such coy games."

"Why did you need a copy?"

"My master did not wish for the keepers of the cloth to know it was appropriated."

"Stolen, you mean."

Mahmoud waved his hand and smiled.

Crispin glanced at the dead crossbowmen. "Don't tell me *you* killed Walcote, or whatever his true name is?"

Mahmoud frowned, but his face wore amusement. "We wanted him dead, but we would not be so stupid as to kill him *before* we got the cloth back."

Crispin wished for half a heartbeat that he was still holding the cloth and that it could tell him a lie from the truth. But he was also a good judge of men and a good judge of lies.

"Strangely," he said, "I believe you."

"I am gratified," Mahmoud said.

"Yet this cloth that you so fiercely desire does not seem to belong to you?"

"Not strictly speaking, no."

"Then we have nothing to discuss."

"I think we do. My employers wish to make you an offer that you will find difficult to decline."

"Oh? And what is that?"

Mahmoud rose and sauntered toward the door. His hand never left the pommel of a curved dagger in its intricately patterned sheath. "Give us the Mandyllon or the girl dies."

A wave of panic seized Crispin, but his face only showed practiced indifference. "What if I were to negotiate directly with your masters?"

Mahmoud's mouth flattened. "That would be ill-advised. My masters do not bargain amongst the lower classes." He said the last with relish. Crispin fought the urge to frown.

"Would it surprise you to learn that your master is already negotiating with me?" The look on Mahmoud's face more than made up for his last comment. "It seems he effectively cut you out of the entire process. Unless . . . he isn't the master you speak of. I believe you said 'masters.'"

Mahmoud shut his lips and strolled across the room. He stared down at one of the dead men. "That is all of little consequence," he replied quietly.

"Truly? Will this not displease your masters, whoever they are? That at least one of them was forced to negotiate with me? That *you* failed?"

The Saracen looked up. "The end is still the same."

"The end." Crispin chuckled and leaned against the doorpost. "Indeed. The *end*."

Mahmoud rushed him. He snarled, his hand on his dagger. "What have you told them?"

Crispin blinked slowly, enjoying it. "Only what I needed to."

"They don't know about the girl," he growled. "I do. I suggest you surrender the Mandyllon to me before I get to her."

"You don't know where she is."

Mahmoud cast his glance purposefully about the room. "Don't I?" He saluted Crispin and rolled out of the doorway.

Crispin cast a glance at the dead men again before he dashed for the door. He got two paces on the landing before he stopped sharply.

No one was there.

"What the devil—?"

Just that moment Jack and Philippa passed the eclipse of light and shadow at the bottom of the stairway. They trotted upwards when Philippa looked up and raised a startled hand to her chest. "Crispin!"

"Didn't you see him?"

She ascended to the landing where Crispin stood, peering past her. "Who?"

"Mahmoud. You must have just passed him."

Philippa turned to Jack who had come up beside her. "We saw no one."

Like smoke. Mahmoud's threat still hung in the air. Crispin's voice remained calm but his heart hammered against his ribs. "Where have you been?"

"Jack went with me to get some food."

"Where did you get the money? Jack, haven't I told you a thousand times—"

"It wasn't him," she said, putting a hand on Jack's drooping shoulders.

"You said you didn't have any money." He looked at her hand resting on Jack. "You pawned your wedding ring."

She covered the empty ring finger with the other hand. "What any self-respecting servant would do."

Jack chuckled. "I like her," he said.

"Now that you're back we must go."

"Go?" she cried. "Go where? What did Mahmoud want?"

Jack groaned. "She was going to cook, Master Crispin. No offense, but I am tired of your cooking, and mine."

"She hasn't the time." He took her elbow and steered her down the stairs.

Dejected, Jack stood holding the poultry and sausages. "What should I be doing?" he asked.

Crispin stopped. "Oh. Jack, call for the sheriff. If he has any questions . . . well, it is certain he will, and I will answer to him anon. But . . . not at this moment."

"Call the sheriff for what?"

"Those men in our room. I'm afraid they are dead."

"What?"

Without looking back, he ushered Philippa away, but she dragged her heels in the mud and brought him to a halt. "Crispin! I will not take one more step until you tell me where we are going! And what did that terrible man want?"

"You are going to a safer location and stay with some friends of mine."

"But Crispin." She melted naturally into his arms. Her touch brought an instant response. "I thought you wanted me all to yourself."

He wanted to kiss her, but the reality of their public surroundings sunk in. He gently pushed her back. "I want you alive." He glanced up and saw a few turned heads. It took all his strength to step back. "You have enough scandal to contend with without talk of your living with a man."

She set her jaw and planted a fist at her hip. "What's the matter? What tidings have you heard?"

"Mahmoud threatened you."

She laughed, a hearty, throaty sound, one that made him tingle with desire. He had felt that laugh tremble against his chest only last night. It almost made him lose his resolve. "He can't have me any-more," she said triumphantly. "That game is done!"

"He wants the cloth."

"You didn't give it to him!"

"No, nor will I. It is a tangled tale, to be sure. There is more than one syndicate at work here. Yet there is one thing I am certain of. Neither killed your husband."

"But they must have. Who else could it be?"

"I'm afraid it puts the murder back on you."

"Crispin! I did not kill Nicholas!"

"Others will not see it that way. Who else knew about Nicholas Walcote's true nature?" He gently steered her up the road toward the Boar's Tusk. They picked their way over the rutted, muddy lane. Shopkeepers' apprentices called out their wares. A boy—a servant—was holding up a coney by its back feet and waving the limp creature to the passersby. The long ears flopped from side to side.

"Adam did," she said reluctantly. "He found out accidentally. He overheard us talking."

He pulled Philippa out of the way of a cart moving quickly up the street toward Newgate Market. "What did Adam do?"

She shrugged. "Nothing. He is very loyal."

"To you."

She glanced sideways at him. "Jealous?"

Crispin ignored the comment. "He could have made trouble for Nicholas. It could have come to a head."

They reached Foster Lane and the smells of the fish market swelled like a tide of the Thames. Some boys, hefting a basket of eels between them, stopped at the nearest seller and began to bargain. A woman nearby, having just left the steps of a well, lifted a dripping water-bouget to a man astride a draft horse. He fitted it behind him on his makeshift saddle.

"No, Adam is no such man," she said, watching the handsome man on the horse lean down to kiss the water girl farewell. "And I doubt he knew about the secret passage."

Crispin brooded. Adam Becton could easily have discovered such a passage. He was the household steward, after all. It was his business to know the doings of the house. That would also give him access to the ledgers.

"Why do you believe that murderer Mahmoud?" asked Philippa. "He did try to have you killed."

"That was business. I don't take it personally."

She looked askance. "Is that the sort of business you are in?"

"What did you expect? A nice little shop with a shingle above my door? The business of murder is ugly, populated with equally ugly people." She said nothing to this. A cloud shadow moved over them, dimming the street and bathing it darker than its usual gauzy gray.

"Where are you taking me? Is it truly for my protection? Or yours?"

He looked back at her and stopped. There was something different to her demeanor, something cautious; a tilt to her shoulders that protected her, a dull sheen to her eye.

"I told you. You won't be safe at my lodgings. I'm taking you elsewhere."

"A moment ago when I was in your arms, you seemed almost embarrassed."

Crispin set his jaw and stared somewhere near her feet. "I am unused to such public displays of affection."

She shook her head. Her hair was coifed in its two looping braids again, but a loose strand fell over her forehead and lifted in a timid wave with a passing breeze. He watched it rise and fall. It was easier than looking in her eyes.

"You mean it ain't proper."

He shrugged stiffly. "As you like."

"Suddenly I wish I had that Mandyllon right now," she said. "Then you'd speak the truth whether you wanted to or not."

He wanted to speak, to say something that would put that spark back in those eyes. His lips twisted on words that might have brought a smile and another kiss from her mouth. But there was too much to say, and he was ill-equipped to utter any of it. Perhaps Jack could have done. But not him. He could never say the words she wanted. He was glad the Mandyllon was gone. He had no more desire to peer into his true image than at the one etched on that bit of muslin.

"I can't change who I am," he rasped. It wasn't quite what he wanted to say, but it was all he had.

Once animated, her face now became stony. Her lids drew down as they were used to doing, but not in a seductive manner.

"No," she said soberly. "I don't suppose you can." She hugged herself, whether from the cold or the coldness of his words he could not tell. The stray thread of hair lifted again and fell across her eyes, forcing her to blink and look away. A mercy. It prevented him from having to say more.

THE BOAR'S TUSK LOOMED before them, white daub speckled with mud and timbers dark from dampness. The great door—wide and arched, its size and splendor fit more for a church—welcomed all comers. The Boar's Tusk had seen better days. Now it was the kind of place where men sought solace in bowls of wine and beakers of ale, not in one another.

Out of the corner of his eye, Crispin watched Philippa straighten her clothes and brush the dirt from her skirt before they entered.

Crispin scanned the room and spotted the tavern keeper, Gilbert. "Come along," he said huskily. This was exposure he'd rather not have. His feelings had been his own for so long, he didn't like waving them about like a banner.

Gilbert spied Crispin and hailed him. He approached with a lumbering gait and looked pointedly at Philippa.

Crispin made the introductions. "Gilbert, this is Philippa. Can you give her work and lodgings?"

Gilbert stared at Philippa before turning a questioning glare at Crispin, an expression that seemed to say "you must be mad!"

Philippa took on an entirely different demeanor for Gilbert. She was not the haughty lady nor the sultry lover, but now the self-effacing servant.

Chameleon, Crispin mused.

Gilbert's gaze brushed down her clothes. "That dress will not do. Have you other clothes?"

She glanced at Crispin before looking away. "No, this is all I have. And even this is not mine to keep."

"I see," Gilbert mumbled. "Well, my wife will surely have a gown for you. Ever done kitchen work?"

"Aye, sir. I was a scullion for ten years."

"Well then. Go on in and ask for the mistress. I'm certain she'll show you what needs doing. Tell her"—he glanced at Crispin—"tell her Crispin sent you."

She smiled. "Bless you, Master. I am grateful for your kindness."

"Nothing to it," he said, wiping his hands down his apron for the hundredth time.

Philippa disappeared through the kitchen curtain. Both men watched her go. Crispin cleared his throat. "I, too, thank you, Gilbert. I feel she will be safe here."

"Crispin." Gilbert took him aside and spoke into his shoulder. "That's Philippa Walcote!"

"Very good, Gilbert. I thought I'd have to explain."

"What goes on with her? What about the murder? All of London is saying she did it."

"She didn't. I know her."

"Begging your pardon, Crispin, but you have been wrong before. Especially about women."

Crispin's jaw tightened. "Are you implying something, Gilbert?"

"No, only that your judgment may be clouded. She's a beautiful woman. Sometimes that's the only weapon they need."

"If you don't want her here then say so."

"That's not what I'm saying."

"Then what *are* you saying?"

Heads turned at the raised voices and Gilbert took Crispin's arm to steer him to a darker corner. Quietly he said, "I'm saying 'be careful.' I don't fancy the idea of your getting hurt over this."

Crispin rested his hand on his dagger. "I take every precaution."

"I don't mean that. I mean here," and he put his hand on Crispin's heart.

Crispin sighed from his depths. "I am defenseless in that quarter."

"Aye," Gilbert sighed in return. "As are we all. But I don't think it a good idea. She's trouble."

Crispin's smile curved his lips. "When have I ever run from trouble?"

They both looked back toward the kitchen doorway as if Philippa would emerge from mere mention of her. "She is a fair lass," Gilbert admitted.

"Yes," said Crispin with a sigh. He began to feel that stupid feeling again and he turned briskly away. "I have much to do now. Send for Jack if you need me."

He was out the door before Gilbert could stop him.

Crispin stood in the muddy street, glazed momentarily by his many thoughts. A horseman rambling past startled him awake, and he jumped out of the way, but not before kicked-up mud spotted his cloak. He looked down at the spatters and thought of blood. Blood on the floor in the secret passage. Someone lying in wait for the man everyone knew as Nicholas Walcote. Someone who viciously stabbed him in the back. If the death was an assassination, as the Italians wanted, a slit throat would suit better. No chance of noise, and with the victim's back to the killer, it kept the culprit's clothes clean.

But this was a stabbing, a crime of passion. And who was passionate enough in the Walcote house to do such a deed?

"Adam Becton is in love with Philippa," he muttered.

He stared at the road before him. Gutter Lane. The Walcote manor was at least a quarter of an hour distant but worlds away from the inhabitants of Gutter Lane and the Shambles. Was there such a thing as justice for the likes of Philippa or even Crispin? He had dedicated the last four years of his life to that very ideal. Justice for all. His knightly code professed as much. But never before had it seemed to encompass those on the mean streets of the London he thought he had known those many years ago, this seamy side of the city he was only beginning to truly know.

"Justice it is," he said. If not for himself, at least for the dead merchant.

He stepped into the street and headed south at a trot. He could save some time by taking the shortest cuts through alleys. He knew them all. He had learned the ins and outs of the city well. And a man on foot could easily find ways to elude anyone following him. More so than a man on a horse. He had learned that much in the eight years he was barred from court.

Crispin turned down the first alley he came to, barely the width of two men walking abreast. He ducked under a line of wash hanging low across his path and hurried through, taking another quick turn down a dark close seldom used by anyone except cutthroats clever enough to trick their victims down the secluded corridor.

Crispin lurched to a dead stop.

Three menacing figures blocked his path. They stood as black silhouettes against the sunlight of the street beyond.

His pulse raced. Their broad shoulders and wary stance did not signal to him that they were merely passing through. He looked behind, wondering if it wasn't too late to retreat, when one of them spoke.

"Master Crispin?"

Crispin glanced swiftly around the narrow alley for weapons. Nothing looked in the least useful.

"Yes," he said, his hand making its stealthy way toward his dagger. "You found me. What of it?"

"We want a word with you." The man's tongue twisted over the unfamiliar English. Crispin got the impression Italian was easier.

"Very well, then. Come see me at my lodgings—"

"We will see you now. You will come with us."

"My apologies, but I'm on my way elsewhere. Later, perhaps."

The unmistakable sound of a sword sliding out of its scabbard echoed within the tight passage. "Now, I think."

Crispin felt the shadows closing in. With reluctance, he shrugged. "I think you are right."

2 I

CRISPIN DIDN'T BOTHER ASKING. The three men didn't appear very talkative and he wasn't interested in deciphering their grunts.

They followed every dim alley snaking through London and finally came to a row of abandoned stables. They urged him forward and Crispin listened to his steps echo along the narrow cobbled lane. Rickety structures stood on either side, their tiles drooping like a whore's hair in the morning. One of the men motioned Crispin toward an open doorway.

Crispin's heart pounded and his blood coursed hotly through him. If only his dagger would do him any good. His hand itched to grab it, to spin with it and see how many chests he could slash or how many ears he could slice off. But there were three of them and they had swords as well as daggers. He only hoped he wasn't to expect another midnight swim in the Thames, because this time he didn't think they'd make the same mistake twice.

Dark ahead and dark behind. Though long abandoned, the stable still smelled of manure and moldy hay. Crispin's eyes slowly adjusted to the dimness. A cloaked figure appeared in the gloom. Only a smattering of daylight filtered through the broken roof, and he could not clearly see the man's face.

A hand on Crispin's shoulder told him to stop.

"That is close enough, *Signore* Guest." A voice harsh and raspy, sounding as if he'd screamed himself hoarse, with an Italian lilt to the precise intonation.

"I suppose it would be foolish to ask who you are," said Crispin.

The man chuckled, a surprisingly soft sound. "Would I go to such elaborate lengths if I intended to introduce myself?"

"I'm interested to know—"

"I know what you want. But first I must apologize for my men. The two who tried to kill you. You see, we thought you killed Nicholas Walcote."

"So I've been told."

"We assumed you crossed us for the Mandyllon. Those who cross us do not live."

"But now you're convinced I didn't kill him?"

"That is so. We aren't interested in the details. Only in the Mandyllon. My men made an offer. Do you accept?"

"And if I don't?"

The man laughed outright. He shook his head, which moved the hood from side to side. "You have an excellent sense of humor."

Crispin forced a laugh. "Yes, so I do. Well then, eight hundred pounds for turning over the Mandyllon."

"That is the agreement."

"When do I get paid?"

"When you turn over the cloth."

"Before I do, I'd like to know something about Nicholas Walcote."

The shadow shrugged. "The man you know as Nicholas Walcote was paid to make a copy of the Mandyllon."

"Yes, I've been told as much."

"So? By whom?"

"Your Abid Assad Mahmoud."

He shook his head. "Not mine."

"He's not working for you?"

"At one time, *si*. I understand he still represents himself as such. We will put a stop to that."

Though the menace was bereft from the man's voice, it sent a chill down Crispin's spine. "You never met the real Walcote?"

"No, we had nothing to do with him nor he with us."

"How did he die?"

"I think"—he tapped his finger against his shadowed lips—"we mistook the true Master Walcote for our thief. Careless of us. I was told they looked remarkably alike. It created quite an opportunity for this thief, no?"

"All this trouble merely for a holy relic when there are so many to be had. One wonders if there could not be more to an Italian presence in England."

Silence. Then, "Do you accept the offer?"

"I'd be a fool not to."

Crispin turned at the steps of the men beside him. Apparently the interview was over. "Just one thing more. Is your master Bernabò Visconti? Professional curiosity."

The man in the darkness glared at Crispin. At least Crispin thought he did. "We will pay you for the Mandyllon *and* your silence. It isn't too healthy to meddle in these things," said the man. "Stick your nose in too far, *il mio amico,* and you might awaken in an alley with the rats gnawing on your flesh."

"I see. How vivid." Crispin looked behind at the henchmen closing in. "Well, I thank you for meeting with me." He turned his back to leave, then pivoted. "By the way. Your Saracen operative Mahmoud does not seem to be playing your game. My thought is that he had a master other than yours. Perhaps he has another buyer for the Mandyllon."

The shadowed man said nothing. His silence was perhaps the most fearsome thing about him.

"If I were you," Crispin offered, "I would investigate." Let Mahmoud worry about his own skin for a change.

The henchmen surrounded Crispin and forced him to leave. They escorted him almost all the way to where they first encountered him before they fell back, turned without a word, and left him in the street.

Crispin heaved a sigh between relief and exhaustion. An interesting interview. And unusual. No one was taking any chances. This Italian head of English operations did not want to be recognized, which meant he might already be known in places—like at court. Crispin wondered how long he could stall them. He wanted it to take long enough to discover the players and what exactly they were up to. But the longer it went on, the more danger Philippa was in.

Philippa. Why was he such a fool to let her into his heart? Didn't he have enough problems? Jack was a handful. Just making the rent was a weekly challenge. A woman only complicated things.

Oh, but in such ways!

He closed his eyes and exorcised Philippa Walcote from his thoughts. There were other pressing matters. A killer still on the loose. He opened his eyes and took a moment to reckon his location. He remembered what he planned to do before the syndicate's men waylaid him. "Adam Becton." Now more than ever he was convinced that the syndicate bore little responsibility for the imposter Walcote's death.

Crispin straightened his coat. The action helped to ground him in the here and now. He looked in the direction of the Walcote estates and headed there.

CRISPIN WAITED FOR THE door to open and was greeted by a servant. There was comfort in the familiar, and strangely, the Walcote manor felt a little like home. Crispin stepped inside. "Where is Adam Becton?"

The servant eyed Crispin and shook his head. "He is at his duties, good master. Who do you come to see, master or mistress?"

"Neither. I want to talk to the steward."

The short man squinted at Crispin. "He is unavailable, sir."

"Then make him available."

Crispin pushed past him and made his way unaccompanied to the parlor. He stepped across the threshold before he discovered too late that Maude Walcote was there. Just as he decided to back out unobserved she looked up. And scowled. "Why are *you* here?"

His crooked grin returned and he strolled in. "Why does everyone in this house greet me thus? I am a congenial fellow. Truly I am."

"You are a nuisance," she said. "And I fear you are also a menace."

"You clearly do not know me, Madam."

"Don't I? I know your character. There's something velvety about you, but your nap runs the wrong way."

He chuckled at the imagery. "Perhaps it does."

She stood and flicked out the creases in her gown—they dared not wrinkle. "And you are insolent. Who invited you in here?"

"I told you. I am investigating a murder. I want to talk to Adam Becton."

"He is busy."

"And I don't care. I'll talk to him anyway." Crispin strode to a chair and sat.

Maude seethed. *"Lionel!"* She tossed her sewing aside and marched from the parlor.

Crispin sunk down with relief. *God's Blood!* These Walcotes were nothing but arrogant children, but he couldn't help but feel a slight twinge that he saw a bit of himself.

Gazing at the fire, he brooded. If Adam killed Nicholas for love and status, all of his plans have gone for nought. Philippa was cast from the house and disinherited, and her love belonged to another.

Crispin's smile faded.

He shot from the chair and paced.

The squinting servant returned and sloppily bowed to Crispin. "My lord, I cannot find him."

"What do you mean you can't find him? Is he here or is he not?"

"I do not know, my lord."

"I am not a lord," he grumbled and pushed the man out of the way.

"Adam Becton!" called Crispin. He walked out of the parlor and looked across the checkered floor of the hall. He strode through the empty hall to the door to the kitchens and opened it. "Becton!" he called into the passage. A rosy-cheeked boy little older than Jack poked his head from the kitchen doorway and ducked back inside. No one else approached.

Crispin grunted. He reversed his steps and stood in the hall again, glancing up to the gallery above and to the solar, the site of so much mayhem. The servant came up beside him, sputtering in an attempt to confine his untamable guest, but Crispin slid past him and headed for the stairs.

He grabbed the ornately carved banister and climbed the steps two at a time, the servant following vainly behind. Crispin searched behind curtained alcoves, finding one occupied by a sleepy maidservant, catching a nap on a straw-stuffed cushion.

A few paces down the gallery, the solar's door, repaired and as sturdy as before, hung ajar, and Crispin turned to the befuddled servant who arrived breathlessly behind him. "Has Walcote been buried yet?"

"Aye, my—I mean Master. They buried him in the churchyard just as quick as a wink. It weren't right, that. He might as well have been Master Walcote. He were good to us."

"No doubt," Crispin said distractedly. He closed upon the solar and noticed one taper burning within. The room seemed strangely empty without the funeral bier, but then Crispin noticed it. The drapery on the wall was torn aside and the secret passage door stood open. The empty box that once contained the Mandyllon lay cast across the floor. But more than that, he saw the body of Adam Becton lying on the floor in the opened doorway of the hidden passage.

22

CRISPIN WAITED IMPATIENTLY FOR the servant to return with Lionel and Clarence Walcote. He had already checked the window— still barred. But the murderer could have come through the secret door, from the kitchens, or from the front door for all he knew. There was little struggle. He was captured from behind, much like Nicholas Walcote.

There were muffled voices and hard footsteps coming from the stairs. Crispin waited by the body as the brothers entered and gasped at the sight at Crispin's feet.

"He's been garroted," said Crispin.

Clarence's face shone bone white in the torchlight. He eyed Lionel, who tapped his keys on his front teeth.

The servant who had tried to rein in Crispin stood in the doorway, grasping tightly to the doorpost. He looked as if he would faint. "You there," said Clarence.

"Matthew, sir."

"Matthew. Go and fetch the sheriff. Make haste!"

The servant turned and instantly obeyed. They all listened to his feet hit each step and then slap across the hall.

Lionel glared at his brother, probably for such impertinence as to supersede his authority.

Crispin knelt by the body. He pulled away the rope from Adam's neck, tossing the instrument aside. He straightened and glanced about the room. Adam faced away from the secret passage, but judging from the new footprints in the dust, he'd plainly been inside it. One of his shoes had fallen off in his struggle and lay near the empty box.

Crispin retrieved the shoe and stepped back into the passage. He found a clean footprint with dried drops of blood and placed the shoe atop it.

Didn't fit.

He let the shoe drop and examined Adam's body. He found long, fair hairs clutched between his fingers. In his last act to try to save himself, he must have reached behind, grabbed the assailant's head, and plucked them out. But of course, it had done him no good.

"What is all this?" Lionel bellowed.

Crispin walked across the room twice, looking over the body, the box, the open portal, and finally the two men who stared at him. "As near as I can make it, Adam found something here he never expected to find: this portal."

Crispin stepped over the box and reached the passage. He turned toward the brothers. "But you two knew it was there. Didn't you?"

"I remember it now," said Clarence. "It's been a long time, hasn't it, Lionel?"

"Yes," he said. "But what of this box?"

"It contained something else Adam also knew nothing about. Something that our friend, the false Nicholas hid in it."

Lionel edged closer, nudging the overturned box with his foot. "Is that why he was murdered?"

"That's what I thought at first. But not now."

"Oh? Then what's on your mind, Guest? Spill it."

Crispin eyed the two. "I don't think I'm ready to say just yet."

Lionel advanced on him but Crispin was spared further explanation when the sheriff arrived.

"Damn this family!" cried Wynchecombe. He swept in without

ceremony and planted his feet in the room, his back to the doorway and to Crispin. "What have you done now, by God?"

Crispin took the opportunity to slip from the room and into the gallery. Wynchecombe's muffled voice boomed in the background, becoming a low rumble the further away he got.

Crispin made it downstairs to the hall. A small boy stepped out onto the hall's painted floor, but when he saw Crispin, he ducked back in the shadows. Crispin swooped and nabbed him by his shoulder cape.

"Jesus mercy! Help! I'm being killed!" The boy struggled and squealed like a captured piglet.

"Stop that noise, boy. I'm doing nothing of the kind." He set the boy down and crouched low to look him in the eye. He jerked his thumb behind him. "I'm not part of that crowd upstairs."

The boy hesitated. He ran his grimy finger under his moist nose. "Are you the sheriff's man?"

"No, I'm my own man. I am the Tracker."

As if a taper lit behind his eyes, the boy beamed with pleasure. "You're Crispin Guest, ain't you? I heard of you."

Crispin repressed a blush by nodding his head. "Yes, I am Crispin Guest. Now can you help me? I need to find the servants of Lionel and Clarence Walcote. Can you tell me where they are now?"

"What you want them for?"

"I merely want to talk to them."

The boy seemed small in the harsh light of the nearby torch. His smudged pug nose sat between close-set brown eyes. The wrinkling of his nose indicated that this was perhaps one of the most important questions he had ever been asked.

"Well, if you only want to talk with them. They're in the kitchens. Everyone's there now, talking about Master Adam's murder."

"Much thanks," he said, and patted the boy's shoulder.

Crispin followed the boy to the kitchen close and clambered through the narrow passage, making sure he ducked for the low beam.

When he emerged into the kitchen the buzz of conversation stopped and all turned to him.

"Greetings," he said. "I am Crispin Guest. I am not with the sheriff, but I am investigating these murders. If you will, I would speak with the valets of Lionel and Clarence Walcote."

No one moved or spoke. Crispin wondered if they trusted him as much as the boy did. When his gaze roved over the closed faces, every eye seemed to avert from him. Who was Crispin, after all? As far from their like as could be, he supposed.

After a long, strained silence, a man moved out of the crowd. He was thin with a stick neck and long hands and fingers. He looked over his shoulder and motioned to someone. "Come on, Harry. It won't do any harm to see what the gentleman wants."

Harry sidled out of the crowd. He was of average height and girth, with an equally nondescript nose, and small beads of eyes. His mouth was petite and rosy. "Why'd you go and roust me out, Michael?"

"Hush, now," said Michael. "This here is Crispin Guest. Haven't you heard of him?"

"No. You go and put importance on people that don't deserve it."

"He's that Tracker they talk about."

"I don't often come to London," said Harry. "Not like you."

"Gentlemen," Crispin interrupted. "Please." Those in the crowded hall did not move and many in the back strained forward to hear. "Let us go to a private location and discuss this."

Michael motioned with his hand and Crispin and Harry followed him to a door. A pantry; a stone edifice of arches and mews. Harry lit a candle but it did little to light their conversation.

"Now Michael," said Crispin. He and the other two leaned toward the candle, a coven of faces in flickering gold light. "You say you and your master come often to London?"

"Oh aye. Every two or three months it seems."

"Were you here when the man known as Nicholas Walcote was killed?"

"No, sir. We did not yet come."

"Was your master here before you?"

Michael's face elongated. "Well now! How did you know that, sir?"

Crispin's grin gleamed in the candlelight. "A good guess." He turned to Harry, whose features were all angles and planes in the small light. "Was your master at home?"

"Aye, sir. I remember when the messenger came from London to tell us."

"A *messenger* from London?" Crispin rubbed his jaw and realized he hadn't shaved. He turned to the other. "Michael, when you valeted for your master after the death of Nicholas Walcote, was there a stain on one of his leggings?"

"Aye, sir. On his knee. It took a devil of a time to clean it proper. That were a stubborn stain."

"I will wager, Michael, that your master is Lionel Walcote."

"Right, sir. How did you know?"

He smiled but did not answer. "How long was he in London?"

"He left 'bout a sennight ago."

"When he came to London, did he ever visit his brother?"

"Oh no, sir. He and Master Nicholas never did get on well."

"He *never* visited his brother?"

Michael nodded. "Master Nicholas always refused to admit him. It's a sad thing when grown men cannot put their past hates aside."

"Did he hate Master Nicholas?"

Michael glanced at Harry. "Well now, hate is a strong word. I don't know if I meant that—"

"Never mind," said Crispin. "How is Master Lionel's business? Is that why he came often to London?"

"Funny you should say. I probably shouldn't speak of it," said Michael, looking behind him, "but it is rumored that he is all but ruined. And it must be so, for there have been no feasts in the household for nigh on two years now. And he sold off much of the household goods."

"Indeed. And how fares Master Clarence?"

"Well and good, sir, as far as I can tell," said Harry.

"Did he know of Master Lionel's plight?"

Harry looked at Michael and chuckled. "I doubt it. They never have nought to do with one another."

"Then how do you know each other?"

The two men exchanged glances and smiled. "We're brothers," said Harry. "We don't carry on like them Walcotes, though we was raised in the Walcote household. We've seen much, I dare say."

Crispin nodded. "I dare say you have." He felt at his purse for the customary gratuity, but realized he had nothing to give. He cleared his throat and reddened while he bowed instead. "I thank you both."

They returned to the kitchen where the men immersed again with their brethren. Crispin scanned the crowd, missing what he was looking for, and climbed the stairs, ducking the low beam. With money scarce, Lionel no doubt thought it was time to get rid of the rich brother. Even though he would share the inheritance with Clarence, it was bound to be an enormous sum. Crispin's steps slowed as he considered. Perhaps Lionel stalked him for some time, but since Nicholas never left the house, Lionel would never know it wasn't Nicholas. Lionel knew about the passage, though, and could make his way to the solar without detection. A perfect murder. Even with a wife, there was bound to be something in the will for the brothers, or they could contest the will and seize all from the wife.

Crispin reached the bottom of the stairs of the main house. He looked up the staircase and still heard Wynchecombe bellowing.

But discovering that Nicholas was an imposter was even better. There would be no difficulty at all now in inheriting his estates. Philippa would have no claim.

Crispin slowly climbed the stairs. Lionel imagined himself free and clear. So why kill Adam Becton? It made no sense, especially as the Mandyllon apparently played no role in the imposter Nicholas Walcote's death. But it might have played a role in Adam's murder, else why was the box strewn on the floor?

He waited for the answer to click in his head. Still a missing piece. He was close, though. As soon as he found that piece, he knew all would make sense.

Crispin peered into the solar. Adam's body was removed and the sheriff was bearing down on a servant with all the malice in his being—until he glanced up and saw Crispin. As if tossing aside a well-gnawed bone, Wynchecombe abandoned the servant and made for Crispin.

"You!" The sheriff pointed a gloved finger at him.

Crispin steeled himself.

"I want to talk to you."

"I am at your serv—" But Wynchecombe grabbed Crispin's arm and yanked him along down the stairs before Crispin could fully reply.

Still clutching Crispin's arm, the sheriff rumbled across the courtyard to several horses held by a page. William, the sheriff's man, held his own tether loosely and grinned when he beheld Crispin being dragged across the gravel.

"We will talk on the way to Newgate," said Wynchecombe. He jabbed his boot into the stirrup and hoisted himself up.

Crispin frowned. "Must I trot alongside you like a dog?"

The sheriff's scowl drooped his beard and mustache. "William. Give him your horse."

William's grin fell away. "*My* horse? Lord Sheriff—"

"Give it to him!"

William glared daggers before he threw the tether at Crispin.

Crispin's amusement was overshadowed by the sheriff's severe expression, and he mounted silently.

It was good to feel a horse under him again. He couldn't recall the last time he had been in a saddle. The feel of the reins in his hand, the saddle beneath him. Wasn't this where he belonged? Looking down upon the populace from a high seat?

He barely listened to the sheriff, and pulled himself back from the deep memories. Crispin kept the corner of his eye on Wynchecombe's stiff form. They rode knee to knee.

Without looking toward him, the sheriff asked, "Discover the murderer yet?"

He adjusted his seat on the saddle. "For Adam Becton? Not yet. As for Nicholas Walcote, yes. I know who it is."

"Oh? Who?"

"I believe it is Lionel Walcote. He was here in London at the time."

"What was his reason?"

"His business was failing and he had no love for his brother. He knew about the secret passage—"

"As did you, I see. A fact you did not share with me."

Crispin shrugged. "I have been busy."

"So, he knew of the passage."

"Yes, he waited therein to surprise his victim. After Lionel stabbed him, he saw it was not his brother."

"Hence the halfhearted stab to his shoulder."

Crispin nodded.

"So why Becton?"

"He did not kill Becton. A garrote? That is not common fare for a merchant, even a devious one. A garrote shows planning of another sort."

"I agree." The sheriff fell silent and hurried the horse. Crispin jabbed his heels into the side of his own mount to keep pace.

"I shan't arrest him yet."

Crispin stared at Wynchecombe. "Why not, Lord Sheriff?"

"Not by your word alone. Especially when you are so dewy-eyed for the woman. His guild would have me drawn and quartered."

Crispin slumped and fisted the reins. *The fool. Can't he put his faith in me yet?*

They rode under Newgate's gatehouse arch and clattered into the courtyard. Two men rushed forward, each to take a horse as

they dismounted. They eyed Crispin but he ignored their stares and
followed the sheriff into the building, up the stairs, and into his
chamber.

Wynchecombe stripped off his gloves and dropped them on the
table. He unfastened his agrafe and tossed the cloak aside. He sat with
a dissatisfied huff and glared. "Much thanks for helping with this
murder."

"It is my duty, my lord."

Wynchecombe sat back and folded his hands on his belly.

Crispin watched him as a cat watches a mouse hole. He hadn't
long to wait for the rodent to emerge.

"Tell me what was in that box."

Crispin changed his weight from one foot to the other.
Wynchecombe hadn't offered him a chair and it didn't seem likely he
would. "What box?"

"The box on the floor in the solar."

"I don't know. What was supposed to be in it?"

"Crispin, Crispin." Wynchecombe shook his head and rose from
his seat. He sauntered around the table and leaned against it. "You are
a very poor liar."

"My lord—"

Wynchecombe backhanded his face. Crispin was unprepared and
cocked his own fist in retaliation before he remembered where he was.

Wynchecombe growled a chuckle. "Any intentions you may have
had better be put to bed."

Crispin cleared his face of all expression. His hand shook while he
unwound his fingers and lowered his arm.

"I'll ask you again—and you'd best think carefully about your reply.
What was in the box?"

Crispin clenched his teeth. "I don't know."

Wynchecombe shook his head and bellowed for his scribe. "Bring
in two of my guards."

Crispin refused to rub his inflamed cheek.

"I think you know there was a cloth in that box," said the sheriff. "And I think you know where it is now."

Two men shouldered into the room. Both were tall and burly; each possessed big hands curled into fists, their knuckles crosshatched with scrapes and scabs.

Crispin debated with himself how much to conceal.

"It's a special cloth," Wynchecombe continued. "But you know that already, don't you? You know that a man cannot lie in its presence."

"I do not know your meaning."

Wynchecombe moved to his sideboard and poured himself a cup of wine. He drank for a moment, savoring the liquor, before he nodded to the men.

This time Crispin was ready. He may not be able to defend himself against the sheriff, but he was damned if he was going to let the sheriff's lackeys make sausage of him without resistance.

He blocked the first blow with his forearm and landed his own punch into the man's gut. The guard tumbled back and slammed against the wall.

The second didn't waste any time. His fist swung upward and caught Crispin on the side of his head. Crispin's sight exploded in stars and he lost his balance, but only momentarily.

By then the first man recovered. He nabbed Crispin's arms and in a struggle that left the man's shins bruised, managed to pin Crispin's arms behind his back. The second man snapped his fist at Crispin's chin and the stars fluttered about him again. Crispin hit the floor like a sack of turnips.

He did not see Wynchecombe signal, but the men eased back. Crispin clutched his head and crawled toward the wall, leaning against it.

"I want it, Crispin. More important, the king wants it."

Crispin raised his head and squinted. "The king?" he managed to say. "So that is who is behind your summons."

"Yes, and you will obey or I will be forced to place you under arrest."

Crispin laughed, though it was a chalky sound of sputters and wheezes. "The king wants it, does he? Well he can go begging for it, can't he?"

"What does it matter who has it? You told me before you do not believe in the power of such relics. Then what harm would it do to turn it over to his Majesty?"

"I won't give him the satisfaction." And if there was the least possibility that the Mandyllon did have the ability to compel the truth from those near it, Crispin didn't dare take the chance that Richard might possess that much power.

"You were once condemned for lese-majesté," said Wynchecombe. "Do not force the king to look your way again. For all he knows, you may be dead."

"He knows I am not dead."

"Not yet, but soon, maybe." Wynchecombe smiled without humor. "Crispin, I have done my best to keep this situation from occurring, but you have been stubborn in the extreme and refused to listen to my good counsel."

"Were you counseling me?" Crispin rubbed his chin. "Just now, for instance?"

"Damn you, Crispin! Are you going to tell me where that cloth is or not?"

Crispin licked his dry lips. "I can't help you, Wynchecombe."

The sheriff straightened. His hand fell to his sword hilt and the fingers drummed. "Then you give me no alternative." He motioned to the guards. "Crispin Guest, I hereby arrest you in the name of the king."

23

CRISPIN STUMBLED AFTER THE guards. Each took an arm to drag him down the passageway. *That son of a whore.* The sheriff was the king's tool, after all. But Crispin assumed he had more character than that. Wynchecombe hadn't the stomach to stand up to Richard. Few men did and lived, he supposed.

The guards lugged Crispin a long way and tossed him into an empty cell. He rolled once along the straw-cluttered floor before righting himself. They said nothing and closed the door. He heard the key scrape in the lock, then their footsteps receded down the long passageway.

He sat on the floor, which seemed the most convenient, and gingerly palmed his head and then his chin. His head throbbed and ached. Feeling woozy, he stared at the blackened maw of the empty fireplace and willed it to ignite. When that failed, he laid back against the wall, the cold stone chilling his back.

"Why do I seem always to be on the wrong side of the king?"

He closed his eyes. It made the room seem less slanted.

The air thickened with the stench of frightened men. The last occupant of the room left behind his own odor of fear, marking the cell with a distinct haze of despair. Crispin tried to ignore it. No telling how long the sheriff would leave him here. When Crispin had been imprisoned for treason, he had languished in his cell for five months.

He allowed his heart its drumroll for several minutes before taking a deep breath. He was done with fear. Hadn't he suffered enough humiliation? If they wanted to kill him then it was years overdue.

Bracing his back against the wall, he inched upward. "I'll stand, thank you," he said to the shadows. "I will die indeed before I ever give Richard the satisfaction of defeating me."

"Ah, Lord Crispin," came the voice from outside the door.

Crispin stiffened. He felt a curse rumble up from his throat.

Keys clattered and dug into the lock, dropping the pins into place. The door creaked and hung ajar, spilling a swath of irregular light across Crispin's chest. The guard Malvyn stood in the doorway and blocked the rest of the torch's flame.

"So," Malvyn said, fat arms crossing over his chest, "you were never going to be a prisoner in here again, were you? You know, you weren't very polite to me a few hours ago."

Crispin managed a grin. "You're not going to hold that against me, are you?"

Malvyn scowled and eyed him up and down. "You're a high-and-mighty bastard, aren't you? Born into court society, eh? Title, riches. Where are they now? Who will help you now?" He stepped into the room. His footsteps made a hollow sound. "Do you remember the fun we had eight years ago?" He took a short whip from his belt. "You never once cried out, did you? Let's see if we can't change that."

Malvyn raised the whip but never brought it down. Crispin kicked it out of his hand and it skidded across the room.

Standing half a foot taller than the gaoler, Crispin straightened. "I tolerated a great deal then. I don't now." He slammed his boot down on Malvyn's foot. The gaoler howled in pain and bent toward the floor. He never got there. Crispin's fist reached his jaw first. The punch met flesh and tooth, tearing the former and cracking the latter.

Malvyn lost his balance. Crispin lunged at him for more—until spear butts jabbed his chest and stopped his progress.

He stumbled back and looked up at two guards. They raised their spears, but he lifted his open hands and backed away from the door. They hauled out the barely conscious Malvyn and ticked their heads. "He'll make certain you get a beating for that, Master Crispin," said one of the men.

Crispin rubbed his scraped knuckles and smiled. "Yes, but it was worth it."

The sound of Malvyn's heels scraping against the floor and the door closing for the second time filled his ears before all fell silent again. The profound stillness echoed throughout the chamber and rumbled down the passage.

Crispin listened to the silence for a long time. He remembered it well. He used to hum to himself to keep the quiet at bay, all the songs he knew. He tried now to think of a song to hum, but he did not much feel like singing.

As the time crawled by, he felt more and more alone. How much time had passed? He wasn't certain. Only an arrow slit of a window allowed him to measure the sunlight. But with heavy cloud cover, even that was an uncertain sundial.

In the utter quiet, his thoughts caught up to him. He slid down the wall and sat. He scowled, thinking of the king; scowled further thinking of Wynchecombe; then lost the scowl completely when his mind lighted on Philippa.

Resting his throbbing head against the stone, he closed his eyes. "Philippa," he whispered, liking the sound of it in the empty chamber. She should be quite safe with Gilbert and Eleanor. It surprised him that he missed her. Women passed through his life like the seasons, and though he knew he was susceptible to a woman in peril, he did not consider himself a fool where they were concerned. "Well," he admitted with a lonesome chuckle, "not too much a fool."

He remembered he still had her portrait and jammed his hand into the purse. The light was poor but he cupped the portrait in his hand and gazed at it. Her face peered back at him with a mischievous expression that seemed to say she had a secret.

He frowned and lowered the portrait to his lap. Too many secrets.

The fact that she was a chambermaid—no, worse, a scullion—should have struck down any emotions and concern. What he was, what he was born to, was in the blood. He couldn't change. He didn't want to.

"I don't like to fall in love," he said. The hollow sound of his lone voice gave poignancy to his assertion. "But I—" He shook his head. "It's no good. There's no place for her. Hell, there's no place for *me* in my useless life!"

His dizzy brain ran through the memories—of jousts and duels, of all-out combat. He had been alive then. Worth something. "What am I now?" he asked the portrait. "The Tracker. What the hell is that?" He'd cobbled the vocation himself from shards of his former knighthood tied with the string of concocted peasant chivalry. Little better than a mummer in a play mouthing verse written by another, a minstrel strumming an instrument. No more real than the tattered honor that he struggled to believe he still possessed.

"My 'true image' indeed! If I owned a shred of my true self I should have fallen on my sword years ago. If I *had* a sword. Is it cowardice that keeps me alive?"

He glanced at the portrait before tossing it across the room. "She is truer than I. At least she knows what she is."

He heard his own voice and touched his tender head. "What's the matter with me? Must be a fever. Indeed, I do not feel well."

He rocked his head in his hands for a time before raising his face. A chill breeze breathed over him from the window, feeling surprisingly refreshing to his beaded forehead.

The tiny portrait lay facedown among the straw. A crescent edge of frame gleamed. "I will not entertain the possibility," he said to it. "I will not!" He glared at it, almost waiting for a response. The silence overwhelmed again, fell away with an echoed cry somewhere down the passageway, and welled again like something solid, encasing him in its shell. He stared again at the little portrait until a crack in the mortar of his defenses crumbled, only a little, and he crawled across the floor to recover the little painting and cradled it again in his palm. She still smiled at him. "You do not care about your past." He shook his head, partly in wonder, partly in self-loathing. "How is it done?"

He gazed at the portrait for a long moment before embarrassment stiffened his shoulders and he stuffed the miniature back in his purse. He heaved a sigh, stood, and decided to start a fire in the hearth.

One of the better cells designed for nobler occupants, it boasted a fireplace and a bed. The other cells had no such luxuries. Most of London's thieves and murderers shared a communal dungeon where food was scarce and warmth a mere memory. That Wynchecombe bothered to retain any proprieties and place Crispin in such a cell surprised him, but maybe the sheriff simply did it on instinct. Surely if Wynchecombe remembered, he'd move Crispin to a less hospitable place.

He found in the hearth small squares of peat left behind by the previous occupant, but the tinderbox was damp. He might ask the guards for dry tinder when they revisited, though if it were Malvyn who returned, he knew he could kiss a fire farewell.

"Well," he said. "If I freeze to death then my worries are over."

He decided to try to ignite the fire and covered the peat with the driest straw he could find. Spotting Malvyn's whip, he took particular delight in tossing it on the fuel. Taking the tinderbox, he tried to ignite the straw.

He worked diligently for half an hour before the dry straw smoldered. Bending forward, he puffed a breath across the small flame. The peat began to burn but it was a cool fire. He sat with his back to it and rolled his shoulders into the small portion of warmth and watched the light from the arrow slit turn gray and slip slowly up the damp wall.

He stared at the wall opposite the fire—each carefully laid stone

one more piece in the edifice that was Newgate, all flush against one another—and one irregular stone that refused to lay as flat as the wall.

"Christ!"

He rushed to the wall and felt the dried mud with his fingers. "I'm in the same damn cell!"

Behind that crude mortar that he placed himself lay the Mandyllon.

Peering through the spy-hole in the door and seeing no one in the passage, Crispin reached for his knife before remembering the sheriff had taken it. Instead, he used his fingernails to pry the stone loose and dropped it into one hand. He thrust a hand into the hole and touched the cloth with his fingertips. Dragging it out, he stoppered the hole again with the stone.

His thumbs rubbed the smooth cloth and he turned toward the fire and sat before the weak flames. Unfolding the cloth he first laid it on his lap and then raised it. The reflected light caught the image, so faint it was barely recognizable, yet it was recognizable enough to Crispin.

The Mandyllon. "*Vera icona*. True Image," he snorted. If there was one thing he couldn't afford to know, it was his true nature. Not now. "What are you?" he asked. His voice echoed softly in the dimming cell. "Is this truly the image of God?"

He ran his rough fingertips over the image, feeling nothing different in its texture. "If this is what everyone thinks it is, then what would you have me do with it?" He raised his face to heaven, but all he saw were dusty, wooden rafters. He looked back at the fire. "I would rather burn this than have it fall into the hands of the king— or any other villain. Tell me now, Lord, what you would have me do. Would this relic not be better out of the greedy hands of man?"

He waited, listening to the silence. He wasn't certain if he expected a reply, but he caught himself holding his breath and expelled it unevenly. "Does your silence indicate affirmation? After all, I cannot speak an untruth in the Mandyllon's presence. If this cloth is not of your doing then nothing is lost. If it is, then I say it is better destroyed." He thrust the cloth toward the meager flames and waited.

He scanned the room. The gloom descended as the sun lowered. "You know how invincible Richard would become, he whose vain favorites rule the court. And these wretched Italians. Would you unleash them on the world?"

His hand clenched the fabric. He felt the smoke curl around his fingers, felt the warmth of the fire grow warmer on his wrist, but still he held the Mandyllon.

"The truth is not a blessing. It is a curse. Speak, Lord! Tell me! There is little time left."

A clatter. A scrape. The key turned in the lock.

Crispin scrambled to his feet and thrust the cloth behind his back. The door whined open and a silhouette blocked the door's light. "Well, Crispin?"

As close to the voice of doom as he had ever heard.

24

SIMON WYNCHECOMBE PLANTED HIS feet wide apart. Crispin braced for an attack and flicked his glance toward the edge of the doorway.

No guards? The sheriff alone? What was Wynchecombe playing at now?

"Are you ready to talk?" asked the sheriff.

With one hand Crispin dragged his cloak over his shoulders, a poor substitute for dignity. "What shall we talk about?"

Wynchecombe strode forward and stood before the fire. He watched the small flames sputter for a moment before turning his back to it. "You know I will be fair with you."

"I know no such thing."

Crispin knew that his hair was mussed and his coat was spattered with dots of blood from the guard's fists. His face was a quilt of purple and yellow bruises from old wounds and from the newest assault. Nothing lordly about him anymore, except his manner and his mind. But even those slipped under the weight of time and poor living. What did Wynchecombe see when he looked at him, he wondered. Was it a former knight or just another beetle under his boot?

The sheriff nodded grimly. "We are often at opposites sides of a dilemma, are we not? I am under the auspices of the crown, and you very decidedly outside them. I make no secret of the fact that I know on which side my bread is buttered. And I like buttered bread." He crossed his arms over his broad chest and looked down his nose at Crispin, who stood shorter by half a foot. "If that makes me a tool of the king then so be it. When all is said and done, kings come and go. I plan to remain."

Crispin said nothing. His fingers slowly bunched the cloth into a tight ball behind his back.

The sheriff grinned. "I know more than you think I do. About this syndicate, for instance."

Crispin raised his chin. *I'll wager you don't.* Aloud he offered, "If that is so, then why didn't you speak of it before?"

"Why didn't you?"

"It's complicated."

"The girl, Crispin? I'm surprised at you."

"I'm a little surprised at myself."

"We have known about this Italian syndicate for some time," Wynchecombe went on. "We think they are responsible for a conspiracy to forestall goods, thus raising the prices. And for piracy. The king is not pleased. He has charged me with breaking up this ring. What can you tell me about it?"

"I have connections, my lord. What will it be worth to you to have this matter settled quickly?"

Wynchecombe's face elongated with disbelief. "Are you trying to extort me?"

"'Extort,' my lord? That's such a strong term. I prefer 'negotiate.'"

Wynchecombe laughed, a deep, rolling sound that rambled along the walls and trickled out the open cell door. He wiped away his laughter tears with a gloved finger. "Crispin, if you weren't such a traitorous bastard, I might actually like you. Very well. I might consider forgoing your surety."

"My good Lord Sheriff, surely putting the king's mind at ease is worth more than that! I am looking for coins."

"You want me to pay you?" He laughed again. "And what good are riches if you rot here?"

"Good point. My freedom, then. *And* the gold."

Wynchecombe's smile fell. "I don't believe you. I do not think you have these 'connections.'"

"Oh, but I do. For instance, I happen to know that the duke of Milan is behind this syndicate."

Wynchecombe scowled so deeply his mustache completely covered his lips. At last he exhaled, blowing out the cold, foul air in a plume of fog. "I will cover your surety, I will give you your freedom, and I will pay a *small* amount of remuneration. After all, I cannot be entirely certain that you are telling me the truth."

Crispin clutched the cloth. "You can be certain that it is *all* the truth."

"How then does this cloth, this Mandyllon, cross paths with the syndicate?"

"They stole the original and commissioned a clever thief to make a copy."

"And this clever thief? Where is he now?"

"Dead. The man erstwhile known as Nicholas Walcote."

The sheriff whistled. "Christ's toes."

"Indeed."

"But you claim they did not kill this mock Walcote."

"Yes. The cartel killed the real Walcote by mistake. This thief—similar in appearance and age, apparently—simply took his place and ran off with the original Mandyllon. The syndicate wanted it back—for themselves, I imagine—and pursued him for five years. They finally caught up with him, I would say about six months ago. But they did not kill him. They wanted the Mandyllon back first."

"And this cartel . . . run by the duke of Milan, is it? What does it hope to accomplish?"

"They want to stop our war with France in exchange for a deal for control of Calais. And on top of that, they want to bankrupt our wool market."

Wynchecombe's lips parted but he said nothing. He paced in a circle, head down, hands behind his back. Finally he stopped and looked up. "This cloth seems to be in the center of all these unholy tidings."

"Yes," said Crispin. "The Mandyllon has caused a great deal of the grief we now see. Were you able to discover its history?"

"No. Only that men die when associated with it. Wouldn't you rather just hand it over?"

"Should I subject the king to such risks? What sort of loyal subject would I be?"

Wynchecombe merely stared at him, his fist at his hip.

Crispin shrugged. "So I am not so very loyal. Everyone knows that. But Simon, if it is authentic, do you honestly want the king in possession of such a powerful tool? He would be virtually invincible."

"I don't want it in the hands of Visconti. Should I not want my own king to be invincible? And how many times do I have to remind you not to call me Simon?" Wynchecombe regarded Crispin a long time before he dropped his gaze. "I have no great love for Richard either." But after he said it, his face broke into surprise and he looked up. He clamped his lips shut and turned his glare on Crispin. "That is a private admission. I do not expect it to leave this cell."

Crispin bowed. "As you will, my lord."

Wynchecombe stepped toward the bed and sat.

Crispin edged toward the wall and leaned against it, keeping the cloth behind his back.

They said nothing to one another for a long interval. Wynchecombe fingered the sleeve of his houppelande. "The king will be furious when he discovers your involvement in this," he said quietly.

Crispin fisted the cloth tighter. "No more than he already feels for me."

"His games are no longer your concern, Crispin. Court politics. I would think you were well rid of them."

"It is true that in some instances I do not miss it. The backstabbing, the lies. But in other ways . . ." He lifted his free hand in a gesture of futility and let it drop again to his side.

Silence again. He felt Wynchecombe's concentrated stare and raised his eyes to it.

"Why, Crispin? I have always wondered."

"Why what?"

The sheriff's countenance softened. It was something Crispin had not seen before. "Why treason?" The word, as always, caught him off guard. Crispin took a deep breath and stared up into the rafters. "I'd heard of you, of course," Wynchecombe continued. "This when I was just a man of business. As alderman, I was rising in the ranks. And so, too, were you. We'd all heard of you. Protégé to Lancaster. Some were saying that they expected you soon to be part of the king's Privy Council."

Like a wound stripped of its protective scab, Crispin flinched at the raw memories. "I might have been," he answered in a coarse voice. "For Prince Edward, of course. He loved me well. As much as his brother Lancaster. And I would have counseled him to rein in his wife and son, who were not above their own plots or at least those they favored had a liking for such. But I was not yet that trusted to voice these concerns in public. I was still green. Oh how green! And then . . . Edward died."

"Yes. Did it gall you that much for Richard to be king? That you would lose so much?"

Crispin snapped his head toward Wynchecombe. "It was never that! How little you know me. It was for England! Not myself. What did I care for myself if my country failed me? Lancaster was the better man and Parliament knew it, though the whoresons were too cowardly to set him on the throne. A boy of ten! Untried. Underaged."

The sheriff ran a hand over his beard. "But he was the rightful heir." There was an uncertain tint to his words. He grunted and flexed his hands. "He *is* king and we are his subjects. There . . . there is no argument."

"But he wasn't yet king when I . . ." Excruciating, uttering the words even after eight years. He left the rest unsaid and allowed the echo of his voice to die away and leveled his gaze on the small window.

The sheriff cleared his throat. "Alas, Crispin. These are matters for philosophers, not men such as you or me. It is not for me to set up King Richard as emperor of the world, nor to decide against it. What are simple men like us to do? I must obey or I'd be where you are now."

Crispin snorted.

"You blame me for arresting you? I had to do my duty. At least I had to try."

Crispin rubbed his jaw. "And the beating?"

Wynchecombe smiled. "That was for me."

Crispin grinned back. Then he removed his hand from behind him and eased toward the light of the hearth.

Wynchecombe rose. "God's teeth, Crispin. Is that it?"

The smile fell from Crispin's face, and he looked at the wad in his hand and nodded. "Yes."

The sheriff's foggy breath snarled from his nostrils and tangled in his black mustache. His hand fell lightly to the sword pommel. "Surrender it."

Crispin raised his head and scanned the room. Quite possibly this could be his final domain.

Slowly, he shook his head. "Only to Hell." He raised his arm and tossed the Mandyllon into the hearth. The wad of cloth followed a perfect arc and landed squarely on the burning peat.

Wynchecombe drew his sword but not on Crispin. He pointed it toward the fire and made as if to grab the Mandyllon.

But then he stopped.

Nothing happened right away. Smoke seemed to simply rise through the cloth. But soon the white cloth browned and the threads curled and ignited and then the smoke took hold of all of it in a white breath of curling clouds.

Wynchecombe's blade hovered. Any moment now Crispin expected the sheriff to scoop it out of the flames. But he made no move to retrieve it. Instead, he stood silently and watched it burn.

Wynchecombe sheathed his sword at last. "That was a stupid thing to do."

"Yes." Crispin's bruised cheeks glowed with a momentary flare from the cloth. "It might even be blasphemy. Why didn't you save it?"

Wynchecombe could not draw his gaze away from the flames. He shook his head. "I don't know." He rubbed his beard.

"Then you agree. It's too dangerous to pass this about from hand to hand. Better it were gone."

"And your freedom along with it?"

"The cloth was not part of our bargain."

"Wasn't it?" Wynchecombe walked to the other end of the room. He pretended to look interested in the window and its narrow band of dying light.

Crispin folded his arms over his chest. "What will this cost me?"

Wynchecombe angled his face toward Crispin. "You can forget about the gold."

"And the surety?"

"For you, I'll forfeit—half."

"So all that is left is my freedom, which costs you nothing."

"Works out well, doesn't it?"

"What of the king?"

Wynchecombe frowned. He seemed to remember he was in trouble, too. "I don't know. Maybe he can be told it never existed."

"Will the king accept that?"

"He must." Wynchecombe moved back to the fire, leaned down, and kicked the gray ashes with his foot. "He doesn't have much choice now, does he?" The sheriff leaned against the hearth and considered Crispin. The silence stretched between them. "Did it make me say it, Crispin?" he said quietly. "Did it make me speak treason?"

Crispin kept his eyes on the sheriff's. "See how easily treason is spoken. Best not to dwell on it."

Wynchecombe's frown deepened. "Indeed! Best not to dwell on it. Yet the king will still be angry with me, and I do not relish that."

"But you will be the one to break this cartel. As well as solve the murder of a prominent citizen."

Wynchecombe looked interested. "You'll give me the credit?"

"Where credit is due, Lord Sheriff. My only desire is to make certain you get all you deserve."

"Ho, ho! I'll wager you do!" He chuckled to himself until his gaze fell on the remaining ashes of the Mandyllon. He looked at it a long time. "Then I would say we have a bargain." His features sobered. He took Crispin's dagger from his belt and offered it to him. "We took many turns today, you and I." The last scraps of cloth glowed portentously with angry red edges. "I'm releasing you, you whoreson. You have a lot to do. Don't forget to do for me what you promised."

Crispin turned toward the open doorway with a mixed sense of relief and anxiety. He sheathed his dagger, stopped on the threshold, and offered a beleaguered smile. "I would feel safer with the Mandyllon in my hands."

"A moot point. You just burned it."

Crispin stared at the ashes and smiled.

25

CRISPIN OBTAINED A PIECE of muslin from a puzzled Eleanor and used a bit of charcoal to fashion a face very lightly on the fabric. In the right light, it looked very close to the one he destroyed.

Whenever he thought about the real Mandyllon curling and blackening in the fire, his gut twinged. He could never be certain whether he had done the right thing or not. Even if he did not believe in its power, he felt a wave of anxiety at destroying it. High-handed and perhaps petulant, he nevertheless knew he could never turn over such an object to the king.

He had to get to the Walcote manor. He wanted the box that contained the Mandyllon. It would give it the authenticity he needed. There were many fish to catch, and the bait needed to be as enticing as possible.

Crispin arrived in the misty courtyard and approached the front door. The nervous Matthew recognized him, grumbled a greeting, and led him to the parlor.

Crispin turned to the sideboard and poured himself a bowl of wine as Clarence Walcote strolled through the archway.

"Well, don't stand on ceremony," Clarence said sourly. "Go on, make yourself at home."

Crispin did not turn. He tilted back the bowl and drank its contents.

As good as he remembered. He poured another before he looked over his shoulder at Clarence. "I warned you I'd be back."

"But you didn't say you'd be taking up residence." Clarence snorted.

"Well, why not? The more the merrier." He joined Crispin at the sideboard and gestured to an empty cup. "Never drink alone, friend. Fill it up."

Crispin obliged and set aside the flagon.

"Besides," said Clarence, knocking back the bowl, a draught worthy of Crispin, "that bruised face of yours looks like it could use it." He belched and shouldered Crispin aside to pour another. "Wish these cups were bigger," Clarence muttered.

Crispin listened for the customary sounds of servants moving about and the conversation and laughter of the manor's wealthy occupants. But this house seemed smothered under an eerie quiet. "How fares everyone here in the Walcote manor?"

Clarence eyed Crispin from over the rim of the bowl. "It's crowded. And chilly. It looks like Clarence is one too many brothers for this household."

"Oh? Why do you say that?"

"Because my dear brother and his wife would happily settle here rather than return to Whittlesey. They've all but packed my bags."

"Are you going?"

"And let Lionel get all the inheritance? Not likely." Clarence moved to a chair and sat, sliding down to stretch out his legs. "I'm afraid I'm having a bit of sympathy for that chambermaid we rousted out of here. I'm beginning to know how she felt." He ran the cup's rim against his lips in thought. "She was a pretty thing. No wonder that impostor took a liking to her."

Crispin stood stiffly near the sideboard, opening and closing his fists.

"I'll say one thing for her," Clarence went on. "She knew how to run a manor right well. Maude doesn't know a blessed thing about it."

Clarence wiped his lips with his fingers and looked over Crispin as if remembering his purpose. "So, still investigating these murders, are you? Come to arrest someone?"

"Maybe, but I have a question—and a favor to ask."

Clarence tightened his shoulders and stared down his nose at Crispin. "Oh? What's that?"

"That box found in the solar—when we discovered the steward. What happened to it?"

"Maude took it. Using it for her jewelry."

Crispin measured Clarence before turning back to his bowl. "You do not seem to have much love for your brother nor his wife."

"Why should I? They are a pair, those two. Meant for each other. He's the jackal and she's his bitch. They're poison, they are. Poison to everything they touch." He lifted the cup to his lips. "Maybe it's best I do get out of here before something happens to me."

"Do you think something will happen to you?"

He chuckled. "That's only talk." The cup stopped before it reached his lips. "Hold. You don't think Lionel—"

"Don't I?"

"By my Lady!" He gnawed on his lip. "You know," he whispered and gestured with the cup, sloshing the wine on the floor. "He just might have done it at that."

"The both of you were aware of the secret room. It's obvious the murderer entered and exited from there. And Lionel was here in London at the time. Or should I suspect you?"

"God's wounds! You are an impudent fellow, aren't you?" Clarence's hand wandered toward his dagger but then lost impetus. He scowled instead. "What do you want me to say? Plead my innocence? Very well. I so do. I did not kill that insolent fraud. I admire the hell out of him." He saluted with his wine, tilted the bowl back, and drank it down.

"No one knew he was a fraud. Not until you and your brother denounced him."

"That's right. No one knew. So why—if Lionel—"

"Lionel thought it was Nicholas. Too late he discovered he was a fraud. By then, of course, it didn't truly matter."

"He thought it was Nick." Clarence stared into the room with a haunted expression. "How proud Father would be. What a den of wolves are we." He rose and approached the sideboard, reaching for the flagon again, but paused halfway and lowered his hand. He dropped his cup on the sideboard. The bowl spun, wobbled, and finally stopped. His face grew long, and though his eyes seemed lazy and saturated with drink, Crispin noted a change in his mood and the first sincere expression he'd seen Clarence wear. "I think we Walcotes deserve each other," said Clarence softly.

"I need that box, Master Clarence. Can you get it for me?"

He faced Crispin and seemed to slowly rise from his melancholy. "That will make Maude madder than a wet hen." He smiled. "I'll gladly do it." He marched toward the archway, but before he crossed under it, he turned to Crispin. "By the way, what happened to her? That chambermaid?"

Crispin stiffened and scowled. "She's found temporary employment. But I fear for her safety."

"What? Why? She's got nothing."

"She is a pawn in a much larger game. That box might help her."

"An *empty* box?"

"Just trust me, Master Clarence. I know she harmed your family. She perpetrated fraud. But I do not think you would wish to see her killed, especially for something for which she is entirely innocent."

Clarence screwed up his mouth and toyed with his dagger. He nodded and left the parlor.

Crispin felt the need to pace and made several circuits of the room. Philippa. He wanted to concentrate on Mahmoud and the Italians, but such thoughts proved impossible once her image slipped into his consciousness.

She looked so forlorn when he left her at the Boar's Tusk. Why didn't he take her in his arms? Why make such a fuss about a kiss? Plenty of men kissed their women on the streets. Plenty of plain, hardworking men.

Knights kissed women on the streets, too. But those women were last night's conquests at stewhouses, not courtly women.

He looked up at a wall painted with a family scene of people romping in a garden. Painted servants worked nearby dyeing fabric in vats. The wealthy family was turned out in their best furs and scarlets. The female servants cavorted, barefoot, skirts hitched up, ankles and calves revealed. Hounds of high pedigree frolicked with the wealthy patrons, while mongrels nipped at the heels of the drunken male servants toting bolts of cloth under their arms. The peasants hung on the necks of the donkeys pulling carts, while the rich merchants held delicately to the reins of their sleek, white horses.

Try as he might, he could find no pleasure in the antics of the riotous peasants gamboling across the wall. He knew in his gut that he belonged to the sedate and wan faces of the wealthy; painted with just as many brushstrokes.

The candle flame shifted at the same time a floorboard creaked. Crispin was suddenly aware of someone behind him. He cocked his head and saw Clarence. Crispin guiltily adjusted himself, feeling as if his thoughts were spattered across the wall.

"Oh the fuss she made," snorted Clarence. He presented the box to Crispin. "I knew it would be worth it. Of course, I did not tell her the purpose it was being put to. She would have tossed it in the fire for spite."

"Yes. It is foolish to burn things for spite."

Clarence crossed to the sideboard, but stopped midway. He angled his head to look at Crispin. "I'm curious. About you."

"Oh?"

"Yes. I mean, your clothes. And you've got this strange title—what is it again?"

"The Tracker."

"Yes, that. Just who are you, anyway?"

"A man of many talents—and none of them for riches and success."

Clarence laughed. "Yes, I am your brother in that."

"Does not the cloth business suit you?"

"Oh yes, I do well enough. Nothing like Nicholas did, rest his soul." He glanced around the parlor. "Or even this fellow who played at him. I suppose I haven't the head for business. Lionel's right, I reckon. I would have run the business into the ground."

"I hear he has done no better."

Clarence snapped his head up. "Eh? Where'd you hear that?"

Crispin said nothing.

Clarence nodded and smiled. "I see. Part of those many talents of yours, eh?" Clarence grew thoughtful and toyed with the flagon but never quite poured from it. "If Lionel is guilty of this murder," he said slowly, "what will happen to him?"

"He will most likely be hanged."

Clarence shivered. "Christ's toes." He seemed to freeze on the spot, looking nowhere in particular, nor moving his hand to pour wine. "That's a hell of a way to inherit all."

"It is legal. It is better than murder."

"Yes," he said softly. "Better than murder." He looked at the flagon in his hand as if seeing it for the first time and decidedly set it down. He wiped his hands down his coat and ambled toward the arch, never quite looking at Crispin. "Does he . . . will he . . ." He closed his eyes. "Master Crispin. I am unacquainted with the doings of the law. Will it be swift, or will he endure in prison a long time?"

"Were he a high-ranking nobleman, he might well languish in prison. He is a wealthy merchant, which makes him nearly as important, though I should think that all shall move swiftly. Your inheritance will be awarded just as speedily."

"No, no. It isn't that. It's just that I'm actually feeling sorry for the bastard."

Crispin shifted forward. "Best not to say anything to Lionel, Master Clarence. Or to anyone. The sheriff would be very displeased if the culprit should be warned. And don't feel too sorry for him. He could easily turn on you, too."

Clarence raised his head and nodded. "Yes, it has occurred to me. God keep you, then."

"And you. If I were you, Master Clarence, I'd lock my door."

Clarence's face drained of color. He glanced up the staircase and its dark shadows and even darker secrets. He rested his hand on his scabbard and took to the stairs as if they were a gallows.

Clarence. Such a man made Crispin wonder what the real Nicholas must have been like. Was he gruff and all business like Lionel? Or did he have a sensitive side as indicated by Clarence's surprising sobriety? Crispin cast a glance about the chamber. Its riches were evident in every corner, every stick of furniture. No doubt Nicholas was as ruthless as any lord. No one got this rich doing kind deeds.

He wanted no more of the Walcotes and their ceaseless bickering. He'd take care of Lionel soon enough, but this business with Visconti overrode all, and time was running out. When he turned to leave, he nearly smacked into a boy, the one from the kitchens he'd talked to before.

"Master Crispin."

"Yes, lad. What is it?"

"Master Hoode would speak with you, sir. He's awaiting you in the kitchens. He says it is very urgent that he see you now."

"Very well. Much thanks."

Crispin followed the boy across the hall to the kitchen close and trotted through the low-ceilinged passage.

John Hoode stood in the flickering light of the large hearth. He looked whiter than usual. The firelight caught the edge of his fair hair and blazed it with light. The others must have gone on to their beds. He saw only another boy sleeping on a pile of straw near the storage rooms.

"What is it, John?"

"Crispin! I think something has happened! There was a message from your man Jack. He said that Mistress Wal— that Philippa was abducted by the Saracen. You are to meet those men—he just said 'those men'—at London Bridge to make the exchange. Do you know what he meant?"

Crispin's bravado sizzled away and his knees felt weak. All he feared. She was supposed to be safe at the Boar's Tusk. How could she have been taken right out from under everyone's noses? And if she was, then where were Eleanor and Gilbert?

He stared at Hoode's desperate face and somehow grew courage from the man's fear.

"Yes, John. I know what he meant. Do me the kindness of telling Jack to meet me at the bridge."

26

CRISPIN HURRIED OUT OF the Walcote estate and trotted toward the Thistle on his way to London Bridge. He praised God when he spotted a familiar ratlike figure lurking near a brazier trying to keep warm while at the same time remaining unobtrusive to the other men warming their hands.

"Lenny!" cried Crispin across the avenue.

Lenny cringed. The others at the fire turned to look at him and edged away.

"Now Master Crispin," he said in low tones. "What you go and point me out like that? I just got them gentlemen to forget all about me."

"I need your help." He grabbed his arm and steered him into the shadows.

"Anything, Master Crispin. You know old Lenny. Always here to help."

"I need you to get a message to the sheriff."

"The sheriff?" Lenny squinted and darted his glance up and down the quiet lane. "Oh, now, Master Crispin!" he said in the hushed whispers reserved for a church. "I don't go to Newgate. Not if I can help it. You'd best send someone else."

"Lenny, you know I wouldn't ask unless it was dire."

He shook his head vehemently. "Don't ask me to do it, Master Crispin. I ain't going to Newgate and that's that."

"Please, I'm begging you. Tell the sheriff to bring a garrison and meet me at London Bridge. Lenny, for the love of God!"

Lenny brushed Crispin's hands away from him. "Don't unman yourself. I won't go to Newgate!"

Crispin straightened. "I see. You're a coward."

Lenny straightened as much as his bent posture would allow. "Aye, that I am. It ain't a fitting place. I spent too many months there."

"So did I."

"Ah, now. Don't be bringing that up."

"What does it matter? If you won't go, you won't." Desperation steeled over him with a hot flush. What could he do? He hadn't any money with which to bribe the man and it seemed as if it would take a great deal. He felt like throttling him. He clenched his hands into fists and trembled his helplessness into his taut shoulders. "I'm done with you, then. Our agreement is dissolved."

"Master Crispin, try to see it my way—"

"I haven't time, Lenny. A woman's life is at stake." He speared Lenny with a last glare and spun. Damn Lenny! Cowards all. Was there no one man enough in London anymore? He stalked away, hearing nothing from the cowering man behind him. He didn't look back. Perhaps Lenny's conscience would get the better of him but he doubted it. So much for honor among thieves.

It was up to him now. He wished he had a plan.

Leaving Lenny far behind, he trotted toward Watling Street and followed his nose toward the Thames. Mist glistened off the slate rooftops and a slice of moon washed it in scattered light, making the roofs look like teeth knocked out of a drunkard's mouth. Crispin trotted through the streets, feet sucking into the muddier places.

A layer of fog shrouded the city. Crispin perceived only dim, looming shapes of buildings on either side of him. A bobbing light appeared in the distance and Crispin slipped into an alley and pressed his back against a damp wall. The Watch. He knew it was well past curfew and he did not relish delay.

He watched the bobbing light pass—for that was all he could detect of the Watch—and waited several beats before plunging back into the street.

Muffled by the smothering weather, he heard the lapping of water and the tide softly hiss against the rocky shoreline. The Thames at last. He looked upward. The rooftops along London Bridge arose from the gray mist. Stone foundations upheld the miniature city within a city. Shops and houses lined the now narrowing bridge, some hanging precariously over the river. He saw glowing lights dulled from the mist in the vague shapes of windows, but for the most part, the bridge's inhabitants slept, oblivious to what awaited.

One street away. Crispin hurried.

He turned at Bridge Street and paused. Ears peeled, he listened for any sound other than the persistent Thames and the creak of sheets pulling on masts and hulls scraping against docks.

He felt it. Someone behind him.

Soundlessly, he whirled and gripped the hapless soul by the throat.

He heard a choking whisper, "Master!"

Crispin released Jack Tucker and tried to see his face in the dark. The torches at the mouth of the bridge's stone gatehouse did little to penetrate the fog beyond a few feet from the portcullis. All he could discern before him were two wide eyes. "Anything, Jack?" he asked, voice soft.

The eyes, like tiny candle flames, blinked out once and lit again. "There's three of them. At the mouth of the bridge. I can't tell who they are. Then there's more up on the bridge. Maybe three dozen. They've managed to raise the portcullis. Either they've bribed the guards or—"

Crispin looked down the street one way and then the other.

Nothing—no sound, no movement. Was Wynchecombe coming? "I suppose we can't wait any longer." Crispin straightened and walked out of the alley toward the gray shapes of the bridge's gatehouse.

He moved precisely and slowly, well aware that they could see him or soon would.

"That's far enough," said a voice.

Crispin stopped. His fingers whitened on the box.

The voice had the wisp of an accent. Crispin thought it was Italian. Not Mahmoud? Then he recognized it as the voice in the stable: Visconti's head of operations in England.

Three dark figures stood before the quiet gatehouse.

"Put the box down and step away," the voice ordered.

"Where's the girl?"

"Crispin! I'm here!" One of the figures tried to wriggle free from between the other two. The one on the left raised an arm. Crispin heard a smack. He jerked forward.

"Don't!" warned the voice.

Crispin clenched his free hand. Definitely needed a sword in it. Four strides and four strokes would do it.

"Now do as you are told and no one will be injured."

Slowly, eyes fixed on the middle figure, Crispin bent and put the box on the ground. He stepped back but not too far.

The man on the left moved forward. He was covered from head to foot in a cloak and hood. The cloak swished about him as he walked and pooled when he knelt at the box.

He looked up once at Crispin. Two-Fingers. Crispin didn't wait. He swung his foot forward and kicked him in the jaw. The man fell back without a sound, out cold.

The voice laughed. "That wasn't very sporting."

"Now it's even. Give me the girl and I'll give you the box."

"I don't give a damn about the box. Open it."

Crispin knelt and did so.

"Now take it out."

"Where's my eight hundred pounds?"

The voice laughed. "A man gets tired of waiting. I'm afraid it's too late for that. Now it's the girl. Unless, of course, I was mistaken and she isn't worth the trouble. Mahmoud was very helpful in telling us how much she meant to you."

Crispin grunted and said nothing. He reached in and lifted the cloth. In the misty light, it was the same color as bleached bones.

"Toss it to me."

"No. Come get it."

The man laughed again. "Why not?"

He dragged Philippa forward. When they got closer, Crispin could see the vague reflection of light on the blade held to her throat. He straightened and stood over the box. They were close enough now for Crispin to see her face. She held herself well.

The man's face lay hidden by the shadows of an overhanging hood. He was tall and the hand that held the knife was long with slim fingers. Only the tip of a nose was visible from the shadows.

Crispin set his jaw in a grim angle and nodded toward the blade. "There's no need for that."

"On the contrary. She can be most vicious when provoked. I have the bite marks to prove it. But perhaps . . . I'm not the only one."

Crispin refused to reply. He was busy glancing beyond them to the figures closing in from the bridge. He thought he recognized one taller shadow as Sclavo. "Had your say yet? It's cold out here and I'd have it done with."

"So bold when I have the upper hand. You are an extraordinarily arrogant man, Crispin Guest. I like you." He shook his head. "I wish that my own henchmen were as clever as you. Oh, don't mistake me. We are a family. But at times we must hire those outside the family, and they are not nearly so clever."

"Like Mahmoud? I expected him here."

"He's been working both sides of the alley, I fear. We did hire him once, but it seems he's been working for competitors. In Constantinople. They want the Mandyllon back."

Crispin's ears pricked, trying to make out any possible sounds in the distance. He stalled. "It comes from Constantinople? What is this thing? I have never heard of any 'Mandyllon' before."

"I'd never heard of it either until a merchant from the Orient told me the tale. Then I had to see it for myself. Once my master heard the legend, he simply had to have it."

"The legend?"

"It is said that, centuries ago, there was a king of Edessa called Abgar and he was a leper. Even in the far reaches of his kingdom he heard of the miracles of Jesus of Nazareth. He sent his personal scribe Hannan to seek out our Lord and bring him back to heal his king.

"This scribe searched all over Judea and finally reached Jerusalem and found our Lord. But he was teaching there and could not come to Abgar's aid. The scribe, desperate to help his master, attempted to paint a portrait of the Savior so that the king could venerate it and heal. But Christ, struck by the man's sincerity, took a cloth and impressed his perspiring face upon it, leaving the image of his glorious features. This is the Mandyllon—the 'little kerchief.'"

The man nudged Philippa forward and Crispin backed away the same number of strides. The man and his captive now stood over the box.

"The scribe returned to Edessa bearing the cloth," the man went on. "With one glance at the cloth, the king was immediately healed and became a devoted Christian on the spot. All in his kingdom were baptized. The Mandyllon was revered for many years until the old king died and his son came to power. The infidel did not believe in our Lord or the image, and returned to pagan ways. The bishop of Edessa, fearing for the safety of the cloth, walled it up in the church.

"Emperor Constantine himself later purchased the cloth for two hundred Saracen prisoners and twelve thousand silver coins. It was most prized by the emperor because it not only possessed healing properties, as with most relics, but it was a very valuable asset to a king, because a man could not lie in its presence. So it is said."

"Do you believe it?"

"*Sí*. I've seen it work." He stepped closer and pushed back his hood.

Crispin's lips parted with astonishment. "*John Hoode?* What the hell—"

27

"I DECEIVED YOU, I know, but it was necessary."

Crispin stared at the man he knew as John Hoode. Gone was the façade of cowardice. He held himself differently; tall, confident. His smooth accent was full of golden, Mediterranean tones, not coarse and full of the smoke of Southwark.

"You're not English?"

"No, and my name is not John Hoode. My name . . . is not important."

"And this syndicate?"

"I work for it. I am one of many. We labor for one man who controls all. I think you know who."

"Visconti. I always thought of him as a wily general, not a master criminal."

"I should do you harm for such a remark," he said without malice. "My master would expect it."

"Visconti has always gotten away with murder. After all, 'successful and fortunate crime is called virtue.'"

"And you quote Seneca. I knew I liked you."

"The plan is soured now. I've discovered it and let the authorities know. Visconti can't stop or even delay our conflict in France. France belongs to England and the crown will get it back. There will be no deal for Calais."

Hoode frowned. "These are distressing tidings. You seem to know a great deal. My master will be very displeased. But at least I can present him with the Mandyllon. As a consolation prize."

"Yes, the Mandyllon. You've come a roundabout way to get it."

"We need not have traveled so far. The Mandyllon was in Rome. Until it was stolen by our thief some five years ago. We had a difficult time tracking him down, I'm afraid."

"How did it get to Rome?"

"Don't you know your history, Crispin? Rome sacked Constantinople a century ago."

"I see. And such feelings still run deep. Is that why Mahmoud tries to return it to Constantinople?"

"Oh, I doubt he will be able to do so—from the bottom of the Thames."

Philippa looked at Hoode. "He's dead, then?"

"*Sì, senorina.* Very."

"I could kiss you."

Hoode smiled, turning toward Crispin. "I like her. Teeth marks and all. Even at the manor, I liked her methods."

"Why did you kill Adam Becton?"

Hoode's eyes glittered in triumph. "You *are* clever. Poor Adam. He found me when I accidentally discovered the secret room. There are many such secret rooms in Italian courts, you see. I tried to bribe him, but he grew suspicious of me."

"I see." Crispin raised his head. His hand itched for his dagger. He wished for one of Mahmoud's crossbows. "You are the customs controller. And accounting clerk, no doubt. You used your master's initials when you made your entries in the ledgers—BV. Bernabò Visconti. Or are they yours as well?"

Hoode shook his head. "You are methodical. You would make an accomplished general."

"Why did it take you so long to find your thief? If he looked so much like Walcote . . ."

"It took us some time to discover he had taken on Walcote's persona. And then he was in hiding for a number of years, living abroad. We did not know when he slipped back to England, but once we knew, he never left his house."

Crispin snorted. "Very well, then. You've got your cloth. Release her."

Hoode looked at Philippa. He shoved her toward Crispin, who reached out and hauled her to him. She rested against his chest for a moment but he had no time to savor it.

Hoode moved forward and took the cloth from the box.

"Jack!" Crispin hissed into the shadows.

The boy crept forward. Hoode turned and caught Jack with his gaze.

Crispin whispered in Jack's ear, "Take her to Master Clarence and *only* Master Clarence."

"Aye, Master."

"And Jack. What of Eleanor and Gilbert? Are they well?"

"Aye, Master," he replied, puzzled. "No harm has come to them as far as I know."

"Mistress Philippa was not at all concerned when her servant John Hoode came for her," Hoode said by way of explanation. "It was a simple thing to get a message to your boy from the Walcote manor."

Jack sneered at Hoode, grabbed Philippa's hand, and rushed her away. She had the sense to keep quiet, though when she looked back, her face told Crispin she had much to say.

"And now we are alone," said Hoode. "Crispin, may I be frank?"

Crispin nodded. He eyed Hoode's men moving closer.

"The reason we as an organization have existed as long as we have is that we recognize opportunities and how to exploit them. We can use a clever man like you. Ever consider becoming a free agent?"

"I belong to England. I will not be hired against my own countrymen."

"Nor kill? There is much money in killing for hire."

"Even less appealing."

"You are not an ambitious man. A pity."

"Ambition has little helped me in the past. May *I* be frank?"

"In the presence of the Mandyllon, you can be nothing but."

Crispin nodded toward the cloth in Hoode's hand. "Everyone wanted that. Looks like no one's getting it."

Hoode frowned. He clutched the cloth. "What is your meaning?"

Crispin listened and waited for the faint sound of Jack and Philippa to disappear. What made him especially smile was the other sound emerging from the distant streets. The heavy footfall of many boots; the clop of horses. He wasn't the only one to hear it. Hoode's men rumbled quickly from the bridge's gatehouse.

"*Signore!* They come!"

"Who?" Hoode jerked his head toward the sound. Over the creaks of boat against wharf, the lapping of the Thames against the rocky shore, rose the unmistakable clatter of armor and weapons. It drew closer and Hoode took a step back, eyes rounding. Faint torchlight illuminated the rooftops of the houses along Thames Street just beyond sight. Many torches.

Crispin felt the hard steps in his gut as the line of men rounded the corner at last with a rider in the lead. Crispin was never so glad to hear Wynchecombe's clear baritone as he was at that moment.

"Hold!" cried the sheriff, hauling on the reins of his skittish horse as it tripped this way and that. "In the name of the king!" The men flanking him surged forward, never slowing until they were no more than a stone's throw from Hoode.

Hoode drew his sword as he backed away from the solid line of men, and the cloth slipped through his fingers.

Crispin ducked, grabbed the false Mandyllon, and slipped back into the mob of soldiers.

The confused Italians were backed against the bridge. There was no signal. With cries lifting into the night—Crispin could not tell from which side they came—swords suddenly clashed and Crispin had only enough time to jump out of the way of a swinging club. He was suddenly in the midst of a melee.

The bridge erupted with swarming Italians like ants on an anthill and the sheriff's men met them with bold battle cries and the clash of steel on steel.

The scattered, foggy moonlight and the flickering illumination of torches made it difficult to see, but Crispin saw the soldiers rush forward, slashing a path over the bridge's broad avenue. Even Wynchecombe, mounted on his dark stallion, pushed his way into the thick of it. He slashed his sword downward into the opposing men. His white teeth shone against the dark of his mustache. He seemed to enjoy himself.

Candles winked on in the many houses along the bridge and the merchants living there were roused to their windows, rushing to open shutters in their nightclothes, shouting down directives to the fighters below. Still others cast open their doors and, brandishing what they could, joined in the fight. Unlike the soldiers who hacked and slashed with precision, the merchants reacted as any angry mob would. They wielded sticks like clubs, and many had swords that they used perhaps not as smoothly as the trained soldiers, but just as effectively.

The king's men tried to gather the Italians to make arrests but soon found themselves fighting off the merchants, who perhaps saw their chance to wreak their own vengeance on the king's men and any others they decided had done them wrong in the past. Like a wave, they gushed forward over the soldiers. Grunting bodies blundered together, and while the soldiers raised their swords, the merchants swung their fists. Blood spattered the cobblestones. Weapons clattered to the ground from wounded hands and more than one man fell headlong into the dark Thames below with a cry and, if they were lucky, a splash.

Crispin, armed only with his dagger, stood motionless. But it was the sound of clattering steel and the coppery scent of blood that made his own blood pound in his veins.

An unmistakable animal scream sliced the night even above the noise of battle. A spear had pierced Wynchecombe's horse and man and beast sank to the ground. Crispin ran and snatched up a bloody gisarme from the mud. He swung it at the head of the Italian spearing the horse and sliced a good portion of his scalp from him. Blood sprayed, flecking Crispin's face. The horse rolled and Wynchecombe yelled as the beast landed on his leg.

"Simon!" Crispin offered his hand and Wynchecombe grabbed hold. Pulling and bracing with the weapon, Crispin yanked the sheriff free. The man stood unsteadily but none the worse.

He stared at Crispin unabashedly. "Much thanks."

"Think nothing of it, Lord Sheriff."

Wynchecombe stomped his leg, testing it. "These damned Italians!" He swiped the sweat from his face and glared at his twitching horse. He drew his sword. A man sailed toward him uttering an ear-piercing shriek and Wynchecombe hacked downward, stopping him for good. Crispin stood at his back and swung the gisarme. A clumsy weapon, one with which he was not familiar, but it felt good to fight again. Too many years had passed since he found himself in battle, and the fact of the matter was, he missed it. The surge of adrenaline; his muscles straining as he swung sword or ax; the fierce battle cries of his fellows urging him on to conquer. Banners, gonfalons. Heralds and pages crossing the lines. That was where he belonged. Not on the filthy streets of the Shambles.

Wynchecombe panted and looked over his shoulder at Crispin. "I never would have believed it if I did not witness it for myself."

Crispin swung again and then jabbed at his retreating attacker. "What is that, Lord Sheriff?"

"You, coming to my aid."

"We are on the same side, are we not, Simon?" he answered hurriedly, straining as he swung the weapon forward to fend off more foe.

"Sometimes I wonder." He drew forward and slashed at a man with his blade, each stroke in time with his words. "And how . . .

many times . . . must I tell you . . . not . . . to call me . . . *Simon!*" At the last, he thrust home.

"Forgive me, Lord Sheriff," said Crispin, aiming his weapon toward a man with a club, who changed his mind and skirted him. "I must have been distracted."

"You annoy me, Guest."

"Oh? What have I done this time?"

Wynchecombe mopped the sweat from his brow with his sleeve. "You put great demands on the office of the Lord Sheriff. Expecting me to come with an army on the say-so of one of your street urchins."

"Lenny," Crispin breathed with satisfaction.

"Nameless beggars, cutthroats, thieves," Wynchecombe went on. "I expect jackals and buzzards next."

Crispin almost laughed outright. But he smiled anyway at the sheriff's declawed banter. It felt good to swing a weapon again, to be useful. "Why did you come?"

The sheriff shook his shaggy head. "I haven't the slightest idea!" He swung his sword two-handed at a man with an ax and laid him low. Crispin felt each shock with his shoulder blades pressed against the sheriff's back.

"Couldn't be that you have come to trust me, Lord Sheriff?"

The man's gloved fist swept back to box his ear. Crispin winced from the blow and glared at him over his shoulder.

"Don't be a fool."

Crispin thought that was sage advice and scanned the crazed scene, searching for Hoode among the fighters.

"There's more work to be done here," said Wynchecombe, sizing up the battle.

"Yes," Crispin agreed, about to offer more when he saw them. There! Sclavo. Moving forward up the bridge along with the roused Two-Fingers. They made their way to Hoode, but their master found himself surrounded by angry merchants and fought for his life. He swung his sword. The blade flashed in the moonlight. His fierce swings cast shorter swords and daggers aside.

"An accomplished swordsman," muttered Crispin. He would have liked the opportunity to go head to head with Hoode, but he hadn't a sword of his own.

Hoode slashed a path to the bridge gatehouse. Once there, no one barred his way and he trotted unimpeded under the shadows.

"I must go!" shouted Crispin to Wynchecombe and pressed forward, thrusting men out of his way. He tightened his grip on the gisarme. He did not need a sword to stop the man. Leaving the sheriff to his own fighting, he took off at a run, zigzagging through the melee.

He skidded under the gatehouse arch and spied Hoode running up the bridge and across toward Southwark. Crispin pursued, and when he got close enough, swung the gisarme low at Hoode's feet and upended him. Hoode fell but kept his grip on his sword. He righted and glared at Crispin. His face was dark from other men's blood, but his teeth caught the moonlight when his lips parted in a smile.

"Well now. What are your intentions, Master Guest? To fight? Don't let my slight figure fool you. My master the duke would never hire a weakling to do his bidding. I have killed more men than you have ever met."

"Then it's high time I overtake that score." He swung the heavy weapon at Hoode's midsection, hoping its blade side would slice him. But Hoode saw it coming and jerked back out of the way.

"You'll have to do better than that."

Crispin raised the gisarme to jab with its long point. Hoode's sword chopped downward, blocking it. Holding the weapon like a quarter staff, Crispin swung the blunt end toward Hoode's head, but the sword backhanded it out of the way. The blade flashed. Before Crispin could elude it, the sword's point stabbed him in the shoulder.

Crispin staggered back a few paces. "Son of a whore!" The pain shot all the way down his body. His fists whitened over the staff. The throbbing wound left his arm numb and his belly sick.

Hoode raised his weapon, lashing sidewise toward Crispin's rib cage. Crispin blocked the blow with the staff and felt the shock run through the wood.

No recovery time. Hoode retaliated with backswings that slashed the air with an unmistakable whistle. Crispin could do nothing but use the staff to block and step back in retreat. Hoode was as good as his earlier boast.

Crispin saw an opening and thumped the staff's blunt end into Hoode's chest. Now it was Hoode's turn to stagger back. He recovered quickly and came at Crispin again with a two-handed blow. Crispin countered with a block from the staff, but this time the wood cracked and broke in two.

Crispin stared at the pieces in each hand. "God's blood!" Without thinking, he used both sticks like clubs, catching Hoode on either side of his neck. Hoode spun away, gasping. Crispin swung at Hoode's unprotected scalp, but even injured and blinded, Hoode managed to fend off Crispin with the blade.

Hoode turned. His face wore a malicious scowl. "You'll die painfully. And you'll also die knowing that the girl's life is forfeit."

"And you'll die knowing that the Mandyllon is no more, and that you failed your master. It's a copy, a fake. I burned the true one."

"You burned it! Are you mad? It's worth a fortune!"

"To keep it out of the hands of madmen like you? It was well worth it."

Hoode's thoughts played across his eyes.

"Yes. You've absorbed it at last. Visconti won't be very pleased with you. What does the duke do to servants who displease him?"

Crispin saw it all on his face. In many ways the Italian courts were far worse than England's. The dukes and princes of Italy were more like thugs with their own code of laws.

Hoode looked toward the sheriff's men.

Crispin could tell Hoode was considering his options: Was it better in an English prison, or the Lombardy court? Hoode decided. He took off at run up the bridge, sword in hand.

Crispin gripped the staff, cocked back, and let fly. With a thump, the long point struck Hoode's calf and he went down. He lost the sword this time and fell face first across the cobblestones.

Crispin trotted to catch up and picked up the sword, aiming the tip at the back of Hoode's head. The gisarme's point pierced Hoode's calf and blood covered the leg. When Hoode raised his head, he encountered the sword tip and froze. "Let's try it my way," said Crispin, panting. "I arrest you in the name of the king."

Crispin yanked him to his feet and lugged him toward Bridge Street and the sheriff.

By now the merchants and the soldiers surrounded the dwindling number of Italians. The English did not give them quarter until Wynchecombe signaled his captains to force a surrender. The merchants seemed reluctant to capitulate until they were convinced by a party of archers approaching over the hill. Wynchecombe warned the merchants in a loud voice that carried beyond the bridge that he would have no compunction about allowing the archers to fire at will. The merchants pulled back and allowed the sheriff to do his work.

Hoode's feet dragged along the pavement, the broken spear dangling from the wound in his calf. He made no protest, made no sound at all. They met the sheriff directing his men.

Sweat ran down Wynchecombe's face and blood stained his coat where the material was slashed. He turned toward Crispin. "What's this?"

"The feather in your cap, my Lord Sheriff. Visconti's right-hand man in London. And Adam Becton's killer." He tossed Hoode to the ground where he stayed. Hoode twisted and groped for the broken spear but dared not yank it out himself. Crispin dropped the sword behind Hoode.

"Indeed?" Wynchecombe turned toward a bloodied William.

"Shackle him," he ordered. Wynchecombe nodded toward Crispin. "Weren't you here to rescue your chambermaid? Where is she?"

"She's been rescued. All that remained was for the king's men to clean up these Italians, and that you have done. Much thanks to Lenny."

Wynchecombe shoved his sword into his scabbard. "Damn you, Guest! I'm not your lackey." But there was little of the former sting to his words.

"No, my lord. But you have accomplished much tonight. You've made the Italian cartel ineffectual here. You've arrested his minions. I'm certain the king will be pleased."

Wynchecombe's grimace opened into a grin. He glanced about the square again, at the soldiers securing what was left of the Italians. "Yes, that he will be. Perhaps even pleased enough to forget that fantastical relic, eh?"

Crispin pressed his hand to his wounded shoulder.

"You'd best get that looked at."

"There's no time. I must still capture Walcote's murderer."

"You do not forget our bargain?"

"No, as long as you do not forget your part in it. You get the credit, I get my freedom. And my surety is paid."

"Ha! I said half."

"Oh, but my lord—"

"Very well, very well." Wynchecombe waved his hand. "This fight has put me in an agreeable mood. I agree to default all your surety. Now begone before I change my mind. And Crispin." There was a sincere glint in his eyes. "Good luck."

Crispin patted the false Mandyllon beneath his coat. "I'll need it."

28

LIGHTS STILL BURNED IN the Walcote manor. The harried Matthew in rumpled clothes answered Crispin's knock. The servant thrust the candle forward, casting its yellow glow on Crispin's face. The man admitted him without a word and led him to the parlor, but Crispin headed toward the stairs. "Tell Master Lionel to meet me in the solar. I can make my way alone."

The servant's mouth compressed to an agitated line, but he ducked his head and hurried into the shadows to comply.

Crispin took his time ascending the dark stairs. He strolled to the solar and shivered in its darkness. Embers still glowed red in the hearth, and he stirred them with an iron and tossed more sticks on it. When they flared to life, he took a straw and lit the candles, one on the desk and another two in tall floor sconces. Vaguely he wondered where Philippa might be and warmed his hands at the flames, watching the fire lick up at the hearth's blackened walls until he heard footsteps on the landing. He turned and crossed his arms over his chest before the twinge in his shoulder stopped him. He grasped his left arm instead.

Lionel, red-faced and brusque, crossed the threshold. He was dressed hastily in a gown, the material bunched inelegantly over his sword belt. A few loose threads trailed from the gown's hem. His pilgrim's badges clung haphazardly to his sleeve. Crispin smiled at them.

Lionel pushed Crispin out of the way and shook his shivering shoulders in front of the fire. "What is this? Do you think I keep baker's hours? This had better be worth my time."

"Oh, I assure you it is." He strolled to the other side of Lionel and continued to warm his hands. "I am concluding my investigation of the murder."

"Are you now? Very well, then. There's been far too much death in this house. I think it is cursed." He turned from the fire and reached for the wine jug on the sideboard. "Have you found your man?"

"I believe I have." Crispin waited until Lionel poured his wine and took a swig. He did not offer Crispin any. Lionel stared into his cup, but when Crispin said nothing more, he turned and scowled.

"Well then?" Lionel finally took in Crispin's appearance, the blood on his shoulder, the scrapes on his face.

"In a moment," said Crispin. "First, I'd like to show you something." Crispin unbuttoned the last few buttons on his coat, pulled the cloth free, and shook it out. He handled it tenderly but in such a way that the light glowed from behind its faint image. "Do you know what this is?"

Lionel shook his head and took another drink. "Of course not."

"It is called the Mandyllon. A very valuable relic. You see here? It is the face of Jesus Christ."

Lionel set the wine aside. He took a step forward, his hand stretching out to touch it. Crispin pulled it back and shook his head as if to a naughty child. "No, no. Mustn't touch. It's very valuable and very delicate."

"Is it for sale?" breathed Lionel.

Crispin scowled. "You *would* think of that, wouldn't you? No, it's not for sale. You cannot put a price on such a thing. So many have wanted this. So many have died trying to get it. Our false Walcote for one. He transported it from Rome. Kept it in this very room."

"You don't say. Kept it here?"

"Indeed." Crispin raised it and looked it over before glancing at

Lionel. "Relics have special properties." He nodded to Lionel's many badges. "But you know that already."

Lionel touched the monstrance hanging from a gold chain around his neck. It looked to Crispin as if the hairs of a saint were pressed against its crystal case. "Yes, they protect us poor souls."

"Yes. Some do. Some heal. Some have other properties. The Mandyllon, for instance. Do you know why it is so valuable?"

"Why, it has the face of Christ!" He took a step forward. Crispin countered by stepping back toward the wall.

"Of course that's only one reason. But it is valued for its power. Valued by kings and princes because a man is incapable of telling a lie in its presence. Curious, isn't it?"

Sweat broke out on Lionel's face. His nose shined with it. "Can't tell a lie, eh? Ha!" A slight hesitation. "That's very interesting."

"Indeed. For instance. If I were to ask you—"

Lionel held up his slick palm. "Now, wait a moment! That's not quite fair, is it? What if I test it on you first, eh? What if I were to ask about you?"

Crispin drew up as straight as he could with a wounded shoulder and narrowed his gaze down his sharp nose. "Then ask."

Lionel edged forward and raised his double chin. "I've done a bit of investigating about you. You are not quite who you seem. You're supposed to be a knight, I heard tell. That right?"

Crispin squinted. "Yes," he said slowly.

"Is it true you committed treason?"

Crispin pulled his knife.

Lionel shrank back and held up his empty hands. Crispin stopped himself and gritted his teeth. Lionel's face filled with fear and that alone gave Crispin enough satisfaction, though a blade in the man's gut would have gone further to cheer his mood. He looked the man up and down and made a disgusted huff before he slammed the knife back in its sheath.

"Well?" asked Lionel, recovering. He panted. "I asked a question.

If that cloth is authentic, you have no choice but to speak the truth. And I can see that you'd rather not."

"It— There was—" He pressed his lips tight before saying, "It's true."

"Lord love me!" Lionel wiped off the perspiration above his upper lip.

"And now *I've* a question." Crispin raised the cloth, holding it between them. "Did you kill the imposter Nicholas?"

For a moment, Crispin thought Lionel might run. His hands fisted, and his knees bent in an attitude of flight. Crispin's body blocked the doorway. He knew he could outrun the corpulent merchant, but it was late, he was tired and wounded, and no one had offered him wine. He almost wanted Lionel to run, wanted to strike him. Looking at Lionel's sweaty face and piggy eyes, remembering the cold-blooded murder, he decided that a little more violence may not be so bad.

Lionel unwound his fists and straightened. "Ha!" he said half-heartedly. He seemed to take courage from the sound of his own voice. "What does it matter if I say so to the likes of you? Even if that damned cloth makes me say it, who'd listen to a traitor? Not the sheriff. I saw how he talked to you. Doesn't trust you either."

"Did you?" Crispin asked again.

Lionel threw out his chest like a cockerel and thrust his hands into his belt. "Yes," he said at last. "I did." He gestured toward the cloth clutched in Crispin's hand. "That cloth, eh? Confession is good for the soul." He walked slowly toward Crispin. "I thought the man was Nick, of course. Haven't seen him in a score of years. When I saw it wasn't, well. I thought his death would complicate things. Until I realized it made it easier."

"Did you do it for the money?"

"Oh, yes. My business is no more. And Nick always had the best of everything. The best house, the best cloth, the best clients. And he was a true bastard about it. Well, no more. I reckoned he was already dead somewhere or this imposter couldn't have taken his place. So good riddance to him. To the both of them. And I inherit all."

"Not quite all. There is Clarence. Or do you plan to kill him, too?" Crispin raised the cloth.

"To tell the truth," he said, eyeing the cloth, "I haven't thought about it. But there is that possibility."

"You *are* a right bastard, aren't you?"

"I suppose I am. But I'm a rich one. And now." He pulled his sword before Crispin could react. "I'll take your knife and that cloth."

Crispin looked at the cloth in his hand, and tossed it to Lionel. He lifted the dagger from its sheath and held it a moment.

"No tricks," said Lionel. "Kick the dagger to me."

Crispin did as told and the blade rumbled across the plank floor.

Lionel chuckled and raised the sword blade until it was level with Crispin's chest and maneuvered Crispin away from the door. Lionel closed and locked it and then backed Crispin toward the window. "Now what's to be done with you? I don't suppose a man such as yourself would be missed too much if you vanished. And I know the perfect place to hide you. Just so happens there's a passage in this room that takes you down to the garden where I can easily bury your remains. No more Nicholas Walcote and no more Crispin Guest."

"You have no morals whatsoever, do you?"

"None at all."

"You'll hang, you know."

"Only if I'm caught. Clearly you don't have enough evidence or you wouldn't have resorted to this Mandyllon." Lionel clutched the cloth to his chest and inhaled triumphantly before he stuffed it into his scrip. "This needs safekeeping. I can't risk your making me confess in front of someone important."

The wall creaked and the secret panel whooshed aside. Lionel jumped back. His red face turned a crabapple color and his double chins seemed to double again, quivering.

The sheriff stepped into the room and placed a fist at his hip. "Am I important enough?"

Lionel snapped his head toward Crispin and glared. His bushy brows seemed to reach out for him. "You son of whore!" He raised the sword and lunged, but Wynchecombe swung the bejeweled hilt of his sword at the back of Lionel's head. Lionel's momentum propelled him forward and he fell facedown on the floor. His sword flung from his hand, skidded across the planks, and slammed with a clang against the wall.

"Two murders are quite enough," growled the sheriff.

29

WHEN CRISPIN RETURNED FROM Newgate, he was grateful to find Jack waiting for him at his lodgings with a decent fire and a bowl of wine.

Crispin took the bowl and settled in the chair. Jack shrieked and fussed at Crispin's wound. He peeled the coat off and pulled back the shirt to dress the angry gash as best he could before he knelt at Crispin's feet and pulled off the muddy boots. Crispin wiggled his toes toward the hearth, luxuriating in the feel of the warmth on his feet and the wine in his belly. He closed his eyes and leaned back. His shoulder throbbed, but the pressure of the dressing minimized the pain.

"What happened at the bridge? How about that John Hoode being an Italian! Did you get him, Master Crispin?"

"Yes, Jack. I got him. Whether he is poisoned by Lombardy spies or executed by English justice, his fate is sealed."

"What about Master Lionel? Did the sheriff arrest him?"

"Indeed. All in all, Wynchecombe was pleased by the night's proceedings. Not only did he foil a foreign conspiracy but he caught the killer of a rich merchant."

"Him? He didn't do nought. It was you!"

Crispin waved his hand. "I care not. I have my freedom and that is enough."

Jack settled on the floor by the fire and rubbed his upraised knees. "Blind me! They'll hang him, won't they? That will make Master Clarence the master of Walcote manor, then."

They sat for a time listening to the timbers creak and the fire whisper in the hearth.

"In the morning," Crispin said softly, "I shall see how Philippa fares. You brought her to Master Clarence safely, I trust."

"Oh aye, Master. But it is already morning." He rose and cracked open a shutter and looked out at a misty dawn. He shivered and closed it again and returned to the fire. "What of that cloth? Who's got it now?"

" 'An offering made to the Lord by fire.' " Crispin smiled. "It's been offered back to God. I burned it."

Jack stopped rubbing his hands and stared at Crispin. " 'Slud! Master! What made you do such a thing?"

Crispin stared down into his empty bowl. The wet wood gleamed, seeming to ask for more. "You know I don't believe in such things, Jack." Though even as he said it he remembered with a shiver his hours in the cell. He shook it off and stared into the flames. "So many have died trying to possess the Mandyllon. It seemed more hazardous than holy." He positioned the bowl on his upraised fingers and turned the object, toying with it. "Besides, if there was the least possibility that it did have some power, I couldn't let it fall to the hands of anyone who coveted it."

"Was there no priest, no church you trusted? What of the abbot of Westminster? Or the Archbishop of Canterbury?"

"Not even them. Power corrupts. 'We must as second best take the least of the evils.' So said Aristotle. I made the choice. I stand by it."

Jack took the bowl from Crispin's fingers and refilled it with wine. He shook his head. "I suppose that's the difference between the likes of you and me, Master. I'd never be able to take such responsibility."

Crispin took the bowl and sipped its contents. "You forget. I was trained for many years to be a leader. I led many into battle, after all. And I ran my own estates and oversaw Lancaster's affairs."

"Aye. Far from my like, to be sure. Lords and servants. Miles apart."

Crispin frowned at Jack's words and silently drank, immersing his thoughts and his nose in the wine's tangy aroma.

A knock on the door made them both turn. Jack rose, straightened his frayed tunic, and opened the door.

Philippa stood on the threshold clutching her hood to her face.

Crispin snapped to his feet and pulled his chemise to cover his bandaged shoulder. He felt a little vulnerable in his stocking feet.

"May I come in?" she asked, her voice husky.

Jack looked at Crispin and Crispin nodded. The boy motioned her in and slipped through the door behind her, closing it, but not before Crispin caught sight of his smile in the crack between door and jamb.

Crispin stared at the back of Philippa's head when she'd lowered her hood. The golden hair glimmered with rusty streaks. A tantalizing curl sat at the base of her neck where the hair parted. Crispin thought long and hard about pressing his lips there.

She stared into the fire. Their last awkward meeting when he left her at the Boar's Tusk rose in his mind, and he tingled with the same discomfort.

"Philippa, why are you here? Did Master Clarence tell you to leave?"

"No. He did not. He was most gracious, in fact."

He took a step closer. Her nearness felt like heat on his face. "What's happened?"

"I had to come as soon as I could. The whole house was in an uproar with Lionel being taken away. Maude is having a fit." She said it with a certain satisfied slant to her mouth. "Clarence is ready to cast her out."

"I see. These are quieter surroundings, then. Peaceful."

She turned. The satisfied smile left her and the usual slope of her lids was not there. "There's nothing peaceful about your lodgings."

He moved to stand before the fire but not quite next to her. Smoke rolled over the hearthstone and trembled up his thighs. He smelled the aroma of burnt dreams. "Then why are you here? I intended to come to you this morning."

"This can't wait, I fear." She raised her chin. "You see, Clarence has asked me to marry him."

Something seemed to rush past him. He wasn't entirely certain what it was. He felt it like a blizzard of ice crystals stinging his face or the slap of a woman's hand. "These are . . . sudden tidings."

"He'll inherit all the family wealth, you see. And he—well, he says he trusts me to help him run the house and the business, since I knew it so well. I think also he took a fancy to me."

"I see. It makes sense." His chest was tight. He forgot to breathe. "It's practical. You will retain your riches and your home. You will not do better than Clarence Walcote."

She faced him squarely. "I haven't had any other offers."

He didn't mean to, but he looked at her. Her face was harder than before. He owed it to all her recent experiences.

She opened her mouth and her red lips snapped down on the words. "Why don't you tell me not to marry Clarence?"

"Why would I do that?"

"You could make an offer yourself."

He turned his face away.

"Have you no feelings about me at all?"

He felt her glare on his cheek. He stiffened. "Is it not enough I confessed that I loved you?"

She shook her head. "The Mandyllon made you say it. But it can't make you act on it."

"Women," he grumbled under his breath. "They want it all and only on their terms."

"What other terms are there?" She smiled briefly. "Why did you not kiss me when I first came in?" He said nothing. She turned her back on the fire to look at him. She stood that way a long time. "Of course," she

said, sobering, "the true reason you will not make an offer to me is because knights don't marry chambermaids. Ain't that it?"

"I'm not a knight."

"Oh aye, you are. In here," and she tapped her chest. "Always. It is
your true self and you can't shake it. I saw it when you took me to the
Boar's Tusk. You couldn't stand for people to see you hold me. What
would they think, after all?"

"That's not true."

"You call that man Gilbert Langton your friend, but you can
barely stand to be there. Oh, it's a fine place to drink, because that is
the purpose of such a place. But it's not because of Master Gilbert.
It's because you can hide there."

He turned assassin's eyes on her. "Are you finished?"

"I thought *my* life was wretched. But yours is far worse. You've
chosen a lonely life, Crispin."

His frown deepened. "Not chosen."

"I'm not so certain."

He made a furious sound and walked in a circle, holding out his
arms. "Look around you!" he burst out. "This is no great manor, no
palace."

"I didn't ask for one."

"No? Then why consider Clarence?"

"Because he asked me." Her blunt answer stilled his tongue. "If
you don't want me to marry Clarence, then say so now."

"Or forever hold my peace? I've already told you. This is no fit
place to bring a wife."

She made a defeated nod. "It's a shame," she said. "You might have
been happy. But truth to tell, I don't think you want to be."

She turned to go and almost reached the door when she stopped.
She pulled a small pouch from her scrip and placed it with care on the
table. "It's your payment. What the sheriff took and what Nicholas
owed you. It's only fair. You did find the Mandyllon and you saved me
from Mahmoud. That makes you paid in full now, doesn't it?" Her

fingers lingered on the little pouch and then drew away. Her hand slid across the table till it fell flat against her thigh. "I don't need palaces," she whispered, not looking at him. "Neither do you."

She hesitated, waiting for him, but his lips pressed grimly together.

With a sigh, she pulled open the door and walked across the threshold. Crispin lifted his head in time to see the tail end of her train ripple over the floorboards.

The door hung open and he stared at the empty hole for a long time, not thinking, not feeling, until Jack's head poked in. "Master, may I come in?"

Crispin answered by dropping heavily into the chair and laying his arm on the table. He stared past the little pouch.

Jack slid into the room and closed the door. He stood for a moment at the doorway before he moved toward the fire. Toying with a folded parchment, he looked up at Crispin and handed it to him. "A messenger came and delivered this for you."

Crispin turned it over to look at the wax seal, but it bore no arms. He let it rest on his thigh.

"I couldn't help but hear through the door—"

Crispin stared at the pouch on the table with jaw clenched.

"Master. Why don't you go after her?"

Crispin's jaw relaxed and he sighed, feeling the years on his shoulders. He reached forward and touched the pouch. "Because I can't dispute anything she said."

"You ain't a mighty lord now. What difference does it make who you marry?"

"Because it matters, Jack. She was right. It matters to me and it always will. The veil has been drawn aside and I was forced to look into myself. I'm not certain I liked what I saw."

"Can't a body change?"

"No. At least—it may take a very long time." They both fell silent. Crispin remembered the parchment in his hand. He rose, strode to the fire, and flicked his thumbnail under the wax seal. He unfolded it and read:

> *His Majesty was pleased that his taxes are safe again. Rest assured he knows to whom the credit truly falls. Perhaps the king will not stay angry forever. I counsel patience, Crispin. But in the meantime, I caution you from coming to court again.*
> *God keep you.*

The letter was unsigned but Crispin recognized Lancaster's hand. He read it over once more and lowered the paper.

With his free hand he drew Philippa's portrait from his purse. He cradled it in his hand and gazed at it. He looked toward the fire. For a moment he thought about tossing the painting in. Let the flames consume it as they had the Mandyllon. He had thought that burning the cloth would remove the truth. But it was never easy escaping the truth for long.

He glanced at the letter and then the miniature portrait, ran his finger along its gold-leafed frame, and slowly slipped it back in his purse.

Afterword

Why "Medieval *Noir*"?

There is something about the dark, the seamier side of things that attracts me. This is realized in the precise prose and staccato dialogue of such specialists as Raymond Chandler, Dashiell Hammett, and Dorothy B. Hughes. Their fiction centered on a different slice of reality, one of starkness, harsh lighting, deep shadows, manly men with their own code of honor. And of course the women. Always in danger or always dangerous.

It seemed to me a perfect fit to drop a hard-boiled detective in the middle ages, even though the notion of a "private detective" was still centuries away. While there seemed to be a plethora of monks and nuns in the field of medieval mystery, my goal was to offer something different. I wanted to bring something darker and edgier to the genre. Here is a period rife with intrigue, codes of honor, mysterious doings, and dim, shadowy light. It screamed for a detective more like Sam Spade than Brother Cadfael.

A note on some details: Sheriff Simon Wynchecombe was in reality one of two sheriffs of London at that time (who could make up a name like that?). I also embroiled poor Crispin in all the fractured politics of Richard II's reign. Though there were historical instances—very few—of degraded and disseised (forcibly dispossessed) knights, they were either executed or banished and generally not thrown into the degree of poverty that Crispin was. The fact that he is so depleted from what defined him—his wealth and status—makes for an interesting and sympathetic character: King Richard murders him without actually killing him. The irony—for those students of English history—is that the same fate eventually befalls King Richard himself when, seventeen years later, he is forced to abdicate and is subsequently murdered.

Was Richard really all that bad at the beginning of his reign? History tells us "no," that he was, in fact, looked on as a shrewd young man and handled the Wat Tyler peasant revolt with aplomb. It was only later in his career that he allowed vanity and his many favorites to woo him to poor choices. Crispin, of course, sees the world through the eyes of Lancaster, the father figure in his life. And not unlike other recent political events where those in power are followed blindly—never mind the law or morality—we see how extreme loyalty can make even a discerning man like Crispin a little stupid. I have no doubt that as the series progresses, Crispin will see the error of his ways, but by then, Richard will begin to prove Crispin right.

Now about this story. Of course there was no "mob" as such in the fourteenth century, but the city states of Italy and the dukes and princes who ran them certainly could be considered "mob bosses." Bernabò Visconti was a ruthless man, as ruthless as any Godfather, constantly at war with the pope and the city states of Florence, Venice, and Savoy. But ruthless men usually get their comeuppance, and Visconti got his . . . by his own family. He was captured and imprisoned by his nephew, whereupon he died in prison. Of *natural* causes? Who can say?

But I digress. Wasn't this story about the cloth?

The Mandyllon or Mandillon or the Sudarium (facecloth) is an obscure relic, one that can never quite be distinguished from the present relics said to have the image of Christ. First mention of any kind of "veronica" came from apocryphal gospels and manuscripts, most notably *Curia Sanitatis Tiberii* and *Acta Pilati*. A veronica was mentioned as early as the second century, but the Veronica's Veil legend associated with the Passion that we know today emerged out of the medieval need to connect legend and artifact.

Most of the Mandyllon's saga was recounted in this novel and comes from an ecclesiastical history written in the fourth century by

Eusebius, bishop of Caesarea and a later sixth century tale told by Evagrius Scholasticus, an ecclesiastical historian. Many relic scholars believe it is the same cloth known as the "Veronica" that used to be housed in the Vatican in a shrine to St. Veronica. However, historians report that the "Veronica" might have been stolen from the St. Veronica chapel in 1600 when St. Peter's was rebuilt, or that it somehow got "mislaid." In 1608, the chapel in which the veil was housed was destroyed. Was it stolen at that time? In 1616, Pope Paul V forbade copies of the "Veronica" to be made. Was it because the original was gone? The eyes on the veil prior to this were opened, but after the events of 1608, all other copies show the figure with eyes closed. However, there is a "Veronica" that is displayed at St. Peter's Basilica on Passion Sunday, the fifth Sunday of Lent. Is this the original or another copy? Some veil scholars believe the original veil from the Vatican ended up in a Capuchin friary in Manoppello, Italy, where, indeed, a veil arrived there at about the same time the veil was said to be mislaid. Pope Benedict XVI recently made a visit to the friary and viewed what many Catholics hold to be the Veronica's Veil. Yet some even think the one in Manoppello is itself a copy. And still others believe the Mandyllon was the folded Shroud of Turin. Was this the Mandyllon? Was there *ever* a Mandyllon? Who knows?

Could the Mandyllon force you to tell the truth? Playing on the theme of *vera icona*—"true image"—it was my fiction that the veil would force you to reveal *your* true self.

In the meantime, Crispin and friends will return in another mystery of court intrigue and assassination plots in *Serpent in the Thorns*.

Glossary

CHEMISE shirt for both male and female, usually white. All-purpose, used also as a nightshirt.

COTE-HARDIE (COAT) any variety of upper-body outerwear popular from the early middle ages to the Renaissance. For men, it was a coat reaching to the thighs or below the knee, with buttons all the way down the front and sometimes at the sleeves. Worn over a chemise. Sometimes the belt was worn at the hips and sometimes the belt moved up to the waist. This is what Crispin wears.

DEGRADED when knighthood is taken from a man, usually because of treason or other crimes against the crown.

DISSEISIN forcible dispossession of land and title/status.

HOUPPELANDE fourteenth-century upper-body outerwear with fashionably long sleeves that touched the ground. As fashion changed, so did the collar, growing in height, the sleeves in length with pleats—often stuffed—front and back.

LESE-MAJESTÉ literally, "injuring the king"; the act of committing treason or other offense to the king.

SHERIFF the word is derived from the *shire reeve*, a man appointed to settle disputes and keep the peace in a region made up of several villages and towns known as a shire. The duties of the sheriffs changed with the times. The sheriffs of London were appointed for one year and served their term with little compensation except that which they could obtain by benefit of their office, that is, what bribes they could collect from those brought to justice. They appointed the juries, after all, and decided what situations would go to trial. They also served as judges.

1. How do you think the London setting shapes the story?

2. There are many small clues dotting the plot. When you look back over the story, what were the significant clues that you missed the first time? And what did you think of the twists?

3. Classism is an important aspect of Crispin's character. How does it affect his relationship with Philippa? With Jack? With Eleanor and Gilbert?

4. What would you like to know about Jack Tucker?

5. Is the sheriff's motivation for violence justified?

6. Does the Mandyllon really have the power that was attributed to it?

7. Upon Crispin's refusal, Philippa quickly accepts Clarence's offer. Why would she do that?

8. What is underlying Crispin and Lancaster's strained relationship? What can be done to fix it?

9. Who are the characters that sparked the most interest?

10. Do you see London as a character? The Boar's Tusk?

11. Are you disappointed that Bernarbò Visconti remains "offstage"?

For more reading group suggestions, visit
www.readinggroupgold.com.

CRISPIN GUEST MUST UNRAVEL A CONSPIRACY TO SAVE NOT ONLY HIS COUNTRY, BUT HIS LIFE.

"A medieval Sam Spade, a tough guy who operates according to his own moral compass and observes with detached dry humor...this book is pure fun."
—*THE BOSTON GLOBE* ON *VEIL OF LIES*

The legendary Crown of Thorns is brought to England as a peace offering...or is it instead part of a French assassination plot against England's King Richard II? When Guest becomes the prime suspect, he must find the true assassin before he falls prey to the king's justice.

AVAILABLE WHEREVER
BOOKS ARE SOLD